Stallion Gate

Martin Cruz Smith is the author
of **Gorky Park**, nominated by
Time magazine as 'the thriller of
the '80s' and subsequently a
memorable film. His being part-
Indian gives Mr Smith the title
and the insight to straddle the
two worlds that make the story
of **Stallion Gate**.

He lives with his wife and three
children in California.

Also by Martin Cruz Smith
in Pan Books

Gorky Park
Nightwing

Martin Cruz Smith

STALLION GATE

PAN BOOKS
in association with Collins

First published in Great Britain 1986 by Collins Harvill
This edition published 1987 by Pan Books Ltd,
Cavaye Place, London SW10 9PG
in association with Collins
9 8 7 6 5 4 3 2
© Martin Cruz Smith 1986
ISBN 0 330 29357 5

Printed in Great Britain by
Richard Clay Ltd, Bungay, Suffolk

For Nell, Luisa and Sam

NOVEMBER 1943

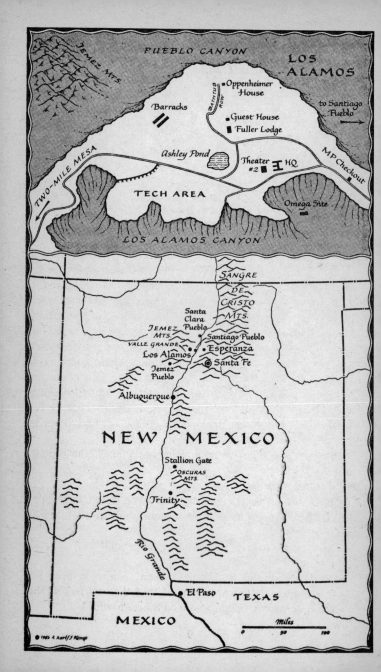

1

The cell at Leavenworth was four feet by eight feet, barely large enough for Joe to sit at one end on an upended pail, but there was room in the dark for a circle of figures. Nearest Joe was a mountain lion, grey and white in colour as a snowfall at night. The cat's spine was a rattlesnake and the snake's scaled head peeked over the lion's shoulder. There was a girl with the body of a bird, a swallow. She had a beautiful, triangular face and her eyes modestly avoided looking at Joe, who was only in dirty GI underpants. Across from her was a minotaur, a blue man with a shaggy buffalo head. At the far end was an officer who had brought his own chair to sit on. He had a long skull and sallow skin and ears pressed almost flat into close-cut, black hair. He wore the patient manner and tailored uniform of a career officer and didn't seem the least bothered by the overhead ring of golden sticks that beat against each other in subdued claps of light.

"You're from New Mexico, Sergeant Peña?" the captain asked.

"Yes, sir," Joe said.

The minotaur hummed softly and rocked from side to side. Joe tried to ignore it and the captain paid no attention at all.

"You know the Jemez Mountains, Sergeant?"

"Yes, sir."

"As I understand it, Sergeant Peña, you're in here for insubordination," the captain said. "But the real fact of the matter is, you were sleeping with an officer's wife."

"Not lately, sir. I've been in the brig for twenty days, the last ten in the hole on nothing but water."

"Which is what you deserve. There is nothing stupider in this man's Army than consorting with the wife of a superior, you'll admit."

"Yes, sir."

"Any ill effects?"

"Some hallucinations."

Joe had started seeing things after the fifth day in the hole. Guards banged on the door every time he lay down, so he hadn't slept, either. The cat had come first. Joe thought the stench of the cell would drive even a phantasm out, but after the cat came the woman on wings. It wasn't a religious experience, it was just crowded.

"You have the feeling you're never getting out of here, Sergeant?"

"It had occurred to me, sir. I'm sorry, sir, I didn't catch the name."

"Augustino."

"You're a defence lawyer?"

"They didn't want to admit you were even in the brig, Sergeant. They've as good as buried you. No, I'm not a lawyer. But I can get you out."

The snake twisted its head and regarded the captain with interest.

"Why don't you tell me how, sir?" Joe suggested.

"You haven't been back to New Mexico recently?"

"Not for years."

"Wasn't too interesting?"

"Not interesting enough."

While the snake watched the captain, the big cat turned its yellow eyes languidly to Joe.

The captain nodded. "I know what you mean, Sergeant. I'm from Texas, myself."

"Really, sir?"

"On my sixteenth birthday I applied for the Citadel."

"Is that so, sir?"

"You get more dedicated officers out of the Citadel than you get from the Point."

"Interesting, sir. Can you get me out of this fucking hole or can't you?"

"Yes. I have the authority to get anyone I want. Sergeant, do you remember a J. Robert Oppenheimer?"

"No."

"Jewish boy from New York? He had tuberculosis? His family sent him to New Mexico?"

"Okay. I was a kid, too. That was a long time ago. We went riding."

"To Los Alamos?"

"All over, yeah."

"He's back."

"So?"

"Sergeant, the Army is setting up a project at Los Alamos. Oppenheimer is in charge and he will need a driver. You are, in almost every particular, the perfect man. Violent enough to be a bodyguard. Ignorant enough to hear classified information and not understand a word. Be liaison."

"Who with?"

"Indians, who else? Most of all, you might be a name Oppenheimer would recognize and trust. I put you on the list. We'll find out."

"If he doesn't?"

"You'll rot right here. If he does pick you, you'll return to your various scams, Sergeant – I expect that. You'll be in glory. But don't forget who found you in this hole. I want his man to be my man. Understood?"

"Yes, sir."

The captain rapped on the door to go. Waiting for the turnkey, he added, "I hear your mother is Dolores the Potter. I have some wonderful pieces by her. How is she?"

"Wouldn't know, sir. I haven't been in Santiago since the war started."

"You don't do pottery yourself?"

"No, sir."

11

"You're not that kind of Indian?"

"Never was, sir."

The captain took his chair with him when he went. Joe leaned back on the pail and shut his eyes on the figures who stayed in the cell with him. He could hear new apparitions arriving. Then he opened one lid and caught the girl with the swallow body lifting her dark eyes and through the murk giving him a wistful look. He laughed. He knew nothing about visions, but he knew women. He was getting out.

DECEMBER 1944

2

Staff Sergeant Joe Peña was playing the piano for the Christmas dance. He had a narrow face for a Pueblo Indian, a deep V of cheekbones, a broad mouth and wide-set eyes. Black-black hair and brows, one brow healed over an old split. His uniform was crisp, the chevron on his sleeve so bright it looked polished, his tie tucked in between the second and third buttons of his shirt. Picking out ballads on the parlour grand, he gave a first impression of a huge, attractive man. Also of damaged goods.

The lodge's walls and columns had the honeyed glow of varnished ponderosa pine. In keeping with the Christmas theme, red and green crêpe festooned wagonwheel candelabras and the open balconies of the second floor. Paper reindeer were pinned to the Navajo rugs on the walls. Atop the eight-foot-tall stone mantel of the fireplace, a porcelain St Nick stood between Indian pots.

"Everyone's here." Foote supported himself on the piano. Foote was a lean and horsy Englishman in a threadbare tuxedo.

"Not everyone," Joe answered while he played.

"You say. Who's not here?"

"Soldiers aren't here, MPs aren't here, WACs aren't here, machinists aren't here, Indians aren't here."

"Of course not, we don't want them here. It's not their bloody bomb. Bad enough that we have the military command. Especially that Captain Augustino creeping around like a Grand Inquisitor."

"I'm ready." Harvey Pillsbury brought Joe a bourbon. In

15

his other hand he carried a clarinet. "I really appreciate this second chance, Joe."

"Just blow. Last time you were silent. It was like playing with a snowman."

Harvey had the contours of a snowman, and downy hair and the high, nasal accent of west Texas.

"Be prepared for quantum improvement."

"Whatever that means." Joe finished the drink in a swallow.

He played "Machine-gun Butch" and everyone sang along. *'. . . was a rough and ready Yankee, He'll never let the old flag touch the ground. And he always will remember the seventh of December, With his rat-tat-tat-tat-tat-tat, and he'll mow 'em down."* The Germans and Italians sang loudest, and the crazy thing was that Joe liked them, Foote included and Harvey especially. Most were Americans and most of the Americans were babies straight from college. The boys had loose ties and sweaty faces. The girls had short skirts and scrolls of hair around broad, polished foreheads. A rent party in Harlem it wasn't, but they were trying.

Harvey had stood through "String of Pearls", clarinet raised and trembling and utterly mute. During "Don't Sit Under the Apple Tree", Harvey licked the reed, forced a squeak, two notes in a row, then three. Halfway into "This Joint Is Jumpin' ", Joe switched to a bass stride, forcing him to blow erratically through a riff like a butterfly flying for its life, and at the end Harvey beamed, red-cheeked and triumphant.

" 'White Christmas'?" he suggested.

Joe groaned. "A little knowledge is a gruesome thing."

There was a stir across the room as Oppy and Kitty arrived. Better than a stir, veneration. The Director of the Los Alamos project was a spindly six feet tall with a close-cropped skull and beak of a nose that emphasized tapered eyes of startling blue. Younger physicists followed him, copying the hunch of his shoulders, his air of distraction. Kitty Oppenheimer had a flat, pretty face, a frowsy dress and dark, thick hair. Her friends were European wives, who surrounded her like bodyguards.

A fingertip slid down Joe's spine There were people at the

16

end of the piano, but they were watching dancers or the Oppenheimers. Harvey was concentrating on his clarinet. The fingertip turned to fingernail. Joe glanced up at Mrs Augustino, the captain's wife. She looked like a cover of *Life* magazine, maybe "*Life* goes to Magnolia Country" with her peroxide-blonde curls, blue eyes and polka-dot dress with ruffled shoulders, and she seemed to be intently watching the couples on the floor, but it was her finger, nonetheless.

"What is this secret project, Sergeant?" she asked in a voice soft enough for just him to hear. "What do you think they're making?"

"Why don't you ask your husband?"

"Captain Augustino took me to a nightclub in Albuquerque last week." Her nail continued like a little knife down the groove of his back. "You were playing. I was struck by how gently you played. Is that because your fingers are so big?"

"Not gently. Carefully. I stay out of trouble." By twisting on the bench to look at her, he managed to dislodge her nail. Sad: nineteen, twenty years old and already a bored Army wife. "What do you think they're doing here, Mrs Augustino? What's your opinion?"

She brushed curls from her face and surveyed the room. "I think the whole thing is a hoax. They're dodging the draft. All these so-called scientists got together and pulled the wool over the Army's eyes. They're smart enough to do it."

"Yeah," he had to agree, "they are."

During the break, Joe had to manoeuvre around some of the "so-called scientists" to get to the bar. The Hungarian, Teller, his eyebrows rising like fans, brayed over a joke by Fermi. A short man, Fermi was fit and balding and wore a rough double-breasted suit and thick-soled shoes that curled at the toe like an Italian peasant's. Physicists called him "the Pope".

Oppy was showing a circle of admirers how to build the perfect martini.

"Firm instructions should always be in German." He had the trick of lowering his voice so listeners leaned forward, and as they did so he poured gin to the brim of the glass. *"Am wichtigsten, der Gin sollte gekühlt sein, kein Eis."*

"Bourbon," Joe told Foote, who, drunk or not, was tending bar.

"Zwei Tröpfeln Wermut, nicht mehr, nicht weniger, und eine Olive." Oppy added enough vermouth to cause an oily swirl in the gin, then he handed his concoction to a woman with red-orange hair. She would have been noticeable simply because she wore black coveralls that suggested she was a member of an army of Amazons, or laboured in a factory of mourners, or had been dipped in ink. It was the sheer intellectual cast of her face that really set her apart. Black hair cut in severe bangs around eyes that were blue-grey with dark edges that dilated with dislike, like a cat's. Strong nose, full mouth and the sort of pale complexion that scorned the sun. She was exactly the sort of female that attracted Oppy and repelled Joe.

"A double," Joe told Foote.

Oppy said, "Joe, meet Dr Anna Weiss. Anna, this is my oldest friend here, Joe Peña."

Drinks in hand, Anna Weiss and Joe dismissed each other with a nod.

"I missed my first year at Harvard," Oppy persisted. "My family sent me to New Mexico for my health. They contracted with Joe's father, a renowned bootlegger."

"That so?" She had a low voice and a German accent and no interest.

"Tell her, Joe," Oppy said.

"My dad also rented packhorses and experienced guides for dude parties," Joe said. "I was the experienced guide. I was twelve. One of the first times I went out, I had a kid from New York. Sixteen and so tall and skinny that the first time I saw him in swimming trunks I thought he was going to die on the trail."

"I couldn't ride," Oppy said.

"He couldn't ride to save his life," Joe said, "but he liked to go out at night to see stars. He was so damned nightblind I had to hold back every branch on the way. One night we got

18

caught in a rainstorm and I got under my horse to stay dry. I heard this guy yelling in the rain."

"I thought he'd left me," Oppy said.

"I told him to come down under the horse with me. He came down, soaked, got under the horse and said, 'Gee!' Because he'd never thought of the possibility of getting under a horse in the rain. That loomed like a brilliant idea to him."

"It struck me as an offer of eternal friendship," Oppy said. "At the end of the rain he led me up to the Ranch School here, to this very place, for some coffee and dry clothes. That was twenty years ago."

Her eyes moved from man to man as if they were describing a previous life as idiots.

"Better switch back to German," Joe told Oppy and took his drink out to the patio. There was a low moon over the mountains and a liquid coolness to the air. By the flagstones was a garden that was deep in the shadow of poplars. "Los Alamos" meant "The Poplars".

What are they doing here? An atomic bomb, a nuclear device, whatever those words signified. He couldn't help but know the terminology from being Oppy's driver and over-hearing conversations in the back seat. As for understanding, it was all a different language to Joe. Chain reaction? Fast neutrons and slow neutrons? Incomprehensible, like Sanskrit. Of course, Oppy read Sanskrit.

Joe set his drink on a flagstone and lit his first Lucky of the day. He still had the habits of a fighter trying to stay in shape, although for what he didn't know.

As Teller came through the doors, he said: "Joe, you could take lessons and become a real pianist. You could play Beethoven."

"Ah, the big-band sound," Joe said. As soon as he could he picked up his drink and slipped away from an analysis of the American jitterbug. Teller had a wooden leg.

Joe was nearly at the doors when his way was blocked by Anna Weiss, the woman Oppy had been instructing in the manufacture of martinis. With her was another émigré. He had a bland and pasty face, straw-coloured hair and rimless glasses. His name was Klaus Fuchs. Joe couldn't remember passing a single word with him. Apparently Fuchs has been giving Fräulein Weiss the usual Los Alamos tour: there are the mountains, there are the mesas, there is the Indian.

"So, you were the one who first brought Oppy here?" she said to Joe.

He nodded. "This was a private school then. A year at the Ranch School cost more than Harvard. The war wiped it out."

"And led you back. That is irony?"

"No, that's pure Army."

The two Germans seemed to stare at Joe from the far end of a scale of intelligence.

"Teller is telling everyone you are musical," she said. "Klaus says you have no actual ability."

Fuchs shrugged. "It should be enough to be a war hero."

"You're kind," Joe said. "Of course, it's important to be on the right side of the war."

"They grow up with rifles here, Dr Fuchs," a voice said from the dark of the garden. "It's a simple thing to be a war hero if you can fire a rifle."

"I have never shot anything," Fuchs said.

"Of course not." Captain Augustino took a step towards the patio, just enough for them to see him. "In fact, we're in hunting season now. I wouldn't go wandering in the woods."

"Naturally," Fuchs said.

"A moon like this, maybe snow, every Indian is going to be out for his deer tonight. It could be dangerous."

"Yes, yes."

Fuchs seemed to regard Augustino the same way he did Joe. The captain was sallow-faced but his short hair was thick and glossy as fur, giving him a half-animal quality which also clung to Joe. A pair of predators, while Fuchs and his Anna Weiss had evolved to the next stage of human development.

"Do you mind if I speak to the sergeant alone?"

"Please," Fuchs said.

The arc of Augustino's cigarette waved Joe out. He couldn't tell how long the captain had been standing, listening.

"Our Germans. I'll say one thing for Fuchs, he's scrupulous about security, unlike some people. Sergeant, are you aware of the improvement in the living standards of the people in the local pueblos since you arrived on the Hill? Cigarettes, tyres from the motor pool, sugar from the commissary. Particularly disturbing is the rumour that Indians have opened some of the old turquoise mines."

"You don't like Indian jewellery, sir?"

"What I don't like is the idea that they're blasting open the mines with high explosive. There's only one place in this part of the country for them to get explosives, Sergeant, and that's the Hill. I'd hate to think any of my men was stealing Army property to sell for personal profit."

"Indians are pretty poor, sir. He can't be making too much profit."

"Then that makes him stupid too."

"If he's that stupid, he'll make a slip. I'll watch for him, sir."

"Do that. In the meantime, General Groves has arrived at the guest house. Wrap up the music. Since you'll be taking the general and Dr Oppenheimer to see the Alamogordo range tomorrow, I want you to get a good night's sleep. The fate of the world will be riding in the car you'll be driving, so it would be nice if you were bright and sober. Agreed?"

"Yes, sir."

"Please be aware, Sergeant, that I am unhappy with the quality of information that you've been giving me lately. We have a deal. You're on provisional assignment to me. That's probation. You go back to the brig any time I say. Now you get back inside the lodge, give them a couple more tunes and send our civilians home happy. By the way, do you know the difference between a nigger playing the piano and an Indian playing the piano?"

"No, sir."

"Funny, neither do I."

Joe tried to concentrate on the music for the last set. He did

21

a little serious work on "I Got It Bad", turning the chorus into bebop flat fifths, followed with the tom-tom rhythm of "Cherokee", then moved into the placid waters of "More Than You Know". The jitterbuggers got one last shot with "The GI Jive" before he U-turned through "Funny Valentine" and slid into the final tune of the night, "Every Time We Say Goodbye". Fuchs was doing a Hapsburg ballroom number with Anna Weiss, as if he was waltzing to "The Blue Danube". She seemed graceful enough in his arms, and smiled as if she found him either amusing or ridiculous. Across the floor, Oppy kept his eye on Fuchs and the girl with a concentration that was unusual even for him. At the same time, Kitty was behind Oppy and watching him and the girl. Perhaps it was the novelty of a new face or her bizarre coveralls, but everyone seemed to watch Anna Weiss; on the dance floor she seemed to be the only one completely alive. It was a trick of the light that followed one person around. Joe had seen the quality before; it was rare, but not unknown.

Every time we say goodbye . . . Porter had written an intimate ballad for lovers parting at train stations, troopships, beds. At previous dances, Fuchs's style had struck Joe as ludicrous; tonight, it was irritating. When he saw Fuchs and his partner heading for a dip, he skipped a bar, went on four bars, inserted the missing bar of music and continued. Fuchs looked like a man trapped by a traffic signal. The girl looked at Joe. The other dancers didn't notice because they were all dancing close and slow. As Fuchs stared at the piano, Joe drew the tune out. It was full of the loveliest A-minor chords. He got Harvey to sustain an E and came down the whole keyboard on the ninths like Tatum, returning to catch Harvey's dying note and stretch it into melody with the right hand while he brought the left softly up the keys like a rabbit. Harvey stopped playing and stood with the reed at his open mouth, eyes big. Joe turned the rabbit into a bebop bopping from chord to chord as softly as a lullaby until he merged the melody again and made it swell until Fuchs couldn't help but start dancing again. When Fuchs was in full spin, he dropped into "The Skater's Waltz", still in

A-minor. The girl was laughing, taking him up on it. Fuchs tried to stop, but she wouldn't let him; Oppy wiped tears of laughter.

Slowly, as if it were a force taking control, syncopation came out of the bass and the waltz became a dreamy rag, then escaped into a comic stride that left Fuchs not knowing whether to put down his left foot or his right until Joe marshalled the notes into a resolute 2–4 and marched them into a proper waltz, where he left them for dead and reprised Porter as if nothing at all had happened, no Strauss, no bebop. Then he cut it short with a nod to Harvey, who came through with a flutey arpeggio. Joe hit a last chord and that was that.

3

In the beginning, Oppy thought he could build the bomb with just five other physicists. They could take over the schoolmasters' houses and eat at the school lodge. What laboratories were needed could be squeezed in between the canyon rim and the little man-made pond that graced the front of the lodge.

After deeper thought, Oppy doubled and re-doubled the number of physicists and added some mathematicians, chemists and metallurgists. The Army brought in the Engineers Detachment to man the labs, run the power plant, maintain the roads and drive the trucks. Two hundred MPs were shipped in for security. WACs came for clerical work. The labour had to be expanded because work that had been expected from the outside world, the real world so far away from New Mexico, couldn't be done there. Volcanic tufa was bulldozed for foundries. Cyclotrons and particle accelerators were jimmied up the canyon road. The British Mission arrived. Dormitories, hospital, school were built and babies born. Soldiers, MPs and WACs were again doubled and needed more barracks, cafeterias, commissaries and theatres. The civilian machinists who cut high explosives would leave if they didn't have their own housing. Civil servants had to be housed. By December 1944, five thousand people were crammed on to the mesa, and they were without streetlights because the Army was still trying to hide its most secret project.

From the dance, Joe cut across the playing field and behind the beauty shop to an area of low, rounded Quonset huts, so-called "Pacific hutments" designed to be thrown up on tropical islands, not New Mexico in the winter. This was where the construction workers who built the housing for everyone else were expected to live. He found the fight by the noise.

The ring was in the day room of the central hutment. Sergeant Ray Stingo was fighting one of the workers. Like Joe, Ray was a bodyguard and driver with security clearance, and had been a fighter, a heavyweight, before the war. He sported a black spitcurl over a beaten-down nose and showed a stomach still hard as a washboard, but he must have had ten years on the kid he was boxing.

Joe edged open the door just enough to see. And smell the deep, sour reek of stale beer and dead cigarettes. The Hill had recruited and suffered through successions of construction men, each group meaner than the one before, as healthy workers without police records were likely to be drafted. The latest bunch were Texans who laboured stripped to the waist but, like a caste mark, always wore their hats. They'd put on their stetsons and pointy boots for the evening's entertainment and stood on sofas and chairs to root their boy on. Ray's backers were MPs, a corps of uniformed thugs who looked nearly civilized next to the Texans. Even with helmets and sticks, the MPs usually stayed clear of the hutments on Saturday night. Joe saw money passing between the two camps. There was probably $2,000 or $3,000 riding on a fight like this.

The boy was left-handed, fast, aggressive. Not much face: a heavy brow, dim eyes, a flat, spade nose dotted with blood. Short, sandy hair and peg ears. In his tank shirt and denim trousers, his most distinctive features were his neck and shoulders of fanning muscle. A natural heavyweight. Twenty years old. Less.

Ray tried to slip the right jab, but the boy pulled it back and snapped it again, moved in again to a chorus of cowboy hoots. There was an old saying, "Poor New Mexico, so far from heaven, so near to Texas." Joe'd always felt it was a combination of the big hats and Texas sun that baked and compressed the Texas brain to the size of a boiled egg. There was a deeper mystery here, though. The Army was drafting men

25

who were missing fingers, toes, other appendages. There was a clerk with two fingers typing in the quartermaster's office. Joe couldn't count fingers inside a boxing glove, but this boy seemed exactly the sort of post-adolescent maniac who should be gutting Japs on some barren atoll. Ray was getting thrashed.

Ray kept circling to his left. which was right into the kid's jab. In New York. Ray had been a solid, middle-of-the-card fighter, a body puncher. Tonight he looked old, the eyes desperate, the muscles puffy. A painful blush spread on his chest and face everywhere a punch landed. He circled into a jab, ducked and moved into a straight left and was down on his ass, sitting on his gloves, his legs splayed. The kid bounced and motioned Ray to stand. The shouts of a hundred men tried to take off the roof.

Joe had already taken a step out into the dark. Through the door, the scene looked smaller, like a cockfight, betters hanging over a pit, some glum, some screaming till their neck cords popped. It depressed him. There was something about war, about murder on the grand scale, that made mere boxing unnecessary.

The cooling night winds blew. Across the valley the range of Sangre de Cristo was a spine pointing south to Santa Fe. At his back the Jemez Mountains were a dark, volcanic mass. In between, the moon looked ponderous, ready to crash.

Why had he picked on Fuchs? Because he was angry and the German was the first easy target to waltz on to the dance floor. Jesus, how shameless would he get before this war was over?

Since he was supposed to be on twenty-four-hour call to drive Oppy and handle any "native" problems, Joe lived outside the barracks, in his own room in the basement of Theatre 2, the enlisted men's general-purpose hall. The basement corridor was a black tunnel of volleyball nets and music stands. Without bothering to turn on the light in his room, he went straight to his locker and opened a new bottle of bourbon and a fresh carton of cigarettes. The glow of the match lit a poster for the Esquire All-Stars, featuring Art Tatum and Coleman Hawkins.

26

Hawkins held a tenor sax. The poster was a door to the past and to the future; it sure as hell wasn't the present. He blew out the flame and on the wall the black men faded and he felt like he was fading himself. Hanging in the centre of the room, barely visible, was a heavy bag. Joe set down his drink and cigarette, pulled off his tunic and shirt. He tapped the bag with a jab and as much felt as saw it wiggle on its chain. The bag's name was MacArthur. Joe hooked it with his left and listened to the satisfying creak of leather and kapok. He hooked again and crossed with his right, and MacArthur jumped. Jabbed, hooked, crossed, bobbed, and crossed again. Air popped from the seams. Over the chain, the ceiling groaned. A heavy bag demanded commitment; hit it tentatively and a man could break his wrist. Joe snapped the bag back, moved in to hit it again and slipped, nearly fell. The bag bounced off his shoulder as he reached to the floor and picked up silk and tulle. The silk had polka dots, like a spotted lily.

"I'll give you a hint. It isn't Eleanor Roosevelt."

Mrs Augustino lit her own cigarette. She had a silver lighter and a silver cigarette case and that was all. Even in winter she had a two-piece bathing-suit tan and she was a genuine blonde. She shut the lighter, but Joe wouldn't have been surprised to see her whole body continue glowing like a neon sign. An Army wife was a dangerous thing. He could almost hear a neon sizzle.

"You shouldn't be here." He was still breathing hard from hitting the bag.

"Try and throw me out, Sergeant, and I'll scream rape so loud they'll hear me in Santa Fe."

"Go ahead, scream." Mostly what he could see now was the glint of her blue eyes.

"Rape," she said softly.

"Mrs Augustino –"

"Call me Celeste."

"Mrs Augustino –"

"I'm twenty years old, attractive. Married to a captain. Here I am, waiting hours for a sergeant to come to bed."

27

"I didn't ask you, I hardly know you."

"Hardly anybody knows me, Sergeant. This is an Army post and I should be at the top of the social pinnacle. Instead, with all these foreigners and scientists, I'm treated like some ignorant hillbilly, like an intellectual embarrassment. I looked around that dance tonight for one man who didn't give a damn for all these geniuses and tin gods and I only found one, Sergeant, and that was you."

He found himself interested. "You think so?"

"I saw you talking to Fuchs. You hate them."

"I may dislike Fuchs."

"And the German girl with him."

"She's not my type."

"That's my point. I am your type, Sergeant."

Well, there was a little bit of truth in that. Enough truth to frighten the lion in his lair, the chief in his tepee. She sat up. His eyes had adjusted to the tiny beacon of her cigarette. Light freckles covered her breasts.

"I'm flattered, Mrs Augustino. Really, but –"

"It's cold out there. Could a lady at least have a drink before she goes off in humiliation?"

Joe brought her the bourbon he'd poured for himself. Tin gods and geniuses? And the occasional sergeant, the one-time fighter but now a man who steers clear of trouble, a man in a long, dry spell of good conduct. Looked at that way, in a desert, she was an oasis of sin.

"Where is the captain?" Joe asked.

"Who knows?"

There was a Victrola against the wall and 78s arranged neatly underneath; he took better care of his records than anything else and he didn't need light to set a disc on the turntable and let the arm down. "Mood Indigo" whispered.

"Then maybe we have time for one dance." He took the empty glass from her.

In her bare feet, Mrs Augustino didn't come to his chin.

"Ready for the dip?" Joe pulled her close.

They bumped into the heavy bag and it wiggled on its chain.

"Was that General Groves?" she laughed.

"No, that's General MacArthur."

"That's a terrible name for a punching bag. He's the greatest American alive."

"That's the one."

4

Snow had fallen like a fine dust during the night. Mrs Augustino stepped delicately through it into the early morning dark.

When Joe went back to his room it was rank with free-floating lust and stupidity. As he picked up the blanket, her cigarette case fell out, cool to the touch, and he knew he didn't want to see her again. Case in hand, he rushed through the basement hall, knocking aside volleyball nets, up the stairs and across the theatre pews that would be turned round in a few hours for Sunday morning services and threw open the side door she had left by. Too late. Nothing but snow and the cold night air. He was only in shorts and icy sweat. Storm clouds had cleared. Directly across the road was Military HQ, an E-shaped building. The roofs were white rhomboids floating on black.

Between two arms of the E, an engine started and tyres rolled. A vehicle crossed the dim gloaming of the road and stopped ten feet in front of Joe. Headlights went on, blinding him. Its engine raced with the clutch in, then shifted into neutral. Captain Augustino stepped out of the weapons carrier and gave a visible sigh.

"Excellent tracking snow, Sergeant." The captain considered the thin sheet-white snow that lay over the road and the prints of a woman's shoes leading from the door.

"For hunting, sir?" Joe held the cigarette case behind his back.

"Just what I was thinking. Better get your clothes on, Sergeant, we don't want to miss the dawn."

"Now, sir?"

"No better day."

"I don't have a rifle, sir."

"I brought one for you. Better get your clothes on."

"I'm supposed to pick up the Director at eleven."

"We'll be done by then."

While Joe went in for his clothes and jacket, he realized his own taste for the expedition. Who was fooling who? If Mrs Augustino was in the bed, could Captain Augustino ever be far behind? Her invitation to Joe became, as soon as he was between her legs, his invitation to the captain, and there was a pure and shining inevitability to the situation that appealed to the blood, as if the blood were rising with the moon. If nothing else, his career as an informer was coming to an end. Though, mulling a different set of ethics, he should stay away from officers' wives. MacArthur jiggled as Joe passed. He deserved to be shot.

The weapons carrier climbed west to the Valle. The snow was deeper in the mountains and the pines made a luminous tunnel in front of the headlights. Captain Augustino's face had its own lunar glow, the intensity of a husband who had not slept during the night's snowfall.

"It's illegal, you know, Sergeant."

"What, sir?"

"Hunting. This is an Army preserve now. Of course, Indians still hunt here."

"Do they, sir?"

"Sneak up here and hunt. Hard for your friends to break old habits."

"Yes, sir."

"It's poaching now, just like in Robin Hood's time. This is like Sherwood Forest now."

"Really, sir."

"You're not a student of history, Sergeant."

"Not really, sir."

"History repeats itself, the first time as tragedy, the second time as farce. It was not an Indian who said that."

31

"Not a Pueblo?"

"Karl Marx. You never heard of him?"

"From New Mexico, sir?"

"No."

"From Texas?"

"No."

"Musician?"

"Maybe the violin in his parlour. You never heard of *Das Kapital* or *The Communist Manifesto*?"

"I'm going to develop my mind some time, sir."

Pines rose like snow-bearing shadows. Augustino was a skilful driver, swinging the weapons carrier wide on a curve without losing momentum or control. A Marlin and Winchester, both lever actions, rattled on the back seat. Also on the seat was a box of .30-.30s.

"At any rate, Sergeant, you don't mind doing something illegal?"

"Not with the right person, sir."

"That's what I thought. You said you were a neck shot or a heart shot?"

"I don't recall, sir."

"I like the spine shot myself. I like to see a big animal drop where he stands, so he doesn't run for a mile and make me chase him. Ever shoot a deer in the ass, Sergeant?"

"No, sir, but I understand it's called a Texas heart shot."

Augustino laughed appreciatively.

"Well, Mrs Augustino's father shot a Mexican in the ass once and chased him ten miles up the Bravo before he nailed him."

"In Brownsville."

"Outside Brownsville by the time he caught him. Maybe it was a New Mexican. You see, Sergeant, our attitude is that New Mexicans are basically Mexicans on the wrong side of the border. Also, it is an idea dear to our hearts that Indians are basically red niggers. That's why they lust so after white women, that's what proves the point. Anyway, I'm a much better shot that Mrs Augustino's father."

Daybreak was when deer and elk were most active. They left the weapons carrier by the road and trudged up a sloping meadow. A pre-dawn blue filled the Valle, and in the distance the higher peaks of the Jemez were flagged with mist. Joe had the Winchester and a pocket of rounds; the captain had chosen the Marlin. In spite of himself, the crisp air and snow excited Joe; it was a perfect morning for a hunt. Ridiculous as it seemed, he saw an identical eagerness in Augustino. They moved quickly upwind to the black edge of the tree line and crouched. Elk would be more likely to cross the meadow; mule deer were louder moving through trees. Joe worked his way along the tree line, further upwind, and Augustino followed as naturally as if he'd hired Joe as a guide. They stopped where the trees formed a spit on the edge of the meadow, commanding 100 degrees of white slope and another tree line facing them only sixty yards away. Their disadvantage was that they'd be in sunlight before the opposite tree line was, but they couldn't have everything. The Winchester's sights were set for 150 yards. He'd aim low on deer coming out of the trees. He might hit nothing; he'd never fired the rifle before and didn't know whether it pulled right, left, up or down.

Augustino pointed to faint dimples in the snow at their feet. Joe knelt and blew the loose flakes away, exposing impressions the shape of dragging double crescents. Heifer? Augustino mouthed. Elk, Joe answered. No more than an hour before.

Not more than an hour before. This was the best part of hunting, the passing of time. Joe had probably been in this same spit of spruce and pines, hunting, twenty years ago with his father.

When solid forms were so faint, it was easy to see into memory. It was a quality of the hour, neither night nor day, that lent every second its weight. Eyes seemed to grow huge and adept even as they were fooled by the nod of a branch. An owl seesawed through the trees. Joe didn't care if deer or light never came. If ever someone was going to shoot him through the head, this was as good a time as any. The captain watched the meadow with the same concentration Of course, mice, shrews and rats ran back and forth all night, and hunters only saw their snow tracks in the morning. At daybreak, a man could only see well enough to shoot something his own size. Shadows clung, half-born. When what was real and what was shadow was uncertain, a man could meet his opposite, Joe thought. Like this white racist officer from Brownsville, Texas. He and Joe could huddle under the same spruce bough.

"Sergeant, tell me," the captain whispered, "have you ever thought of this as the Century of the Jew?"

"No."

"Marx was a Jew, you know. The worldwide communist movement started with Marx. The Russian Revolution was largely led by Jews, such as Trotsky. Every country on earth, even China, is fighting for its soul against Marx."

"Even China?"

"History unfolds like a wonderful and terrible adventure. There are great rhythms and cycles. Each century is different."

"What was the last century?"

"That was the Century of the White Man."

Joe couldn't figure what this had to do with Mrs Augustino. "Sure wasn't the Century of the Red Man."

"No. But now we're all in the same boat, Sergeant. First, Marx overthrows traditional authority and religion, then another Jew destroys every absolute in the laws of science."

"Really?"

"Science was built on absolute laws until Einstein's theories of relativity and quantum physics. Marx and Einstein. Now there's nothing an intelligent man can believe in, either in religion or science. The very word 'atom' in Greek means that which is indivisible, did you know that?"

"No, sir."

Captain Augustino stirred beside Joe. "Which does not mean that they haven't suffered. When I hear of the suffering of the Jews under Hitler, I wish I were a Jew myself. You see, in the Century of the Jew they've taken our hearts, when they already had our minds. You see how it's coming together, all of it, right here."

34

"Here?"

"I'm talking, Sergeant, of the Third Great Jew. Sergeant, what would you say if I told you that J. Robert Oppenheimer was the most brilliant man you or I or anyone here had ever met?"

"Could be, sir."

"Sergeant, what would you say if I told you that Oppenheimer was an agent of the Soviet Union, intent on developing an atomic weapon here only so that he can deliver the finished plans to his Soviet friends?"

Joe didn't know what to say.

"You'd say I was mad, wouldn't you, Sergeant?"

"Have you," Joe picked his words carefully, "passed your opinion on to General Groves, sir?"

"As did the FBI. But the general is in Oppenheimer's thrall. Everyone is. Nobel laureates are his lapdogs and the United States Army has been tied up and delivered as a gift to him. I have felt the allure myself."

"Have you, sir?"

"The most fascinating conversations in my life have been those with Oppenheimer on history. He read *The Decline and Fall of the Roman Empire* on a single train trip from New York to Los Angeles, and *Das Kapital* on the way back. This is a physicist, I remind you."

"True," Joe said. Oppy was always trying to launch turgid conversations.

"Have you ever noticed something hypnotic about him, Sergeant? The way people will go into his office saying one thing and come out saying the opposite? The way everyone imitates him? The way he's made his own empire here? Here at this focal point of history?"

"You're following orders from the FBI or someone in Washington, sir?"

"I don't need orders from anyone. Everyone in Intelligence already sees the obvious connections. It's –"

"Shh!" Joe saw three shapes emerging silently out of the opposite woods; they stopped at the trees' edge. Three large blurs watching and listening. Could be deer, elk or horses. Joe crouched lower. The Winchester had an open sight on a short barrel, one round in the breech and five in the magazine. He wondered how good Captain Augustino was with the Marlin.

The first breath of day was a leaden grey light. Stars dulled and disappeared while the three blurs came into focus. Elk or deer, from their utter quiet, Joe was sure. They were waiting to make sure the meadow slope was safe, just as he was waiting to be certain of his shot. Gradually he saw them. Two bull elks and a pregnant elk cow. Strange a cow would be with bulls at this time of year, he thought. He aimed at the bull on his side, assuming the captain would take the other. The bucks were beautiful, dark heads and big antlers ahead of their soft, tan bodies. A heart shot, he decided. His own heart stood still, waiting, watching the lightening slope of meadow snow growing against the angle of pines. The three elk stood on shadows.

Augustino shot and the elk cow dropped in a heap. The bucks bolted into the woods and crashed through the trees.

"You didn't fire," Augustino said.

"You shot the cow."

"I gave you the bucks."

Joe stood up. "You don't shoot a cow that's carrying. She was carrying, anyone could see that. You said you were a hunter. You're an asshole."

"Sergeant, you missed your –"

"You don't shoot a cow that's carrying. At least I thought you were a hunter. I listened to this garbage of yours about Jews, this fucking drivel, because you're an officer. But you don't shoot a cow that's carrying. You're fucking crazy, Augustino, you know that? This shit about Marx. I lived in New York. I marched for the Spanish Civil War vets. I had two co-eds screwing me for a solid month to teach me about Marx, while you were still beating off in the sheets of Brownsville. And when I was ten I knew you don't shoot a cow that's carrying."

"I'm warning –"

"Don't warn me!" Joe ripped away the bough over Augustino's head and then swung the Winchester against the trunk.

The rifle cracked in half. Barrel and breech flew away while the stock stayed in Joe's hand. He threw it aside. "Don't warn me."

"Go on," Captain Augustino's tone changed. He hadn't budged when the rifle had sliced over his head, though the colour went from his face, making the half-moons under his eyes even darker.

Joe started across the snow for the elk cow. The top of her neck was blown off and her legs sprawled in every direction, but her eyes were still wet and alive. The pregnant belly rose distended and hard above the rest of her.

"Let me tell you," Joe yelled. "Your wife says you have a prick the size of a wet inchworm. It's got to be twice the size of your brains."

He walked faster through the snow, unbuckling his coat away from the .45 that rode inside his belt. He felt Augustino raising the rifle behind him. Heart shot? Head shot? With the .45 free he took the last ten steps on the run. When Augustino shot, he was already diving.

The cow kicked as the second bullet hit. He landed on the other side and rolled back against the elk. Captain Augustino stood, disdaining cover, and levered another round into the breech. Joe rested the .45 on the cow and put the captain in the square notch of the gun's sights, for all the good that would do considering the accuracy of an automatic. He squeezed the trigger. The gun bucked and a branch exploded five feet above Augustino's head. "Shit!" He squeezed off another. Bark blew off a tree next to the captain.

Augustino slipped behind branches. All Joe could see of him was the vapour of his breath and the tip of the rifle. His own breath came like the steam of an engine. The cow was too small. If Augustino started to stalk and come from a different angle, Joe was dead.

The rifle barrel levelled again, but aimed at where the bucks had vanished. Then Joe saw them coming out of pines, two men in blankets and snowshoes, their faces and hands blackened with paint, long hair unbraided and loose. The first was stooped with age, and he led the second with a long cord tied to the wrist, as if he were blind. The man being led shouldered a net stuffed with dead bluejays; the net looked like a brilliant, blue wing. There was one owl in the net, and one nighthawk, birds that could only be netted against a moon. The men must have heard the shots, probably saw them, but they crossed the meadow between the elk and the trees where Augustino hid, neither quickening nor stopping, slowly trudging down the snowy slope with the prizes of their own hunt. Though they seemed to be heading in the direction of Santiago, Joe didn't recognize them. They moved like an apparition, or a short parade from another world. Then they reached a line of aspen at the bottom of the slope and were gone.

"Sergeant!" Augustino yelled. "I've changed my mind. I don't want to kill you. I do want to kill you, but I have more important things to do."

"The hell you do."

"I have duties to perform." Augustino stepped forward into the clearing, his rifle in his left hand, barrel up. "I can't allow myself to be distracted, to enjoy mere personal vindication, to sink to your level."

"It was your idea to come here."

"Shoot an officer and it's your life, Sergeant." Augustino dropped the rifle as he approached. "We came for an elk and we shot one, that's all that transpired. Nothing else really happened."

"Because you missed."

"You're not in a position to publicly accuse me of anything, not a sergeant fornicating with the wife of the officer he accuses. This is an experience to put behind us. A morning's hunt, is all." He stopped twenty feet short of Joe.

"You don't shoot a cow that's carrying." Joe aimed. Head shot? At this range, a .45 could take off the captain's head from the brow up.

"We have to get back to the Hill to pick up the Director and General Groves." Augustino looked at his watch. "Mrs Augustino will be going to Sunday service."

"You want to get rid of me, Captain, why don't you just post me to the Pacific or Europe?"

"No, you serve me better where you are."

"Doing what? Driving? Opening doors? Screwing your wife?"

"The information, Sergeant."

"Useless." Joe got to his feet.

"Not at all, Sergeant. It makes you an informer."

"There's got to be something else."

"Think of it this way. What we're building here is a secret weapon, right? You're my secret weapon. Your other choice is the stockade, if you want to go back there."

"You're a lunatic, Captain."

"What can you do about it?"

Heart shot? At this range, a round would punch out the captain's heart, aorta, half a lung. Joe let the gun hang straight down. Fired. The elk's legs jerked once, like a spasm in a dream. It stretched its neck across his feet. Its eye faded and died.

"I'll expect a report later on anything Oppenheimer says conversations with Groves especially. anything political in particular." Augustino hadn't flinched. He took the deep, satisfied breath of a man turning home. "The usual."

5

The car was a blue Buick sedan with a V8 engine and grey plush interior. In the back were Brigadier General Leslie Groves and Oppy; in front, Klaus Fuchs, a field radio, and, at the wheel, Joe. The inside of the windows beaded with sweat. Outside, all of New Mexico seemed to tip from Los Alamos, mesa turning to foothills of black nut pines, piñons, on white snow.

The general's whole body looked tucked, badly, into his uniform. Groves was a tall man, his grey hair was vigorous and wavy, his moustache bristled and his eyes were bright as steel, but below the collar, starched khaki and overcoat bulged everywhere under the pressure of soft fat. General Groves was fond of Los Alamos. His domain extended from the giant production plants of Hanford, Washington, and Oak Ridge, Tennessee, to the original labs in Chicago, but they were run by Union Carbide and DuPont or the pain-in-the-ass Europeans in Chicago, whereas Los Alamos was his personal duchy and run by his inspired choice, Oppenheimer, and was the real heart and soul of the project, the greatest scientific effort in the history of mankind. The Buick, the best car in the motor pool, was always set aside for him when he came and he was always driven by Joe. Other brass and VIPs who had come from Washington with the general referred to Joe as "Groves' Indian". The story got around that even the President had asked Groves about his "Indian companion".

Oppy wore an old Army greatcoat that could have been wrapped round him twice and a pork pie hat that emphasized the narrowness of his skull. His hands fidgeted because the

40

general allowed no smoking in the car. Klaus Fuchs sat practically at attention in an overcoat and fedora, rimless glasses that seemed to flatten his eyes.

Groves hadn't wanted anyone from the British Mission, they thought Los Alamos was Oxford, but as Oppy said when he picked up the general, Fuchs wasn't really British.

"I'm going to see the President tomorrow," Groves said. "He's going to ask me why we need a test. We have barely enough uranium for a single bomb, and hardly any plutonium at the moment. Why should we waste any of it on a test, he'll ask."

"There are two separate devices," Oppy said slowly and patiently, not because Groves was stupid but because the general was not naturally articulate and these were the simple words Oppy wanted passed to Roosevelt. "There is the uranium device, which has basically a gun-barrel design. We don't expect to have enough refined uranium until July and a little thereafter, but we're confident the device will work. Then there is the plutonium device, which has a complicated 'implosion' design. By July, we expect to have enough plutonium for two bombs, and by August enough plutonium for two more bombs, and by September plutonium for two more, but we have no certainty the design will work. It's the plutonium device we have to test, and it's the armoury of plutonium devices that will end the war, not the single detonation of our uranium device. You can tell the President that choosing a test site is a sign of confidence."

"We're depending heavily on this site being right," the general said. "The alternative test sites are some islands off California, sand bars off Texas, some dunes in Colorado. The last place I want to hide an atomic blast in is California."

"That depends on how big it is, of course," Oppy said.

"Well, how big will it be?" Groves demanded.

"Five hundred tons of TNT is the current estimate of the yield," Fuchs answered. He was part of the Theoretical Group estimating the blast.

"Couldn't it be much larger?"

41

"Theoretically, it could be five thousand tons, fifty thousand tons. Almost no limit."

"Five hundred is a start." Groves was mollified. "I'm going to tell the President we're going to set it off on the Fourth of July."

"Wonderful," Oppy said.

Too bad we missed Christmas, Joe thought. Maybe this was the time to tell the general that the head of security on the Hill was of the considered opinion that Joe Stalin's special agent was Robert Oppenheimer and they ought to pull off the road and get the whole thing sorted out. Even if there was nobody capable of taking Oppy's place and even if test, bomb and ultimate victory had to be scuttled.

Maybe this wasn't the time. Perhaps this was the best time to be a dumb sergeant, the "Indian companion".

As soon as they hit the highway at Esperanza, Joe put his foot down. The wartime speed limit was 35 mph, but the general always preferred to cruise at 85. Petrol rationing had largely emptied the roads and the prow of the Buick could roll on two-lane tarmac, sometimes narrowing to one lane, with wide shoulders for slow-moving donkey trains, carts, wagons.

Santa Fe passed as an electric glow under an ash-coloured sky. An Army hospital was pumping money into the town. Signs offered drinks, boots, curios.

As Oppy and Groves droned on about problems of the isolation of isotopes and allotropic states of plutonium, Joe wondered why he had gone to bed with Mrs Augustino. Was it her he wanted? Some other woman? Any woman?

Like a conscience a state trooper's motorcycle emerged, siren wailing, from behind a sign that said, "War Bonds Are Bullets!"

The general's travels were secret; it was understood he didn't want to talk to any local justice of the peace. Joe floored the accelerator. New Mexican troopers had black uniforms and black bikes. At 100 mph, the dark silhouette became a dot in the rearview mirror. Swaying on passenger straps, Groves and Oppy went on talking about construction schedules. Fuchs spoke only when asked, otherwise he was as quiet as a drawer. Information on hand but only when demanded.

In the fields, the breeze rattled rows of chilli, unpicked because a farmer could walk into Boeing's Albuquerque office and keep on straight to Seattle to build B-29s and draw more money in a month than he'd ever seen in a year.

"Explode. Implode. Two apparently contradictory events at the same moment," Oppy was saying. "I wouldn't suggest trying to explain it to the President. Still, it is a sweet concept."

Past Albuquerque and through the lower valley, crossing the Rio so often it seemed a dozen rivers, Oppy and Groves discussed problems ranging from plutonium assembly to sugar for the commissary. The car pressed against a headwind towards grey clouds that built and receded at the same time. At Antonio, a farming town of dimly lit windows, they left the highway for an eastbound single lane of frayed tarmac, crossed the Rio one last time and entered a vast, tilted basin of scrub and low cactus. There, the clouds moved forward and snow began to fall, lightly to begin with, tracing the wind, more heavily as the sun was covered, packing on the wipers and coating the headlights.

"If Hitler had the bomb . . ." Groves said. "We get reports that this winter offensive of the Germans is just to stall while he finishes some secret weapon. Suddenly he has jet-propelled planes, new rockets."

"If Hitler has the device, he'll use it on the Russians," Oppy said.

"Is that a bad idea?" Groves asked.

Joe swung off the road and stopped the car. Its nose pointed at barbed wire fence and white flakes. The fence posts were split pine, as grey as bones, spaced eight feet apart and leaning from habit away from the wind. There was no proper gate with crossbeam or hinges, just a section with two strands of barbed wire stretched to a stick hung by plain wire to a post, so stick and section could simply be unhung and dragged out of the way. Inside the fence was meagre grazing land, brushwood and sage flattened by the headlights. Yucca spines dipped and waved in the snow.

"Stallion Gate," Joe announced.

"There's no one here." Groves looked up and down the road. "There's supposed to be a half-track and two jeeps waiting for us. You're sure this is it?"

"Yes, sir." Joe pointed to the slightly whiter double track of an access road that ran under the bottom wire. "They would have come to the gate. I'll see if I can raise them."

The field radio was a pre-war crank model with a range in good weather of forty miles, and the answer, when it came, hovered on static. The party from the Alamogordo base had lost a track and lost time, but would still meet them at the fence.

As Groves slumped back in his seat the entire car moved on its springs. "I'm supposed to be in Washington tomorrow and here we are twiddling our thumbs at a barbed wire gate."

"Joe, you're the only one who's ever been here before," Oppy said. "What's your advice?"

"The weather's getting worse. I suggest we wait."

"Sergeant, I have never accomplished anything by standing still." Groves sat forward, decision made. "There's no more than an inch on the ground. We'll meet them en route."

It took ten minutes for Joe to put chains on the rear tyres, untie the gate, drive through and, for etiquette's sake, tie it up again. Everyone got back into the car, slapping flakes from their coats, and they started off on the faint trail that wandered across the field.

Joe drove in second gear, trying to keep his lights on the ruts without getting his wheels into them. Fuchs studied a grazing service map.

"How do you think they lost a track?" Oppy asked.

"Link pins," Groves said. "Tanks, half-tracks, bulldozers, same thing. If they had trouble with a drive wheel, they'd be stopped dead."

Joe shifted to low as the road vanished.

"We're almost in Mexico. How much snow can there be?" Fuchs wiped condensation from the windshield. "They said they were coming to meet us, yes? We should be seeing them any minute."

After a long silence, Joe said, "We should have seen them half an hour ago."

Snow rushed in sheets against the car as it pushed over the rise and fall of the ground. When Joe found the road again, he was happy to lay his wheels in the ruts and try to stay in them. He put his head out of the window to avoid Fuchs' urgent wiping. There were signs of humped earth, craters, moments of impact frozen in the snow.

"It's like sailing." Oppy was delighted. "Same dark sky, same white, same swells."

"I remember my first time at sea," Fuchs said, suddenly talkative. "It was when the British shipped us to Canada as enemy aliens at the start of the war. U-boats attacked the convoy. They sank the ship just before us."

"I didn't know you were an enemy alien," Groves said.

"I'm British now," Fuchs assured him.

"German and British," Groves added drily.

Implode. Explode. Two events at the same time. On the troop-ship to Manila, Joe had watched the ocean. For lack of anything else to do, there being no women on board, and no card-playing either – because the officers were so wound up about going to serve under MacArthur Himself, Joe stood on deck and observed the sea. He watched for big events and little events, from surfacing whales through families of dolphins to haphazard flying fish. One day he noticed something new: contradiction. The wind was stiff and easterly, driving rows of whitecaps from stern to bow. But the ship was plunging, trudging like a farmer in boots, through heavy swells churned up by storms a thousand miles ahead in the west. The surface of the water, the ragged spume, was merely sliding, a deception, over the true internal intent of the sea. The hidden intent. Joe remembered because it was the first moment he realized he and everyone else on the ship might not be coming back from Manila.

"Sir, I think we're there." Joe killed the car engine and lights. An easier snow of fewer, fatter crystals fell.

Fuchs sat bolt upright and said like a vaudeville comic. *"Was ist das?"*

Heading over a rise and towards the car were three men carrying rifles.

"Mescaleros," Joe said. "Apaches."

"Talk to them," Oppy said.

Groves said as Joe got out, "Keep them away from the car so they don't recognize us."

Two of the men were father and son, each almost as big as Joe, both in snowshoes. They had long hair, wool hats, greasy jackets, one sheepskin and the other corduroy. Clothes and hair were dusted with snow and their faces shone with sweat. The third man had a slightly squarer head, shorter hair, a plaid Pendelton jacket, rags wrapped round his hands and feet. Navajo, Joe thought. None of them looked like they would recognize Groves and call Tokyo. But what the hell was a Navajo doing down here?

"See the horses?" the old man asked Joe.

"Horses?"

"Horses everywhere," the old man said.

Joe passed out cigarettes. Apaches were Chinese to Joe. Navajos were thieves. Likewise, Apaches and Navajos thought all Pueblos were women. The Navajo moved close enough to take a cigarette and stepped back. Flakes drifted down. The storm was resting, not leaving. The Navajo's rifle was casually held towards the car.

"They kicked off the white ranchers," the father said. "They", Joe knew, meant the Army. "Still horses, though. If we don't take them, they just shoot them."

"They come over in planes and machine-gun them," the son said. "Sometimes, they bomb them. Day and night."

"Could be Texans," Joe said.

The Apaches erupted. They slapped each other on the shoulder and they slapped Joe. Even the Navajo laughed nervously.

"Those bastards," the son said. "Army planes, they're crazy."

"Army bought the ranchers out," the father confided, "but they made it in one payment so the ranchers had to give it all back in taxes, and if the ranchers try to get back on the land, they bomb them."

"Sheep up north." The Navajo had a high voice and clipped his words in half. "Someone in Washington says an Indian can only have eighty-three sheep. Part of the War Effort. What do sheep have to do with the war?"

"Nothing," Joe said.

"Indian Service comes and kills the sheep. Shoot you if you get in the way."

Joe remembered now. Near Gallup, a gang of Navajos had taken a couple of Service riders hostage and then vanished. Across the state, newspapers were treating it like an uprising. The Indian Service and the FBI were looking for the fugitives all the way north to Salt Lake City. Not south, with Mescaleros.

The young Apache looked speculatively at Joe. "You ever fight in Antonio?"

"Yeah."

"You fought my brother in Antonio. They put up a real ring at the motor lodge behind the café. Kid Chino?"

"He was drunk, he shouldn't have got in the ring."

"He was sure sober when you were done." He stomped his snowshoe for emphasis. "That was the soberest I ever saw him."

Joe recalled the brother, all piss and steam the first round, throwing up in the second.

"Pretty good fighter, your brother."

"A good boy." The old man glared at the son with him.

Joe passed the cigarettes round again. The Apaches examined the lighter, a Zippo. "Battery C, 200th Coast Artillery" was engraved on one side.

"Bataan." The son handed it back.

The father looked up. "Good weather. Bombers can't fly and it's easy tracking in the snow."

Joe didn't see any signs. He was a fair tracker, but he was no Apache.

47

"Better you get the horses than no one."

Finally, the Navajo shivered and lowered his rifle. The four men smoked, contemplating the quiet between the low sky and snow-covered ground. Then the father and son killed their butts and nodded to Joe. The Navajo followed. The three men, the Navajo on the outside, moved off to the north, making a wide arc round the car. Wouldn't that have been an interesting end to the atom bomb, though, Groves and Oppy gunned down in the snow in return for sheep?

Joe opened the general's door. "I don't think they recognized you, sir. I told them they were trespassing on the Alamogordo Bombing and Gunnery Range and would have to leave."

"Seemed a little touch and go," Oppy said.

The Apaches and their friend were already moving out of sight, not so much getting smaller as disappearing between points of snow. The real horizon could be 500 yards away, 1,000, a mile. Oppy emerged from the car, lit a cigarette and lit Fuchs' cigarette, too, with a flourish of relief, as he got out. Groves stepped on to the snow and tilted his head back to perform a professional sweep of the four directions.

Oppy spread the map over the hood. "This is where we are. Latitude 33 40′ 31″, longitude 106 28′ 29″."

"So, where is that?" Groves asked.

"East are the Oscura Mountains." Joe pointed. "South, Mockingbird Gap; west, three volcanoes the locals call Trinity; north, Stallion Gate." Each way was a wall of white.

Where Joe had pinned the map down with his finger, Fuchs made an X with a soft pencil and drew a perfect, freehand circle around the X.

"If this is Ground Zero, the point of detonation, we will desire a distance of ten kilometres to the first control shelters."

Groves set a surveying transit in the snow, planting the three legs firmly. The air bubble sat in the middle of the transit level. Flat ground. Confidence was the general's face; he sniffed the air with anticipation. The errant party from Alamogordo was forgotten.

"Just the way we chose Los Alamos," he called to Oppy, "the top men on the spot."

While Groves sighted through the transit telescope, Joe paced off fifty yards with a tape, flags, stakes. Oppy and Fuchs paced off in another direction.

When Groves waved. Oppy set a red flag at Joe's feet.

"Captain Augustino tells me there's a spy on the Hill," Joe said.

"Did he say who?" Oppy looked up with the eyes of an innocent.

"No," Joe lied.

"No names at all?"

"Let's say the person was just a security risk."

"He'd have to be pulled off the project."

"His reputation?"

"Ruined. No names?"

"Let's say I wanted off the Hill. Say I wanted combat."

"That's an Army matter, Joe. The Hill is an Army base, after all. You'd have to go to the head of military administration."

"That's Augustino again."

"The captain is a powerful man in his own little realm."

"Which is the Hill."

"He really didn't give you any names?"

"I suppose he'd tell you if he had a name in mind."

"True." Oppy was relieved. He gave Joe a conspiratorial grin. "Remember, the captain is an intelligence officer. It's his duty to be paranoid."

With the next set of flags, Oppy and Fuchs swapped places.

"It must be interesting to be an Indian." Fuchs followed Joe's measured steps. "To be free of civilization, to live simply as men and women with nature."

"You mean, go naked?"

"No, I mean defy all bourgeois standards of behaviour. You understand what I mean by bourgeois?"

Joe watched Oppy slowly pacing through the snow. A frail figure, his coat whipping around him. He spread his arms, turning, holding flags. and seemed, in his ungainly way, to be dancing in the snow.

They created a model of the test site to come, red flags for directions, lettered stakes to indicate relative distances to control shelters, base camp, observation posts, evacuation roads, populated areas. By the time they gathered by the transit, the model's Ground Zero, snow had almost stopped. Groves' manner was brisk and expansive, an engineer breaking ground. Waving his hand, he described the test tower, miles of wire, roads and trucks he saw in his mind. Oppy had brought a bottle of cognac, and even Groves, who usually drank nothing more than the smallest glass of sherry, accepted a ceremonial sip. Alone in the car, Joe radioed the convoy that was supposed to have met them hours before. He opened his own flask. Vodka. This was not sophistication. Wartime distillers made vodka from potatoes, corn, molasses, grain. From ethane, methane and petrochemicals. From horse sweat and purified piss. Santa Fe liquor stores wouldn't sell a bottle of anything unless you bought a bottle of vodka. Another subversive communist connection.

He drank from his flask while he fished in the static.

". . . difficulty . . . lost a drive wheel . . . soon, over."

Joe read and repeated his map co-ordinates to the static and signed off. The general would miss his flight; he'd have to see Roosevelt another day.

Suddenly it was colder and darker. Clouds flowed by on either side, and directly above was a stream of evening stars. When Joe returned, he made a fire from cowpats he dug out of the snow. The other three, exhilarated from mapping the test site, were still sharing the cognac. It occurred to Joe that these minutes of waiting for the party from the base probably were the first moments of relaxation, of complete and powerless rest, that either Oppy or Groves had had in years.

"You have to wonder whether the Chinese alchemists who discovered gunpowder," Oppy said, "when they were on the verge of discovering gunpowder, were fortunate enough to have a night as quiet and beautiful as this. Perhaps the Emperor of China had horsemen searching for them, as jeeps are searching for us. Perhaps we'll meet them."

"What do you mean?" Groves asked.

"Einstein says time bends around the universe in a curving line. On that line you can go backwards or forwards. We'll never find this same Stallion Gate here again, but we can always find it on some cusp of time. If we could do that, we could meet those Chinese horsemen, too."

"I'll tell you about going back in the past," Groves snorted and filled his hand with caramels from his pocket. "The bitterest day of my life was when I was ordered to rescue this project. I had just been offered my first combat command the week before. A soldier wants to see combat. My father was an Army chaplain, and even he saw combat. There I was, Army born and bred, ordered to spend history's greatest war at home overseeing a bunch of scientific prima donnas who, as far as I could tell, had sold the President a bill of goods." He popped a caramel into his mouth and ruminated. "Well, I don't run phoney projects that don't show results. A lot of scientists and so-called geniuses tried to sell me a bill of goods on how to make this atomic bomb. The greatest American physicist is E. O. Lawrence. I like Lawrence. He put the cyclotron on the map and he won the Nobel Prize, but he's hardly produced a speck of uranium. Nevertheless, I will make this project a success. It's largely a matter of plumbing, albeit complicated." Oppy's eyes glittered with amusement. Groves wiped his fingers in the snow. "In fact, I have never been more positive of success than I am at this very moment, at this very place."

"This will be your monument," Oppy said.

"Monument?" Groves sighed. "After I built the Pentagon, I calculated that in my career I had moved enough earth and laid enough cement to build the pyramids of Cheops two hundred times over."

"This is a different kind of pyramid," Oppy suggested. "This has different blocks, some steel, some gold, some of water, some so radioactive you can't touch them or even come close to them, and the pyramid must be built according to a blueprint no one has ever seen."

"Let me tell you the kind of monument I want," Groves said. "I've seen the estimates of the casualties we're going to suffer in the invasion of Germany and Japan. I wouldn't mind a monument of a million American lives saved."

Groves' sincerity was ponderous and real and demanded silence. Embers slipped and rose.

"The Hindus say that the final vision of Brahma will be mist, smoke and sun, lightning and a moon." Oppy paced in front of the fire, too excited to be still. "Brahma would be a good name for the bomb."

Joe stood on the arc of the fire's light. Outside the arc were rattlesnakes curled up, cold and asleep under the snow. There was a whole map of winter sleep: mice balled up in burrows, toads suspended in mud, nightjars tucked into the folds of the earth. Memory was out there, a map of women curled up in the dark. Japs. Actually, life was very nice when he got to Manila. Mostly what the Army wanted him to do was box. Tour the airfields giving exhibitions against the local champions. Fight in the annual Boxing Festival at Rizal Stadium. Play piano at the Officers Club. When dependants were shipped out, the officers, like men freed from a domestic garden into paradise, came in with the most beautiful whores, coffee-coloured Filipino girls and White Russians with paste jewels. When the invasion came, three days before Christmas, Joe led a platoon of Philippine Scouts. The first night they made contact was in a banana plantation and in the dark among the rustling fronds he heard, "Hey, Joe! Over here, Joe." He'd figured out that Japs called all Americans "Joe", that the Japs hadn't come across the Pacific for him personally, but the voices were unnerving, like the dark come to life. "Joe . . ."

He wished he could listen to the car radio and hear some big band from Albuquerque or, if the ether gave a lucky bounce, a jazz station from Kansas City. Ellington, like a black Indian in an invisible canoe, paddling through the clouds. Paddle, Duke! Rescue me.

Groves was down to his last toffee. "The big picture is, no one else has the industrial base or the technology. Never forget the inherent inefficiency of the Soviet system. It will take them twenty years to develop an atom bomb, if ever."

There was something in the clouds, dim lights moving in and out, and there was the sound of distant thunder.

"A world without war," Oppy said.

"A Pax Americana," Groves agreed.

Lights appeared in the stars between the clouds. A more diffused glow grew in the snow below the lights. Nearer. The general's final caramel grew sticky between his fingers. Oppy cocked his head limply in the manner of the most ethereal saints. Fuchs stared through the flames reflected in his glasses. Joe counted until he heard thunder again.

"Bombers, about six miles off."

"Here?" Groves asked.

"It's a bombing range, sir. Night practice."

"What do they bomb, exactly?" Oppy asked.

"At night," Joe said and looked at the campfire, "illuminated targets."

He broke for the car, dived into the front seat and cranked up the field radio. Through the Buick's windshield he watched the three men kicking apart the fire. Groves was surprisingly nimble, Oppy disjointed as ever. Beyond, blooms of light moved laterally on the horizon. The radio held a roar of static untainted by any coherent transmission.

By the time Joe returned, all that was left of the camp fire was a circle of soot. Fuchs was on his knees, slapping the last embers. With the fire out, the party could see how the moon had escaped the clouds and filled the range with an opalescent haze.

"Can we get away?" Groves asked Joe.

"I noticed on the way in that they like to bomb the stretch of road behind us. If we blink headlights at them, they'll try to drop a fifty-pounder on the hood. Run without headlights and we'll turn over in a ditch. We may as well stay here."

"What if you're wrong?" Fuchs' face was smudged and his

hair stood up straight. "This entire project should not be put in jeopardy because of a stupid Indian."

"Shut up, Klaus," Oppy said softly.

Joe said, "B-29s."

The approaching bombers were huger than anything he had ever seen in the air. Superforts, twenty tons of steel, twice as big as Flying Fortresses, each of their four engines the size of a fighter. Chutes spilled from the bays, floated, and sputtered into flares.

"Good Lord," Oppy said, "this is beautiful."

Why flares? Joe wondered.

The lead bomber lifted reluctantly and the next in line took its place, settling lower with closer attention to the ground. Why so low? Joe wondered. The belly turret turned, its .50-calibre barrels swinging back and forth. He could make out the green light within the Plexiglass nose. A green bombardier not even bothering with his sight pointed straight down, and as if there were a magical connection with his finger a phosphorus bomb lit the valley floor. From the bomb came running shapes, horses, brilliant with lather and the glare of the bomb. racing under the wing. Mustangs out of the mountains for the night grazing and the mares the ranchers had left behind. Joe couldn't make out individual horses, only the motion of their rocking and straining, urged by the dazzle of tracers, and the way they wheeled from rays of burning phosphorus. At a distance of a mile, he thought he could hear not only their hooves but their breath, although he knew they were drowned out by the various sounds of pistons and hydraulics and .50-calibre rounds in the air. Then the mustangs and bombers moved on together, like a single storm, distance muting the sound, and nothing could be seen except a flash that resembled an occasional faraway stroke of lightning.

What Joe remembered best was what Oppy said when they were alone in Alamogordo, after the half-track and jeeps had finally appeared and towed them to the base.

"It was awful, but it was still . . . beautiful."

JUNE 1945

6

In Santiago, calves were cut and branded in the hour before dawn so that the men could catch the morning bus to Los Alamos, where they worked as custodians and furnace stokers.

Joe was alone in the second corral, where steers were brought in for sale. With meat rationing, there was a market for Indian cattle and it was Joe's job to go over them with a Geiger counter. It consisted of a metal wand, wire, and a case with 20 lbs of batteries and a micro ammeter that was useless in the middle of a herd in the dark. The Geiger counter was emitting the audible clicks of gamma rays. At least from one cow. Joe slipped a rope over its head and led it out of the corral and around a hay rick, where a path led to a copse of cottonwoods and willows. A rare rain had fallen the day before and mud sucked on his shoes. In the middle of the copse were cans, mattress springs, shoes and bones cemented in a great mound of sodden ash. He yanked the cow into the pile up to its knees, put his .45 where the vertebrae of the neck joined the dome of the skull and fired. At the last second, the cow, curious, looked up and the bullet tore through the artery of its neck. Blood shot in a solid, black stream over Joe's chest and arm. He held the animal tight and fired again. The cow dropped like a weight. Joe picked up a can of kerosene and poured it over the dead animal, lit it and staggered back from the blaze. In the yellow flames, Joe could see two things. The cow was mottled, its hide half-bleached. Every canyon around Los Alamos had cattle and every canyon had sites where poisonous isotopes were vented or exploded; either way, the isotopes were sown into the soil and water. Which was why the personnel on the Hill underwent nose wipes, ass wipes and radioactive urine checks, but as for the ignorant animals that wandered the sites, Army policy was "kill them, burn them, bury them", and the perfect instrument was Joe. A hide turned white? That was new. The other thing was that through the greedy roar of the fire he could see that the cow was pregnant. He remembered why he was so upset with Augustino when they'd gone hunting. He'd never thought of it since then. Not shooting an animal that was carrying was an Indian stricture, a primitive taboo. Not against the killing the life, but against killing the seed of life. He started for the cow as if he could pull it out of the flames. Realized how stupid it was. Staggered back. Jesus, what a butcher. The way the cow had turned its large, marble eyes up to him. The sideways fountain of blood. As the pyre burned and crackled, he thought of the second heart within the cow.

One moment he was so close to the fire that his shirt was steaming, the next he was in the tangled dark of the willows forcing his way to the road where he'd left the jeep rather than pass by the corrals, rather than see anyone or have anyone see him. As he stumbled out of the woods, headlights ambushed him, as if the burning cow had risen and stalked him.

The lights swerved. A Buick fishtailed to a stop, its rear end in the mud of the shoulder of the road. Ray Stingo and then Oppy came running to Joe, shouting at the same time.

"You okay?"

"What happened?"

"Doing a little native liaison for you," Joe told Oppy.

"The blood –"

"Why was the cow white?" Joe demanded.

"White –"

"The cow I killed because it was hot."

"Hair can react to low levels of radiation. So it's cow's blood." Oppy stared at Joe. "You should see yourself."

"What are you doing here?" Joe asked Ray.

"We went to the train station at Lamy. Early train from Chicago."

Oppy said, "I told Sergeant Stingo to swing by here on the way back so I could ask you to drive Dr Pillsbury around the high explosive sites today. And remember, you're guarding a party tonight."

"Okay, but I want a weekend pass."

"Joe, we're one month from the test."

"I need a pass."

"Why?"

Joe laboured each word. "To get the blood off."

"I'll do what I can." Oppy looked at the car. "You think you can help us get the car back on the road?"

As the three men walked to the Buick, Joe saw that a rear window was rolled down. Of course, Ray and Oppy had gone to the train to meet a passenger. With the final rush to the test, all sorts of people were coming to the Hill from Oak Ridge, New York, Chicago. In the dimness, Joe recognized her by her cool grey-eyed gaze. Fuchs' partner from the Christmas dance. Joe hadn't seen her since.

"He's all right, Anna," Oppy said. "It's not his blood."

"Whose is it?" she asked.

Joe stopped by the bumper. The rear right wheel had made its own well in the mud.

"Get her out so I can move the car over."

"Dr Weiss?" Ray opened the door for her.

She looked at Joe's shirt and could have been scrutinizing the gore on a beast that walked on all fours. Joe noticed the white azalea in her hair; white azaleas were Oppy's favourite. He could just see Oppy offering it to her as she stepped from the train.

"A real giant would be able to lift me, too."

"Anna," Oppy said, "be reasonable."

"Okay," Joe said. "Stay."

"Joe, if the three of us –" Ray began.

Lift me? Joe gripped the chrome handle of the bumper, rocked the car and tested the suction of the ooze on the tyre. He could lift an elephant and kick its ass down the road. Through the rear window her eyes glittered. On the third push the tyre ripped free of the mud and in the same motion Joe straightened and walked the rear end of the Buick on to the road. When he let the car drop, she laughed, as if nothing he did surprised her, let alone scared her.

"Don't forget Harvey Pillsbury." As Oppy got into the car, he gave Joe a worried glance.

Joe had forgotten Harvey, and the cow. Watching the taillights move away, Joe could have sworn he saw the flash of her looking back.

On Two Mile Mesa, south of Los Alamos, bulldozers had cleared piñon, cedar and cactus to make way for test pads and concrete bunkers. There were photo bunkers with spring-forced steel jaws that would snap shut before rocketing debris reached the cameras inside. There were X-ray bunkers, steel-sheathed and coffin-shaped, that resembled ironclad warships sinking into the sand. Plus gauge and meter bunkers. Magazine bunkers. Control bunkers. On the raw plain, the bunkers fought their own war, firing more than ten tons of high explosive a week.

The Hanging Garden was the biggest test site, an entire hilltop shaved level by Jaworski's crew. It looked like an Aztec pyramid forty yards across at the top, but instead of a bloody altar was a steel pad blackened by carbon and fire, and attended not by priests but by a dozen draft-deferred graduate students in shorts and baseball caps. The overall litter of burned cables and broken glass gave a false impression of disorder. There was a pattern. At the outer edges were the periscopes for the flash and rotating prism cameras that would record every microsecond of a blast. Halfway to the pad were deep trenches for pressure gauges. Nearer to the pad, the buried mother cable emerged from the ground to be attached to exposed detonator cables. Almost nudging the pad was an X-ray bunker with the distinctive aluminium nose cone from which the rays would emanate to take their ghostly pictures. On the pad was a waist-high wooden table stamped USED for United States Engineers Detachment and in the middle of the table was a model of a plutonium bomb, a twenty-inch sphere with a steel shell of bright pentagonal plates bolted together at the edges. The team in baseball caps was connecting black cables to the detonator ports in each plate.

Leopold Jaworski wore suit, braces, a military brush of grey hair and moustaches dyed as dark as arrowheads. He had soldiered against Kaiser Wilhelm of Germany, Tsar Nicholas of Russia and Marshal Pilsudski of Poland. In fact, he was the only scientist on the Hill who knew anything about war.

"You see," he explained to Joe, "a uranium device is child's play compared to this. Simply put half your uranium at one end of a barrel, half at the other end, shoot them together with gun cotton and you have your critical mass and chain reaction. But plutonium has to be brought together into a critical mass much faster with high explosive, at 3,000 yards per second. Explosion is not good enough. The explosive in this device crushes and *implodes* a plutonium core into a critical mass."

"That will take a lot of explosive," Joe said, to sound intelligent.

"The energy released by the nuclear fission of one kilogram of plutonium is equal to 17,000 tons of TNT."

Joe nodded to the model on the pad. "You don't have a plutonium core in this, do you?"

"No." Harvey arrived, puffing; he'd gone back down to the jeep for his clarinet, which he carried around like a riding crop. "Leo wants to blow up the table, not the mesa."

"I used a squash ball for this test," Jaworski said. "I assume the core in the full model will be the size of a croquet ball."

"About," Harvey said.

"About?" Jaworski sounded horrified and delighted at once. "Dr Pillsbury, here you are, head of the schedule committee, and you don't know how large the core will be? Isn't the core your very particular assignment?"

"There'll be enough credit to go around if the gadget fizzles."

"Harvey, if this 'gadget fizzles', no one will ever, ever hear of it. The Manhattan Project will be the American doughnut hole of history."

"What are you testing now?" Harvey asked to change the subject.

"Ah, now? We are testing some new detonators that must fire through a bank of high-voltage condensers in the same one-millionth of a second. We are testing lenses of Baratol explosive to focus the shock wave. And we are testing a flash technique for shadow photography."

"We have thirty days until Trinity. All this information is absolutely necessary?"

Jaworski turned to Joe. "Hitler goes to hell. The devil takes him to different rooms to choose his punishment. In the first room, Goering is nailed to a wheel and rolled through boiling oil. In the second room, Goebbels is being devoured by giant red ants. In the third, Stalin is making love to Greta Garbo. 'That's what I want,' Hitler says, 'Stalin's punishment.' 'Very well,' says the devil, 'but, actually, it's Garbo's punishment.' " Jaworski turned back to Harvey. "It helps to have all the information. Don't worry, I've tested weapons for thirty years. I know the military mind. General Groves wants this bomb. I'm confident he will drop something on Japan."

While Jaworski's team had been connecting cables the sky had been changing. June and July were the rainy season. This year, though, rain was replaced by dry electrical storms that rolled like loose cannons down from the Jemez and across the valley. A pair of black clouds exchanged lightning bolts as they moved in an eerie calm towards the Hanging Garden; the thunder was too far away to hear. The entire mesa was falling quiet because orders were, no testing of high explosives while there was lightning and the chance of a power surge. Unperturbed, Jaworski led his men down to the control bunker for lunch.

"Coming?" Joe asked Harvey.

Harvey held up his clarinet. "Might as well stay here and practise. Then I'll sound the all clear."

"Good place. Next to a bomb on a hill in a storm."

"You said I needed practice. Besides, it helps me think."

On his way down, Joe glanced back. Harvey looked like a duckling beside a grey and ugly egg.

The Hanging Garden got its name from the scarlet gilia, paintbrush and yarrow that had taken root and flourished in the turned soil of the hillside. The wild flowers were a brief, improbable splurge of colours – every shade of red, brilliant orange and madder – that turned and waved in any breeze that crossed the dun drabness of the mesa. They twined round the periscopes, overflowed and made the timber facing of the hill into terraces. Speculation claimed the flowers tapped a broken water pipe. Others said Jaworski came in the night with watering cans. At any rate, the Hanging Garden so thrived that the loading platform of the bunker built into the base of the hill seemed more a bower.

"It's one big 'if'," Jaworski told Joe. "It's like Oppy had invited the greatest minds in the world to come and design the greatest 'if' ever seen. But if it works . . . What was the estimate of the blast?"

"Five hundred tons of TNT. You'd know better than me."

"No one knows. Maybe ten times that. Or twenty times. Or forty times."

Jaworski asked Joe to join the team in the shadow of the loading platform and have lunch. But the Hungarian was a devotee of Spam and all there was to drink was milk. The Army had decided that milk counteracted the health hazard of working with TNT, so it supplied tubs filled with ice and bottles of fresh milk. The bottles said on one side, "Buy War Bonds!" Since the siege of Stalingrad, another side said, "Praise Russia!" Joe stayed alone on the apron, the only place at the Hanging Garden where smoking was allowed.

The two clouds drifted closer. He looked for a bowed veil of rain, but it wasn't there. Just the sudden step of lightning two miles off. On the mesa road he could see MPs on horseback searching for cover. Directly across the apron was a magazine bunker. It had twin four-inch-thick doors and was set at an angle in its own earth mound so that any accidental explosion would be directed away from the control bunker. "No

Smoking", was painted in red above the doors. Joe took out his cigarette and lighter, and walked towards the magazine to check the padlock on the latch. Joe had switched locks months before. This lock was his.

As he brought his cigarette to the flame, he felt the hair on the back of his neck rise. Magazine bunker, mesa, sky fused into one white light. The flames slewed sideways, sucked from the lighter. He didn't have time to look up at the top of the Hanging Garden – that was illusion – but he felt it erupt, the light turning from white to peony red, the fireball rise and expand in the majestic silence of compressed eardrums as even the air in his lungs seemed to fly out. Then the ring of the shock wave moved, the pain of sound returned, a puddle of sand rained on the apron.

"Harvey!" Joe shouted as he ran up the chute to the test pad. He heard Jaworski and the others following, yelling as they came.

The wooden table and steel sphere were gone, erased from the pad. The exposed cables had disappeared and the ground around the pad was baked and reverberating, without a weed or an ant, only a shimmer of the finest particles of graphite and gold. In a wider radius were glass and the metal commas of broken gauges. At the edges of the hilltop, the gilia and sage burned. Overhead, the black clouds were gone, as if blown out of the sky. The mountains rose and fell on heat waves. There was no Harvey.

"It was the lightning." Jaworski caught up with Joe. "An electrical surge."

"Cordite!" someone shouted and everyone dived to the ground.

Cordite was another hazard of the Hanging Garden. There was no more reliable explosive than slotted tube cordite, but it had the habit of blowing free of a blast, then catching fire and detonating at a later test. His face in the dirt, Joe saw smoke sputtering near a cable trench. It was the acetone in the cordite that smelled.

A figure rose from the trench. It held half a clarinet in one hand, half in the other. Its head looked like a sunflower, a carbon-smudged face in the centre of stiff blonde hair, just a touch of red at the nose, like half a moustache. The front of his shirt hung down over his belly, which sparkled with black and gold.

"Harvey!" Joe called. "Get down!"

Harvey dropped the separate halves of the clarinet as he stepped up to the smouldering cordite and, with elaborate fumbling, opened his fly. A pink organ popped into view. He hesitated, scanning the bodies lying around the test pad until he spotted Jaworski.

"I've thought about it. The plutonium core will be exactly the size of a croquet ball."

Then he played his golden stream upon the burning cord to the last faint whiff and the last triumphant drop, then sat down and rolled back into the trench.

7

"The Japanese soldier is fanatical and well trained. And confident. He has seized the Korean peninsula and he has routed the armies of China. He holds sway from Singapore to Saigon, and from Shanghai to Peking, dominating his larger, Asiatic counterparts and surprising the British. But – and this is a big but – he has yet to face the prepared forces of the United States and the Philippines."

Joe and some fifty recruits from the Philippine Army were assembled in the village plaza. Three lieutenants from Mac-Arthur's general staff had come to exhort them, taking turns on the concrete pad that served for the market. Today was market day, and behind the soldiers the vendors patiently waited in the mud. They bent under the weight of pots, knives, sharpening wheels, orange bags of saffron, wicker baskets of fish, bottles of quinine tablets, plaster saints, bolts of Dutch cloth, cages of fighting cocks. Selling coconut, breadfruit, green bananas, red bananas, tins of ghee, bricks of tea and coffee, cosmetics, love potions and douches. The villagers were small, brown, broad-nosed: men in loinclothes, women in grass shawls, babies riding hips. The previous day's rain rose from the nipa huts in a heavy vapour redolent of jasmine, rotting fish and pig shit. Flies swam in a shaft of light. The recruits had been issued shorts and bamboo rifles. Joe wore a flat campaign hat and Sam Browne belt. The lieutenants sported white pith helmets and sharp creases.

"And he has yet to fight American and Philippine Christians. The Japanese – whether Buddhist, Taoist or Hindu – regards life as cheap. His soul is his Emperor's, not his own."

The villagers, vendors and recruits nodded blandly. They spoke Tagalog, little Spanish, no English. Their eyes were on the *barrio teniente*, the village leader. When he nodded, they nodded. A dog wandered up to the pad, sniffed and pissed. In its cage, a cock ruffled and settled into green, iridescent feathers.

"It is your Christian duty to defend the Philippines. You recruits will be trained by the finest instructors in the US Army. They will be equipped with the most modern weapons. They will be led by the greatest general. You will be the bastion of Christian democracy in the Pacific. When the Japanese hordes descend on the Philippines, we will stop them on the beaches, we will push them back into the sea, we will sink their adventure to the bottom of Manila Bay."

The *barrio teniente* held a pet iguana on a string. Around its neck the lizard had a chain of gold with a crucifix. It raised its crest and hissed with each tug of the string and the cross sparkled against scales.

"This American sergeant has come from a great desert over the ocean to help defend your islands. He has been especially assigned to turn your patriotic young men into a great new Philippine Army. Listen to him, obey him, follow him, and the Philippines will never fall. Thank you."

The lieutenants stepped back. The *barrio teniente* hesitated, then clapped. Everyone else clapped, so softly it sounded like rain. The lieutenants saluted. Joe saluted and, at once, the recruits did too. But a week later the Japs didn't sail into Manila Bay: they wiped out the air bases at Clark Field and Iba, landed at Vigan and Legaspi, at each end of Luzon Island, and started marching towards Manila in the middle. Joe remembered one of his recruits who pissed on a bomb, a dud that had torn through the bell tower of a church. It was an act of frustration because the anti-aircraft ammunition was so old and corroded it detonated under 5,000 feet. Mitsubishi bombers flew at 6,000 feet and dropped bombs all day long. So the recruit stood on the edge of the hole this bomb had made in the sacristy and unleashed his personal torrent of scorn down on to the dud. He was big for a Filipino, in a loose shirt, shorts, American boots. Joe was having a smoke by the altar. Only it wasn't a dud, the bomb had a time-delayed fuse. High explosive expanded at about 10,000 feet per second (that's all explosions were, expanding gases), but Joe always believed there had to be some moment, however brief, of shock, understanding and disappointment in the boy's mind before he was dead. Before the bomb turned the church tower into the barrel of a gun and turned the boy into the projectile that was shot up through it. Some moment, some understanding. If brief, at least bright.

Across the mesa, an afternoon caravan of MPs moved slowly, avoiding each rock and possible snake. As the men and horses passed out of sight, Joe slipped out from under a piñon tree and down the chute of the Hanging Garden to the loading apron. He flipped a whittled stick in one hand. The control bunker was empty. He had thirty minutes before he was supposed to be at one of Oppy's rare parties back on the Hill.

When Joe had replaced the padlock on the magazine bunker months before, he'd left a key inserted which the scientists used and meticulously guarded as if they were carrying out strict Army security. He opened the lock with his own copy of the key, squeezed through the door, shut it, turned on a flashlight and set it on a shelf. On both sides were shelves of meters, gauges, film magazines, copper and alloy tubes. In a cage at the back was the high explosive. Joe could make out Torpex, Baratol, Comp B, Pentolite, all TNT-based explosives. Also cordite, Primacord, smoke pots, gelignite, primers and Navy powder. The cage went from the floor to within a foot of the ceiling and its door had a combination lock. He could reach over the cage top and nearly touch the high explosive.

From his pocket Joe took a buckskin strap and tied it to one end of the stick. When he was a kid, he and his friends used to hide along the Rio in the winter and trap juncos. The fat grey birds liked to flock on banks where the snow had melted. The boys tied horsehair nooses to willow branches above the river's edge and caught two birds at a time, singed the feathers off in a fire and ate them hot. Delicately, Joe slid the buckskin noose over a brick of gelignite. The explosive would go to Santa Domingo, a pueblo south of Santa Fe; there were some veterans among the Domingos, some real experts in explosives. The gelignite fell on its side. He shook the stick to draw the noose tight, gently lifted the brick clear of the shelf and brought it over the top of the cage to his free hand. It was cool as clay. The second brick slid loose as it came over the top and Joe caught it waist-high.

The New Mexico National Guard had arrived in Manila in September 1941. They were chosen, supposedly, because New Mexicans were brown and spoke Spanish and would mix well with Filipinos. Rudy Peña had volunteered for the Guard because of his brother Joe.

Joe hardly remembered Rudy. He was ten years younger, pudgy, quick to cry. His black hair stood up like rooster feathers. He was a wetter of the bed he shared with Joe. A longtime crawler, a late talker. During the worst winter, when the Army came through Santiago and threw from their trucks 50 lb sacks of dried milk that were frozen hard as cement bags, Joe dragged a sack in each hand while his little brother clung to his leg and bawled, his face a mask of frozen snot. The harder Joe tried to kick him off, the tighter he held on.

By sixteen, Joe had left the pueblo and all he saw of Rudy were the photos from Dolores: Rudy and rabbits, Rudy on a horse, Rudy in a tie; the soft and surly face developing into a stranger with dark, nearly Arab looks who was growing up in a world that, to Joe, consisted entirely of letters and pictures. After the years of fighting and music in New York, it was a shock to Joe to hear he'd meet his brother in the middle of the Pacific.

Joe was training the newly constituted Philippine Army, and when he got back to Manila the Guard had already rolled out to Clark Field. The history of the Guard was a huge and intricate joke. Coming from land-locked New Mexico, they were trained in coast artillery. On arrival they were given British First World War surplus cannons. Within a week of the invasion, they were fighting as infantry in the jungle. General MacArthur said the Philippines would never fall and President Roosevelt dispatched convoys of ammunition and supplies to Manila. But out at sea the convoys turned round and headed for Europe. And MacArthur slipped away one night in a torpedo boat.

Before Joe ever found him, Rudy vanished on Bataan. The New Mexico National Guard vanished on Bataan. Joe escaped. When he arrived Stateside and toured defence plants, the colonel in charge of publicity called him a walking advertisement for the Army, which seemed illogical to Joe, since he was one of a handful of men who got out of the Philippines while thousands didn't. Dolores seemed to agree with Joe. She wrote to tell him not to come to Santiago because as far as she was concerned her only real son, Rudy, was dead. So, instead of going home, Joe took the colonel's wife to bed and got shipped to Leavenworth.

One trick of the Japs was to tie themselves high up in the fronds of a coconut palm. A sniper would eat a handful of rice, then swallow water from a canteen to make the rice swell and the stomach feel full. A Jap could stay up in a tree for three days. But this Jap had been up for a week or more, tied so tight he couldn't come down. Swaying in the breeze and watching the world go by: planes, patrols, clouds. Joe wouldn't have seen him if he hadn't stepped on a rifle and looked up at the face staring down from the palm. The head was black as a coconut, holes for eyes, hole for a mouth, shirt and stomach burst open. A flying advertisement for Bataan.

Joe often wondered, when at night the Japs called "Hey Joe!", "Over here, Joe!", did Rudy Pena ever think there was some confusion, that they'd come for the wrong man?

Without even trying to be quiet, he closed the magazine bunker door, snapped the padlock shut and followed his flashlight across the apron towards the Hill.

Joe figured he owed the Army nothing.

8

Oppy had taken over the house of the headmaster of the old Ranch School. It was a stone and timber cottage behind a stand of spruces at the end of Bathtub Row. The sun had just set over the Jemez, leaving the sky bright and the mesa dark. Joe had strapped on his Sam Browne belt and ·45. His guard post was the garden.

Through the windows, the cocktail party had the quality of the pages of an illustrated book being idly turned. The Oppenheimers entertained infrequently and briefly, and when they did, only the highest level of the Hill's scientific community was invited, so the guest list was basically European. Their faces were rosy with tension and drink. Joe saw Fermi and Foote arguing, the bemused Italian rocking impassively on his heels while the Englishman gesticulated with a highball. Fermi's wife and Teller's wife, two small dark women, leaned close for a confidence on the sofa. The ensemble of faces changed from moment to moment, but everyone inside seemed to glow.

"Sergeant, you look lonely." Kitty Oppenheimer brought out a Scotch for Joe. With a smile she would have been a pretty woman. Her brown hair was a tangle. She managed to look blowsy and sharp at the same time.

"Thanks." Joe took the glass.

"Shoot to kill."

"I will."

"Shit." She tripped on a boy's scooter and landed on her back in a flower bed. "My zinnias. Nothing's going right. Let me rest, for God's sake." She waved away Joe's hand. "They're singing the 'Marseillaise' again in there. Give me a smoke."

Joe set the drink on the grass, put a Lucky in her mouth, lit it.

He said, "You're pissed as a skunk."

"Goddamn right. I am. Sergeant, what I meant to say when I came out was you look lovely. You do. All dark and Byronic out here in the gloaming. She's pretty, isn't she, Joe? And young. He was engaged to her sister once. did you know that?"

"Who?"

Kitty rambled on. "He was a real hero to Anna, I suppose. Men do that to little girls. Then when the girls grow into women, the men try to stay romantic figures. There are any number of interesting psychological aspects. I have my breath back."

Kitty gave Joe her hand and he pulled her to her feet. The story was that she was part European nobility, related to Admiral Canaris of the Abwehr.

"Can you stand?"

"I must return to my duties as hostess of the Royal Society of Prickless Physicists."

"Can you walk?"

"The funny thing is, at a certain point you don't worry about other women at all. If you're smart, you worry about girls."

"Take a deep breath. Today Germany, tomorrow the world." Joe picked a flower from her shoulder. "You can do it."

"I look like Ophelia." Kitty had a throaty, corroded laugh. "I always thought I'd be Lady Macbeth."

After Kitty returned to the house, Joe poured out the Scotch. The party would be over soon. He'd go to Santa Fe to deliver the gelignite waiting in his jeep and then he'd have his drink. Besides, some guests were wandering into the garden now to take advantage of the evening, the hour between the heat of the June day and the cold of the mountain night. The altitude of the Hill was 7,000 feet. Voices seemed to carry, or maybe voices were louder. In the last month, since the defeat of

Germany and the death of Hitler, all the émigrés seemed wrapped in a rubicund patriotism, as if their Americanism had been confirmed. They'd make Trinity work, no matter what. He saw Kitty inside with Oppy and the woman who had been in Oppy's car that morning. Joe didn't remember her name. Kitty sat on the hearth and the new arrival stood at the far end of the fireplace while between the two women Oppy leaned, almost contorted, at an angle across the mantelpiece. The toe of his Wellington touched Kitty's knee and his long fingers stroked the glass that the younger woman had set on the corner of the mantelpiece. He looked like a poet dictating. Kitty, a toughened muse. The redhead both cool and fascinated.

"One grenade here could change the history of physics, couldn't it, Sergeant?"

Captain Augustino had rolled up to the garden gate and stopped his jeep behind Joe's.

Joe saluted.

"Yes, sir."

"What in the world are they doing now?"

A radio was being handed out through a window. The sound of piano drifted across the garden to the cars. Joe hadn't realized until that second that the mesa crickets were chirping away. Beethoven. A sonata with insects luring the entire party outside, except for Oppy and the two women.

"I think that's the Hill station, sir. I think that's Teller playing."

Los Alamos transmitted a signal that died before it reached the valley. Teller was sloppy on technique, but his playing had a lot of momentum.

"Sergeant, what would you say if I told you that Mrs Augustino was dead? That she was shot by an intruder back in Texas and that the intruder had escaped?"

The Beethoven was coming to a crescendo. No one in the garden could hear what was said by a captain and sergeant at the gate.

"I'd say you were lying, sir. Why would you kill her when you can make her pay for the rest of her life?"

73

"Sergeant, you show real promise. Come closer."

In the garden the music was followed by light static. There was a hush of anticipation as people stood around the radio. The glow of cigarettes in the shadows.

"Sir?"

"Wait," Augustino said.

"Once upon a time in a dark wood there lived three little pigs," a deep voice with a middle-European accent issued from the radio in the grass. Teller again, reading bedtime stories. *"The first little pig was a poet. The second little pig was an artist. But the third little pig was a practical pig who enjoyed working with hammers and saws."*

"Go on," Augustino urged Joe.

"I didn't drive Oppy today. I have nothing to report."

"With Dr Oppenheimer, there's always something to report. He went all the way to the railroad station to pick up a Dr Weiss. They came by Santiago. You met them. What did they say?"

"Nothing. Their car went off the road and I helped them out, and that was it."

"Sergeant, it wasn't the grace of God that got you out of the stockade, it was me. I can send you back to that hole any time I want. We have a deal."

"But they didn't say anything, sir."

"The poet was a lazy pig and made himself a house out of nothing but straw. Straw walls, straw tables and chairs and a straw door he always left open –"

"I have an FBI report that a Soviet courier is on the way or already here. Suddenly, Dr Oppenheimer takes the time to meet this Dr Weiss and personally escort her here. It doesn't make sense. You've seen her?"

"It was dark this morning."

"She's in there with the Oppenheimers right now. It could be a regular communist cell meeting. Wouldn't it be interesting to know what they're saying right now, to know whatever they say when they think they're alone?" Augustino pondered the possibility. He looked up at Joe. "I want you to keep an eye

74

on Dr Weiss. I want you to get close to her. Use your Indian charm. Next time we talk, have something for me."

The captain started his jeep, reversed and U-turned back towards the lodge. There were laughs in the garden.

"Or I'll huff," Teller's voice rose dramatically. *"And I'll puff. And I'll blow your house in –"*

9

Sante Fe was an hour away, but it was the shopping and social centre of the Hill. People went to Woolworth or Sears during the day, and at night they went to La Fonda. Situated on the plaza in the centre of Santa Fe, the hotel was a three-storey mock-adobe fantasy with exposed beams and wooden balconies. For fiesta, a mariachi band played on a balcony. During Christmas, the roof was illuminated by candles set in sand behind paper bags. The hotel had also become, thanks to the Hill, an outpost of the FBI.

It was the task of the Bureau to watch everyone from the Hill who came into Santa Fe. Since everyone went to the bar of La Fonda, the agents stationed themselves comfortably in the hotel lobby. Joe had cut the gelignite into flat strips, wrapped it and the primers tightly in newspaper and tucked them into a folded newspaper. When he entered with this innocuous package under his arm, half a dozen agents stirred, then recognized Oppy's bodyguard and settled back into rustic leather chairs. The agents called anyone from the Hill a "longhair". From Oppy on down, people from the Hill called the agents, identifiable by their straw snapbrim hats, "creeps".

The bar was full. Santa Fe was the state capital and attracted a large number of alcoholics who were legislators or lobbyists, plus oilmen, cattlemen and tourists. The bartender was a strategically placed agent. For once, Joe didn't see Harvey or anyone else from the Hill. It had taken him two hours to get to Santa Fe because he'd had two flat tyres on the Pojaque Creek shortcut to the highway. All he wanted to do was deliver the high explosive and keep on going to Albuquerque and the Casa Mañana.

"A bourbon," Joe said, since he was there.

"That's against the law." A gnome in a white suit hopped on to the stool next to Joe. Hilario "Happy" Reyes waved a Havana panatella as if in the comfort of his living room – which, in many ways, the bar of La Fonda was. "Tsk, tsk, serving liquor to an Indian? I suppose we can make an exception of the Chief."

"No more than you," Joe said.

Hilario was lieutenant-governor of the state of New Mexico. Better, he was legend. He was from Santiago Pueblo and Joe had seen old pictures of him dancing in white buckskin leggings at the Omaha Exposition of 1898. But when statehood came in 1912, Hilario had become "Happy" Reyes, a Spanish politician, and he had served in every state administration, only once falling as low as judge. Since Roosevelt's second term, he'd become a Democrat. He was ancient and vigorous, as powerful as a joker in the pack, a worn but still potent magician.

"To the home of the brave." Joe picked up his drink.

"I want you to fight, Joe. I have a boy from Texas. Natural southpaw. Fast. Knocks them out with either hand. Hasn't had a fight that's gone four rounds. Works up on the Hill with you."

"You're setting up fights again?"

"Joe, it's the spirit of the times. Entertainment. Baseball hasn't stopped. There's a one-armed out-fielder playing for the St Louis Browns right now. Hasn't stopped baseball." After years of wearing his white planter's hat, like a girl holding a parasol against the sun, Hilario's brown skin had acquired a pallor that made his eyes, which were black as tar, all the more startling. "Joe, when you're as old as I am you find out that people lead very short lives."

"I noticed that in Bataan."

"Then the experience wasn't wasted. Now it's time again for fun. I want you to meet a fan of yours."

"Harry Gold." Hilario's friend popped out from behind the

77

stool. Gold was short, swarthy and so fat he looked inflated inside his double-breasted suit. He wobbled on new boots and removed a new stetson to shake Joe's hand. His hair was dark and wavy.

"Harry's a New York Jew," Hilario said.

"I saw you play with Charlie Parker on 52nd Street," Gold told Joe. "And a couple of weeks ago, at the Casa Mañana. I always wondered what happened to you."

"Joe used to be the Indian Joe Louis until that nigger music got to him. Joe, you're still popular. The boy has beaten everyone in the state. You're the only action left."

"I haven't fought for two years, Hilario."

"That's not so dangerous for a fighter of your quality. Anyway, you're like a thoroughbred coming down in class."

"The comeback of Chief Joe Peña?"

"Don't laugh. I can set it up in two days and guarantee you $2,000 just for showing up and laying down."

"I'm looking for investment opportunities in New Mexico," Gold said to Joe.

"Why don't you just put your money directly into Hilario's pocket?"

"That's your problem, Joe," Hilario said. "You don't know how to boost your own home state. Word is, some black marketeer is dealing high explosives to Indians. There are legitimate businessmen who can't get explosives during wartime, contractors and developers, men with money. I want to give you this opportunity, Joe, because that Texas boy is going to beat the shit out of you."

As Joe worked his way back across the lobby, the special agents were re-reading their sports pages. The headline folded over was "B-29s Pound Nips". A circle of ladies in crocheted dresses were retreating from an Indian selling necklaces. His hair was tied back in a single grey braid, his dirty shirt buttoned at the neck. He offered them one arm draped with turquoise strands and then the other. Together, ladies and Indian moved past the poster of a flamenco dancer and through the double glass doors that led to the dining room.

Joe meant only to glance in. There were about twenty tables, enough to assemble a miniature, artificial Santa Fe: society Spanish in heirloom mantillas, artists who had fled New York, cultists who had fled California, lawyers not sharp enough to practise law anywhere else, all sitting in the glow of stamped tin chandeliers. The ladies found a table. The Indian stood at it, holding out silver rings and pins in his hand, and still hadn't seen Joe. From the table nearest the kitchen Harvey waved a clarinet. With him were Klaus Fuchs and the woman from the car, Anna Weiss. They were having after-dinner coffee.

"Back in business." Harvey held the instrument out for Joe's inspection. It was a used PanAmerican with a chrome-edged bell, the basic high school model. "Picked it up in the pawn shop."

"This ought to strike terror in the Emperor's heart," Joe said and handed the clarinet back. "Feeling okay?"

"We had a premature detonation on the test range this afternoon," Harvey explained to Anna. He looked up at Joe. "Just the bloody nose. I'm fine. Sit down."

"The sergeant has other duties, I'm sure," Fuchs said.

Anna Weiss said, "Sit, please."

She wasn't a rosy English fair. Not pallid, either. More of a smooth china paleness, made all the more startling by her hair, black as an Indian's but finer, and rakishly set off by a red lacquer comb. She wore a Hawaiian shirt with red palm trees. The ensemble had a go-to-hell quality that would test the nerve of any escort, let alone a stuffed shirt like Fuchs. At least her accent was softer than his.

"Through his clear thinking and quick actions, Dr Pillsbury saved the lives of a great many men this afternoon," Joe said as he sat. He laid his newspaper on the table.

"You didn't tell us, Harvey," Anna said.

"Tell them, Harvey," Joe said. "How you doused the cordite."

"No, no." Harvey had been drinking. A blush rose from his neck up. "Joe's the real war hero."

"I saw him in action this morning," she said. "He defeated a car."

"It's unbelievable they let him in." Fuchs had yet to address Joe directly, and now he stared at a new irritation.

The old Indian Tenorio stood at the table and displayed his arms laden with necklaces, nodules of blue and green turquoise on knotted string. Cleto was a Santa Domingo man, and the Domingos sold jewellery up and down the Rio and even into Navajo country in Utah. His eyelids were low and his shirt was stained with trails of brown chilli sauce, but the ribbons in his hair were bright and La Fonda not only suffered, it prompted Cleto to approach guests as long as he did so with the minimum of contempt.

"How much?" Joe asked.

"Two dollar." Cleto laid the necklaces on the table.

"Ridiculous." Fuchs picked up a string and held it close to the candlelight. He scratched a stone with his fingernail. "You know what turquoise is?" he asked Cleto.

"Turquoise."

"Turquoise is, in fact, a phosphate of copper and aluminium."

"One dollar." Cleto shrugged.

"See, you didn't even know what you were selling. I just told you, you should pay me. I've seen these stones. They change colour, they fade, they're hardly diamonds. They're stones off the ground."

"Not off the ground." Joe lifted a necklace. "They have to mine them. The old way is to build a fire against the rock, then throw water on the rock. The rock shatters and you see a seam of fresh turquoise like a blue stream of water. It would be easier to use explosives, but they're impossible to get now." He put two dollars on the table and gave the necklace to Anna Weiss. "For you."

"You're a gentleman, Sergeant. Thank you."

She slipped the turquoise string over her head and inside the collar of her shirt. The stones were mixed: evening blue, blue-weed blue, mountain lake blue, corn green. With the shirt and comb, she looked like a ragpicker of all nations. A beautiful ragpicker though.

Cleto quickly gathered the necklaces and money from the table and moved away.

Fuchs took a deep breath.

"Sergeant, sometimes your simpleness seems almost clever. You have what we called in Germany a 'peasant wit'. Do you understand? But there is a great difference between cleverness and intelligence. Where you see pretty stones, I see phosphate. Where you see 'longhairs', I see an elite. To be honest, the war will be won by intelligence, by science, not by soldiers. Not to denigrate anybody's sacrifice."

"Klaus, we're all soldiers fighting for the same cause," Harvey said.

"And we all have different causes." Fuchs turned to Anna Weiss. "Take the necklace off, it looks foolish."

"Willst du lieber einen gelben Stern haben?" she asked. *"Oder einen roten?"*

At the sound of German, the entire dining room fell silent. In the hush Harvey whispered, "Joe, that old guy with the necklace stole your newspaper."

"You're seeing things. You need a cure," Joe said. "Let's get out of here. Let me take you up to some hot springs, some sacred healing waters. You're invited, too," he told Anna Weiss and Fuchs.

"Impossible," said Fuchs.

"When?" Harvey asked.

"Right now," Joe said. "Tonight. I'll lead you in the jeep."

Anna Weiss said, "Yes."

10

High above the Jemez road, a hot spring poured into a well of rock. Pink coralroot crept out of pine needles. Spruce bough and moon floated on sulphurous steam.

Joe was already in the black water. Harvey bobbled like a rubber duck. Anna Weiss laid her clothes on the edge and stepped in. As she sank, her eyes looked directly into his and she said, "Joy through strength." She went under and came up, her hair moulded to the sides of her face.

"Too bad Klaus didn't want to come up from the car," Harvey said. "He's getting a little testy. It's the pressure from Trinity. Only a month to go."

"Why Trinity?" she asked. "Why does Oppy call the test site that?"

"From an English sonnet," Harvey said and mimicked Oppy's hoarse whisper. "Batter my heart, three person'd God, for you as yet but knock, breathe, shine, and seek to mend."

"Doesn't it have a name already?" Anna asked.

"Stallion Gate," said Joe.

"An American name, I like that better."

"So do I."

"This is the perfect example of average temperature," Harvey said. "Half of me is cooking and half of me is freezing, but the average temperature is very comfortable."

Every time one of them stirred, water – pungent. buoyant, black – spilled from the well and over moss soaked with the same sharp smell. Between branches they could see the peaks of the Jemez, some hanging in shadow, some shining with scree. Clouds on an easterly wind made the mountains move forward like a wave.

"There was a volcano here as big as Everest about a million years ago." Joe spread his arms along the rim of the well. "When it blew, it threw rocks as far as Kansas. There's still a volcanic vent beneath us."

"Like a deep-banked ember," she said.

"And all these hills are sacred to the old people. Shrines in the caves. You never know what you're going to stumble into. My father and I were hunting one day, when we both fell into a hole. A hole in the ground, dust swirling around. We'd fallen into an old kiva. We were sitting on the floor of it. All around us were these figures. A man with blue skin, blue as a bluebird, and the head of a buffalo. A purple swallow with the head of a girl. A mountain lion sitting like a man. The kiva could have been five hundred, maybe a thousand years old, but the colours were as bright as if they'd been painted the day before. And in about an hour, they faded. In two hours, you could hardly see them. I couldn't even find the place now. It's filled in with dirt and disappeared, but there are more."

Joe was surprised at himself for telling the story. First, that he remembered it. Second, because it smacked of noble-red-man-seduces-tourist. Maybe that's what he was trying to do.

"What is the religion here?" Anna asked. "Was Adam created on the sixth day? Was Eve created from his rib?"

"Different."

"How different?"

"There are different stories, which I remember poorly. Have you seen the clowns at the dances here?"

"No."

"Well, when the world was new, a brother and a sister set out across the mountains. He was handsome. She was beautiful. As they slept on a mountaintop, he realized that he loved her. When she woke up, she saw that he did. She tried to escape by stamping her foot and splitting the mountain so that a wide river flowed between them. He was so mad for her that he threw himself on the ground, and his face swelled and bled,

83

and she felt so sorry for him that she swam back across the river and slept with him. The incest made them outlaws and their children became clowns. Not exactly the same story as the Bible."

"What about everyone else?"

"Everyone sort of wandered up out of the earth. Hard, finished, completed. I really can't tell you about Indians."

Least of all the Indian steeping in the water. Why the hell was he taking the chance of stealing high explosive to give the stuff to Cleto for nothing when he could make a killing out of the contractors in Albuquerque? Did he want to get caught and sent back to Leavenworth or shipped to the Pacific? There was an element not just of self-contempt, but of self-destruction.

"I can tell you about Indians," Harvey said. "When I was eight, some so-called civilized Cherokees threw me into a water tank. The walls were about six feet high and it was half full. It didn't have the aroma of this water, but it had slime, hence amusement value, the pay-off being what I would look like when I hauled myself out. As I climbed out, I noticed the water level sinking just a little bit. I got back in and the water level went up. I went in and out, in and out, then I calculated the volume of the water displaced and its weight and, from that, my weight and volume. I had recently read in *National Geographic*, between pictures of African breasts, that crocodiles weighted themselves by swallowing stones so they could swim lower and sneak up on those poor African girls. So I shouted from the water for the kids to throw some rocks into the tank. That was my real start in physics. You know, I'm starting to like this water. Does this mean I'm sweating poisons or I'm cooked?" He paddled back and forth between Joe and Anna Weiss. "What are you going to do after the war, Joe? Still thinking about opening a jazz club? I bet you'd need a silent partner."

"How silent? Does this include the clarinet?"

Harvey stopped in the middle of the water.

"Joe, do you think I'm drunk?"

"Are you?"

"Pi to ten places is 3.1415926535. Could a drunk say that?"

"You did."

"He's right." Harvey murmured to Anna. "In the Texas Panhandle we have tent meetings where people roll on the ground and drool and talk in Hebrew, Hittite and Welsh. It's nothing to speak the simple alphabet of algebra or the garbled Greek of physics. But, Joe, Joe, Joe, I don't want to get you into trouble."

"How could you get me into trouble?"

"I wouldn't say anything, but I wanted you to understand if I disappear. Because you're my good friend."

"What are you talking about?"

"Joe, I'm quitting the Hill."

"Quitting?"

"Nobody remembers that we started this project only because Hitler had his project, so he couldn't blackmail us with his bomb. Now it looks like he never made one. Now we say we're going to use it on Japan, which doesn't have any project."

"Hold it. This afternoon at the Hanging Garden, you nearly killed yourself working on this bomb."

"I was undecided then. I thought I'd let Fate choose for me."

"Well, that was a glorious pose, you and the cordite. This still doesn't make any sense to me. If the Japs had the bomb, you don't think they'd drop it on us?"

"But they don't. We do and we have to make the ethical choice. Joe, I didn't leave Amarillo to become a physicist to atomize a hundred thousand human beings. When Oppy came to Columbia and recruited me, it was to make a bomb so Hitler wouldn't use his. That's all I signed up for, that's all anyone signed up for."

"Except the Army, Navy and Marines."

"The ethical choice –"

"It's a hell of a luxury. It's not one that enlisted men have."

"Well, as a civilian –"

"You're a civilian because Oppy got you a draft deferment, so you could come here and build a bomb. I'm your friend and

I'm happy for you. So build the bomb and end the war. Boy, Captain Augustino would love this conversation. Augustino would haul you off the Hill in a car trunk."

"I'm prepared to suffer for my decision."

"Suffer for your decision? There are men dying on shitty piles of sand all over the Pacific. There are men stuffed in the holds of ships heading to Japan for the invasion. I think they're going to suffer for your decision. Who else have you told?"

"Just me," said Anna.

"You helped Harvey come to his decision?"

"I hope so," she said.

"Well, there ought to be room in Augustino's car trunk for both of you. Good luck," Joe said and heaved himself out of the water. Quickly, he picked up his uniform, belt and shoes. This wasn't the idyllic night in the hot springs he'd had in mind, not at all.

Harvey stood as tall and defiant in the water as he could get.

"Are you going to report us?"

"No, but I'll let you geniuses find your own way down."

"Stay," Harvey begged.

"Yes, tell us more fascinating Indian experiences," Anna Weiss said. "Lift more cars. Play more waltzes."

On the road to the Hill, deer dashed in front of Joe's headlights. They were mule deer, five or six of them. He braked and skidded to the edge before he stopped. His lights picked out the scribbling flight of moths, the dart of a nightjar, and then faded over the long drop to the canyon floor.

The world was full of victims, all too eager to take you with them.

11

Light lay in the blue shutters and between the threshold and the door. The house had two rooms, a kitchen with a wood-burning stove and a larger room for everything else. The adobe walls were whitewashed with kaolin. There were a cot, maple bureau, enamelled table and chairs, dusty pails, an open cardboard box full of pots, and a corner fireplace that was black and empty. On the walls were a crucifix, the Virgin, Saints Michael and Christopher (wading through water, the Christ child on his shoulders), photos of Rudy in his confirmation suit, dressed in feathers and bells for a dance, in his uniform and garrison cap.

Joe had heard that Rudy was dead, that the B-17s at Clark Field were loaded with fuel and lined up in rows when the Japs came over. Each bomber blew up the next one, and the last B-17, trying to take off, rolled over a gun battery before exploding. Not that bodies were found.

He sat on the hard bed and smoked, using a pail as an ashtray. He noticed how he didn't look up and he knew it was out of fear. Fear that Dolores would come in from the kitchen with a dishcloth in her hand. Or that Rudy would be standing at the foot of the bed, whining, wanting to box. It was the first time in years that Joe had been in the house and it was just as bad as he'd thought it would be. Smaller. There was nothing so claustrophobic as memory.

Rudy could still be alive. Hiding out in the jungle. In a prison camp. In Japan.

Of course, Fuchs was right. If the bomb worked, all the

Rudy Peñas in the world wouldn't measure up to a single Oppy, Harvey or Fuchs.

Goddamn Harvey and his need for approval. Why tell a sergeant that you're leaving the war? Joe hadn't gone back to the Hill. He'd picked up a couple of bottles at a bar and went out target shooting, looking for unlucky coyotes. He figured he'd wake up in a motel in Esperanza, the Spanish town across the river from Santiago. Instead, he woke up in Santiago, in this house.

At least he'd made up his mind. He was going to tell Augustino. The captain wanted something on Anna Weiss, and Joe would give it to him.

The house groaned, or maybe it was the sound of himself. The kiva in the ground had nothing on this. He dug in his pocket for another cigarette.

The door swung open. Dull, blinding sun filled the room and in the doorway stood a phantom.

"Rudy?"

"Who?" Joe shielded his eyes.

"Mrs Quist. Joe? That's you?" The wraith stepped in and became a tiny lady in a white Lana Turner suit, turban and sunglasses. "You're the last person I thought I'd see here."

"You and me, both." He could see how wrinkled his khakis were, the butts on the floor.

"Pots, Joe. This is always my first stop."

"I'll get out of your way." He heaved himself off the bed. His shoes were still on. As soon as he put the carton of pots on the table for Mrs Quist he stumbled outside to the pump. Her Hudson was parked alongside the jeep.

Morning was come and gone. Around Santiago rose thin columns of black smoke because the noon stillness was a good time for firing pots. In the back yard across the road Sophie Reyes tended a fire of pine, cedar, bits of two-by-four piled around a milk crate filled with pots. Sophie plucked up a piece of wood that seemed to be nothing but flame and put it where the fire seemed sparse. When an ember rolled free, she swept it back into the fire with a brush of yucca stalks. A soot-blackened tin sheet blocked any unwanted breeze. Everything she did was like Dolores. They had been sisters, and Sophie had the same helmet of grey hair, wore the same traditional, one-shoulder dress, smudged apron, Montgomery-Ward shoes.

Ben Reyes came out through a screen door into the yard. His braids hung round a puckered, leathery face. He wore no shirt, only a vest, kilt, trousers and moccasins. Usually his contribution to Sophie's work was to sit in a chair and sort feathers. Today he was head to head with another doddering ancient with a walking stick.

Joe pumped water into his hands. Rinsed his mouth. Combed his hair with his fingers. With the sun directly overhead, the one-storey adobe houses appeared waist-high. The ladders leaning against the rooflines were bleached, the wood twisted; the ladders looked balanced on their own shadows. The pueblo was a maze of dirt roads and alleys, outdoor ovens, corrals and open porches, homes distinguished one from the other by a blue frame on these windows, a green frame on those. The Peña and Reyes houses were at the edge of the pueblo, but an alley ran directly to the plaza and he could see the cottonwood with its tyre swings. He watched two boys run across the plaza, climb on to a roof, gather their courage in a breath and jump to a lower roof, and he remembered making the same heady leap, and the stirring of husks and chilli dust when he landed.

Santiago. Never mind that he'd spent his adult life in New York and toured the entire country, East Coast, West Coast, Mexico and France. Before the war he'd gone to Paris with Big Chief Russell Moore, a trombone player, a 410 lb Pima from Komatke, Arizona. In the Palais des Sports, Joe knocked the French heavyweight champion three times through the ropes and still lost the decision because the French kept throwing their champion back in like an undersized fish. Big Chief had this trombone at the Palais and every time the crowd threw their fighter back, he played a slow, rising slide. That night, Joe and Big Chief drank absinthe from brandy snifters in a café unworried about war because the French had a bigger army than the Germans.

That was six years ago. Now, he rolled like a stone back to where he'd started. The funny thing was that the war had freed most of the men in Santiago, drafted them out of their bean fields, and sent back the one man who'd got away. The mills of the Gods were slow and all fucked up.

Jazz was liberation. Joe had always been a counterpuncher and that's what bebop was all about, hooking off the jab. Charlie Parker claimed to be part Cherokee or Cree. Any dressing room of black musicians was full of would-be Indians. Those were Joe's Indians.

He saw Ben and his friend approaching the jeep. Ben's companion was in dirty coveralls, braids, and the white cotton blanket of a Taos elder, but he wasn't old, just blind, his eyes sunken and shut. Trachoma, Joe thought. Until sulpha, trachoma had been common in the pueblos. No one caught it now, except the sort of fanatic who wouldn't use Anglo medicine.

"Spring's coming, Uncle," Joe said.

"Spring's coming very nicely now." Ben scowled and introduced his friend. His name was Roberto.

The three men spoke Tewa. Tewa was the language of a number of the Rio Grande pueblos and it was expressive in describing the beauty of the clouds, rain, water, corn. Tewa was also the language of a people who had wandered through the wilderness arguing. No pueblo existed for long without splitting into two parts that despised or, at least, suspected each other. So, Tewa was rich in phrases and intonations of derision and scorn.

"Still cold in Taos?"

"A little cooler." Roberto's voice was quizzical, as if he were picking up a new object with it. "You come up to Taos much?"

Taos thought it was the top of the world, maybe one step below the Hopi, but very close to heaven. It occurred to Joe that what he didn't need at the start of the day was a religious nut; what he needed was a coffee or a cold beer.

"Not since the war started, actually. Always mean to. Uncle, I never got a chance to thank you. December, you stumbled into a hunting party. You must have been out trapping in the snow. You came through at the right time."

"Thank Roberto, not me. Wasn't my idea."

"Ben said the other hunter was hunting you," Roberto said.

Joe remembered that the two men coming out of the woods into the light of the dawn were connected by a rope or a thong. Ben and a blind man.

"Then, thank you," Joe told Roberto.

"He was hunting you?" Roberto asked. "He was crazy."

"He was an officer. Smoke?" Joe felt for his cigarettes. His pocket was empty.

"Have one of mine." Roberto took a thick, hand-rolled cigarette and stuck it into empty space.

"Thanks." Joe reached. The things always tasted like dung, he thought. Roberto put one in his own mouth and Joe lit his, then his own. "That's some smoke." Joe coughed.

"From Taos."

Roberto held on to the side of the jeep. He had a long Spanish nose. His hands looked surprisingly strong, the nails caked yellow. So that was how he got by; mixing adobe by hand. It was something a blind man could do. Roberto wouldn't be able to make much adobe, but what he did make would be fine stuff.

"We know what you're doing up on the Hill and we want you to stop it," Ben said.

Neither Joe nor Roberto paid attention to him.

"I met your mother once," Roberto said.

"Yeah?"

"I guess you were in New York. She was a clan mother, wasn't she? Winter Clan?"

"You're a Winter Clan?"

"Summer."

"She was winter." For Christ's sake, everyone on this side of the pueblo was Winter Clan. Then he remembered Roberto was blind. "This is mostly Winter Clan here."

"We want you and the Army to stop it," Ben said.

"Well, Ben," Joe said, "I doubt very much you know what's

91

going on up on the Hill, but if you want to stop it, you tell a general, you don't tell a sergeant."

"Your mother made great pots," Roberto said. "She had that special clay."

"Yeah, the white clay."

"You were the only one besides her who knew where she got it, she said," Roberto told Joe.

"Her and Sophie."

"You're making poison," Ben said.

"Ben," Joe asked as softly as he could, "Remember Pearl Harbor? Bataan?"

"You play the piano, she said," Roberto told Joe. "And I met your brother Rudy."

"I am telling you now to stop it."

Joe was trying to control his temper.

"You really ought to take your case to Roosevelt, Ben. Or maybe to the boys from Santiago who are out fighting right now. Or to their mothers."

Ben spat in front of the jeep.

"Talking to you puts me in mind of the worm. The worm has no ears and no balls."

"Well, Ben, your contribution to the war effort, sitting and farting and sorting feathers, is known and appreciated by all."

"It's been a good visit," Roberto told Joe. With his walking stick he hit Ben on the shin to locate him.

"Any time," Joe said.

Ben acted like there was a whole lot of conversation yet to be had, but Roberto gripped the old man firmly by the arm and, blind or not, led Ben across the road to Ben's yard.

Crazy. First Harvey, then Ben Reyes.

"I'll give you a dollar for each one," Mrs Quist stood in the doorway and brushed dust off her white suit.

She'd been coming from southern California to Santiago as long as Joe could remember. Once she'd been a visible woman, a little more tanned each year. Now she was wrapped up like an ambulatory burn case. Her voice was nasal, as if it were burned. Joe followed her into the house.

92

Five pieces were lined up on the table. A polychrome pot with a plumed serpent chasing itself so closely there was no leaving from tail to jaw. A plate as black and shiny as coal but perfectly round and decorated with a ring of a hundred finely-drawn feathers. A brown pot grooved like an acorn squash and as smooth as polished stone. A tall wedding pot with elegant, twin necks. A little black seed bowl, round as a ball, with a small hole.

"This house is a mess. If Dolores saw it . . ." Mrs Quist sighed from aggravation and waved away the dust.

"A dollar each?"

"I'll lose money. If you take in the expense of my travel, the ration cards for gasoline, hotel, food, closing down the shop, there's no way I'll see a profit. I've been sick, you know."

"You did say a dollar."

Mrs Quist carefully put the squash pot into a box padded with newspaper and wood shavings.

"I can't sell them in Santa Fe. There aren't any tourists, just soldiers. Soldiers buy postcards, not pots. Probably, by the time I get back to Los Angeles, half of these pots will be broken, so I'm paying five dollars for two or three pots."

She wrapped the plate and dropped it gently into the bottom of another box, then wrapped the polychrome pot and set it on top of the plate.

"I may not be able to sell any of these. The war changed everything. People are coming back from France and Italy, they've been all over the world now. They're going to want fine art, going to want to collect paintings, Picassos, Monets, not Indian pots."

"That sounds tough."

"That's the way of the world, Joe."

He couldn't see her eyes through her dark glasses. Her mouth was a lipsticked oval. He'd grown up with the annual visits of Mrs Quist, with her annual lament. He couldn't remember when there'd been a good year for selling pots.

"Most traders are only working on consignment now, in fact." She packed the tall wedding pot with special care. "They wouldn't give you any money at all and then you'd have nothing."

"Nothing instead of five dollars?"

Mrs Quist packed the bowl last, and then she laid and smoothed a dollar note on the table where each piece had stood.

"There."

The notes crinkled. One slowly spun.

"Aren't you going to pick them up?"

"Later."

The breeze was nothing more than warm air drifting into a cool adobe house. The spinning dollar drifted to the table's edge.

"Well, it's your money, you do what you want with it."

"Oh, I'm only doing what Dolores would have done if she were here, Mrs Quist. She would have listened to everything you said and she would have taken a dollar a pot. You're going to make $20, $25 apiece? You've always made that kind of money out of Dolores. She always knew, I used to tell her, but she was too embarrassed for you to say anything. She was embarrassed for your greed. But she said you could have the pots, so you can. Except this one." Joe removed the seed bowl from the box. "Now, that's your dollar bill on the floor and you can pick it up if you want." Joe hadn't meant to frighten her, but Mrs Quist stepped back as if he were going to hit her. "No? Then let me help you go."

Joe carried the boxes to the Hudson and carefully laid them on the back seat. He held the door for her while she got quickly behind the wheel, put in the ignition key and pressed the starter. Her sunglasses trembled until she caught her breath.

"Joe, if I were you, I'd pick up all that money and clean up that house before Dolores sees it."

"Dolores is dead. Died last year." Joe pushed the car door shut. "I thought you knew."

A Cadillac was squeezing through the alley along the back fence of the Reyes' yard, and Joe paid no more attention to Mrs Quist as she pulled away. The Cadillac was a white coupé with chrome louvres and it manoeuvred like a fighter plane up to the pump. The driver's window rolled down and a thin, black arm hung jauntily out. A diamond ring winked from the pinky.

"Hey, you are back home, Joe. I looked for you last night at the Casa and you weren't there." Pollack grinned and shook his head, expressing separate emotions at the same time. "Someone said they saw your jeep outside here. That's good. It's good to go home." Pollack had a sly, yellow smile, wide nose and a flat forehead that curved into tight grey hair with blue-black scalp shining through. When he spoke, his hands had the sort of fluttery movements that put Joe in mind of fans at gospel meetings. When he got excited, his eyes looked like they would pop with emotion. He always dressed in a silk shirt during the day and a tuxedo at night. Altogether, he gave the impression of an alley cat who had achieved a dignified old age. "It's good to see you back here."

"You drove all the way for the sight?"

"I was looking for you. I can't go up that secret mountain to get you, I've got to catch you when I can. I could've used you last night. Had a piano player must've been German. All he knew was polkas. Must've been a POW."

"Sorry."

"It's your club, too, you know."

"I haven't heard you say that for a long time."

"You don't share the profits, mind, because your daddy Mike never put any money in. But we were partners. His name is on the papers. He was going to buy in, but he never had the chance. I always sent a little money this way to your mother, you know. I didn't have to, but I did. What is that you're smoking? Smells like it collected in a hoof."

"I know." Joe dropped the homemade and stepped on it.

"Thing I learned was always be sharp. A person in the public eye has a responsibility to look sharp."

Joe stepped on the running board. "What are you leading up to? So I didn't get to the Casa last night."

"I'm selling it." Pollack was pleased with the surprise.

"The Casa Mañana?"

"Yeah. Eddie Junior's coming home from Italy. I'm going to set us up in a nice club in Harlem."

"That's too bad. I mean, that's great for you and Eddie, but the Casa was the best club in the state."

"The only one with the authentic big band sound. One hundred thousand dollars. That's including kitchen, tables and chairs, liquor, liquor licence, plus parking lot. Practically an entire block. Albuquerque's going to boom after the war, you know."

"Why doesn't Eddie come here?"

"He grew up with his mother. All he knows is New York." Pollack's eyes wandered off in thought.

"And Italy."

"Italy, yeah." Pollack brightened. "A war hero like you. A veteran. Wouldn't it be great if you came to New York and played in our new club? One little thing, Joe. A matter of clear title. I'm going to need your signature on the papers, you being Mike's heir."

"Me being his heir? To what? I don't have a share of the club, you said so."

"It's a nicety."

"The nicety is, I'm a partner without a share?"

"There'll be a consideration."

"Money?"

"A consideration."

"A definite sum?"

"Considerable."

"Give me a number. A hundred dollar consideration? A thousand dollar consideration? Give me the range."

"I can't say."

"I can say. How badly can I fuck up your bill of sale?"

"Joe, we're friends, we're partners."

"I'm just finding out." Joe studied Pollack's aghast face. He slapped the top of the car. "Fuck it. Bring round the papers, I'll sign them. You don't have to bring any 'consideration'."

"You scared me." Pollack still looked grey.

"I'm sorry. Just . . . gravity's got me down today."

"Well . . ." Pollack didn't dare say much else.

"You ever wonder what they're doing up on that secret mountain? On the Hill! What would you say if I told you they were making a machine to end the world? To blow up the whole thing?"

"Now I know you're fooling." Pollack started the engine, eager to get away.

"Yeah."

"Well. Now we got that settled, Joe, I best be going. Good to see you back in your own home."

"Yeah."

Pollack backed up, U-turned and eased between the Reyes' yard and the goat fence that served as the boundary for out-houses, compost heaps, cornfields. With his eyes Joe followed the Cadillac in gaps between adobe walls, past the Winter Squash kiva, into the plaza and under the cottonwood. He looked back to the dirt road between the outhouses and the homes. He hadn't noticed before that Mrs Quist's Hudson had stopped halfway into a cholla cactus. Her door was open and he could see her hands over her face, although he didn't realize she was crying until her dark glasses fell on to the ground. As she leaned to retrieve them, she almost fell out.

It was unbelievable. Mrs Quist had been robbing Dolores as long as Joe could remember; for years she'd paid Dolores a dollar a pot, fifty cents a pot, a fraction of what she could get in Santa Fe or LA. When Joe thought of the money Mrs Quist had made out of Dolores . . . It was a predatory relationship. It was like watching a cat cry over a mouse. It was insane.

He went into the house. On the table was the black seed pot, a dark moon with a seed-sized hole on top. In the air, released from the newspapers, was the dust of the pots, the starchy smell of dry clay and overwhelming scent of memory. Dolores was there in the chair by the table and all he had to do to see her was raise his eyes. She was a small woman with fine features and unlined skin and complete concentration. Her hands worked quickly, moving her polishing stone over the pot. Starting from the bottom, she drew a straight line up to the lip, and a line beside that, and a line beside that, using only enough pressure for the clay to rebound brighter until the surface of the pot was faceted by hundreds of lines like the iris of an eye. Then she gave the pot another pass, following the infinitesimal ridges between the lines. He couldn't make out what she was saying, but he heard the sound of her voice, which was musical. He pressed his back against the wall and looked.

No Dolores. Only dust motes stirring slowly in the light above the table, chair and pot, the last and only piece of hers he had. He snatched it up and ran out of the door.

The Hudson was gone. Coming along the outhouses and fences was a jeep, Sergeant Shapiro at the wheel and Corporal Gruber with him. The MPs had helmets, guns and clubs, so they were on duty. They were weightlifters, mouth breathers. Gruber had blunt, ceramic features, Shapiro a slack, blue jaw. His face was screwed up into something approaching passion or desperation. Joe had never seen them on the reservation before.

The jeep skidded to a stop in front of him. Gruber looked disgusted. Shapiro had trouble finding words. "Chief, did you see me the other day?"

"When?" Joe was still glancing around for Mrs Quist's Hudson.

"On patrol, walking my horse."

"No." Joe brought his attention back.

"It was the day the high explosive was stolen at the Hanging Garden. You didn't see me on patrol?"

"What day was that?"

"It was bad enough the bunker was broken into. Augustino saw me. Captain Augustino says I learn to ride or I go into the infantry and he's personally going to see I go to the Pacific. He says I'm going to be in the first fucking boat that hits Japan."

"The first asshole in the water, the captain said," Gruber reminded him.

98

"You taught Dr Oppenheimer how to ride, you can teach me to ride," Shapiro told Joe. "Tomorrow's Sunday. My life is in your hands."

"I'm working tomorrow."

"Chief, I'll make it up to you. Anything you want. You'll see."

"Maybe in the afternoon."

The Hudson still hadn't crossed the plaza. It seemed to have just disappeared. As if Mrs Quist had gone straight to heaven to buy from Dolores direct.

12

Sunday morning. While Oppy was in Washington, Joe was assigned to the workshops on Two Mile Mesa. They were nail-bright sheetrock structures; inside was a general sense of panic over the one-month deadline of the Trinity test. In the casting building, the commercial sugar kettles in which high explosives were melted had broken down, the stirring ladles clogged with a brown "fudge" of Baratol, a TNT derivative.

Cast 200-pound wedges of explosive were carted in red Radio Flyer wagons designed for small children. When axles collapsed, everyone jumped. Replacement wagons were in a stockroom called FUBAR, for Fucked Up Beyond All Repair. Besides a shortage of wagons, there was a shortage of Bar Top varnish. To prevent them from chipping, castings were always painted with Bar Top; there was nothing more fragile than explosive.

Rough castings of high explosive were trimmed with bronze saws to minimize sparks. Joe hosed a casting while a machinist delicately cut the riser tabs left from the mould. Both men noticed the spark at the same moment. Joe hosed the casting furiously until he was sure only a single crystal of Baratol had sparked and didn't propagate. The machinist was soaked through. "What I like about this job," he told Joe, "is I can piss my pants and no one knows."

Afternoon. A basalt canyon topped with cedars. Below, a stream, moss, violets and a single Apache willow. Joe watched

Shapiro anxiously balance on a twelve-year-old mare named Dixie.

"That's much better," Joe said and walked around the horse and rider. "Here's the secret. Dixie's not going to fall down. She's just going to follow the horse ahead of her. You never go first, you never go last. She is the sweetest, slowest horse in the MP stable. From now on. she is your horse. You are her sack. Be a sack for her."

Shapiro frowned. "Oppenheimer, he gallops, he jumps his horse."

"His horse's name is Crisis. You want to ride a horse with a name like that? You get friendly with Dixie. Take her carrots, apples, sugar lumps every day."

Shapiro sagged in the saddle a little more confidently.

'Back in Brooklyn, my brother kept pigeons," he said.

Joe got an image of Shapiro in a rooftop pigeon cote, feathers and blood on his hands.

"Nice. Well, you get friendly with Dixie like that."

Overhead, the cedars were a gallery of cut-outs against the sky. Joe thought he saw something watching from above. Could have been a crow.

"Chief, you want to do me a real favour, you'll help me fight. You see Ray Stingo fight the kid from Texas?"

"Yeah."

"I'm fighting the kid."

"He'll kill you."

"It's southpaws." There was agony in Shapiro's voice, as if he were talking about an incurable disease. "The first thing I ever learned was to circle off the jab and counter with the right. That moves me square into a leftie's cross. I don't see it coming, I never see it coming."

"Maybe you have a chance."

"Augustino's behind it. He's betting on the kid. Those fucking Texans stick together."

"Get down."

"I really appreciate this, Chief."

Shapiro dismounted and both men removed their caps, web

belts and .45s. They assumed boxing stances. Joe put his right foot forward as if he were a left-hand boxer.

"Your right hand is low. Better. Let me see you move." Joe hung out a lazy, open-handed jab in the air to see Shapiro's reaction. "Don't move that way. Duck and move to your left. Keep the right up. Again. Now, hook with your left." Shapiro bored in, hands pumping like a maddened milkmaid. Joe put out another slow-motion jab. "Duck, move and hook." Joe caught Shapiro's hook on the arm. The moss was springy, dappled by sun that broke through the willow.

"You think I have a chance, Chief?"

"Let's see."

Joe shot a right jab more at full speed and slapped Shapiro's chin. Reflexively, the MP moved to his right and into a slap from Joe's left hand. Joe slipped a couple of Shapiro's jabs, then slapped Shapiro's chin and cheek again. As soon as he saw anything coming his way, Shapiro locked into his old habit, moving counter-clockwise into another slap. Joe blocked two hooks, ducked a jab and slapped Shapiro again. The MP's right cheek turned from blue to stinging pink.

"Forget it." Joe grabbed Shapiro's wrists.

"Forget it?" Shapiro's muscles bulged with frustration.

"You can't win. Sorry."

"Help me."

"How many rounds is it?"

"Six."

"Kid's an amateur, basically. He's probably never fought longer than three rounds. I hear he knocks everyone in two."

"Swell."

"That means if you can get to the fourth round, this kid is punched out. You can count to four? Good. So, don't move left, don't move right, don't move back because you're not fast enough. Just move in. You'll get hit on the way in, but you take it. Then you wrestle. Catch my arm, come on. Lean on it, yank it. That wears down the shoulders. Keep moving in." Joe backed away, slipping to one side and then the other. "Three rounds is nine minutes. You wrestle him for eight of those minutes, he's only killing you for one. When you grab him, don't butt. You've got scar tissue, like me. You'll cut before he does. Move in, move in." Joe was disgusted with himself because he was enjoying the trickle of sweat down his ribs, the concentration, the peripheral dance of boxing. Ducking a branch, slipping a jab. When Shapiro stood still, Joe waved him in again. "You dumb palooka, move."

Shapiro looked over Joe's shoulder. Joe turned and saw someone standing outside the shade of the willow. He had to squint because she was so dark against the sun.

"Klaus is climbing a mountain," she said. "It was boring watching him climb a mountain, so I left."

He had to take her from the edges in. Back-lit trim of short-sleeved white shirt and trousers. Hair cut in a page boy, ink-black and straight. Grey eyes making a study of him. No lipstick, but full lips. And the expression of a person looking into a bear pit.

"The Chief was teaching me how to ride," Shapiro said.

"An old Indian method?" Anna Weiss asked Joe.

Sun, white-hot, edged her cheek.

"At least with the Indian method, nobody gets bored," he said.

Where basalt had broken off in storeys of black columns, wrens darted head first into the canyon rim, into their nests.

Far below and behind, Shapiro rode alone in the opposite direction, letting his horse follow the stream back to the Hill.

"I told you," Joe said, "some of the land here is still used by the local people. Which mountain was he climbing?"

"Not so much a mountain as the next valley."

"Canyon?"

"I forgot. You have no valleys here, only canyons. And gulches."

At the top, through the fringe of cedars, the Jemez spread out ahead. High peaks surrounded by pines, the range smoother to the south and building like an ocean swell to the north. Anna turned, exhilarated by the climb, taking in mountain meadows coloured extravagant purple by mariposa lilies. She turned the way children turned, Joe thought, as if the world turned round her.

"You'd think you could see anything from here," she said.

"You're going back to Chicago?"

"Soon." As Joe stepped in front of her, she asked, "Shouldn't the lady be first?"

"Rattlesnakes." Joe nodded to the rocks along the path.

She fell in behind him. "So, Sergeant, these mountains are your home."

"According to the Army."

"You don't like the Army."

"I don't know anyone sane who likes the Army."

"That's not a direct answer. Captain Augustino seems to like the Army."

"Stay away from Captain Augustino."

"You told him about Harvey?"

"Nothing to tell."

She had a light step; she was more athletic than he'd thought.

"Tell me about Mrs Augustino," she said.

"Mrs Augustino left the Hill months ago."

"In a hurry, people say."

They came to a stop. She seemed to be studying him as if he were stuck with a pin against the sky.

"What else do people say?" Joe asked.

"They say you have a weakness for officers' wives."

"For women."

"You think I'm rude, Sergeant?"

"No, I think you're interested."

Wind lifted a wing of her collar and rubbed it against her hair.

"Perhaps we'd better look for Dr Fuchs," she said.

The path descended into a spring-fed canyon where water had cut through tiers of pumice, pink sandstone, limestone. Box elders grew at the canyon floor, ponderosas up the sides. Much of the Jemez pines had been cut for timber. Not this canyon. These ponderosas were deep orange, diamond-plated, over a hundred years old. In the soft stone walls over the tree tops, jays and dippers made their nests. In the highest and least accessible reaches of the walls were the pockmarks of handholds and the shadows of rock shelves.

"This is where Fuchs went climbing?" Joe asked.

Anna nodded. "It was very dull."

Joe picked a crow's feather off a twig and the feather left a grey smudge on his fingers.

"Could be fun by now."

At the base of the wall behind a screen of pines was a rough ladder with more feathers. Joe told Anna Weiss to stay on the ground. He scaled the ladder and was climbing the niches in the stone when he heard her following.

"Why should I miss the fun?" she asked.

The pines as they swayed brushed his back. Sixty feet up, Joe climbed above the tree tops and reached a rock ledge about ten feet wide and fifteen feet deep carved out of soft tufa. The low roof and floor were blackened with soot mixed with feathers. Klaus Fuchs, his shirt torn and dirty, sat facing Roberto, the blind man from Taos.

"Gott sei Dank, du bist hier," Fuchs said when he saw Anna.

"It's me, Joe Peña," Joe told Roberto.

"I heard you coming," Roberto said. "Come in."

Roberto's hair was long and unbraided. He had his blanket over his shoulders and it wasn't until Joe helped Anna up that he noticed that Roberto was holding a Marlin double-gauge shotgun with its muzzle nestled firmly in Fuchs' crotch.

"We're not disturbing anything, are we?' Joe asked.

"Not you, no," Roberto assured him.

"I am a guest of the American government, on American government land, with American government protection, is this not so?"

Fuchs' neck was covered with finger smudges, so there'd been a scuffle. His hair stood up with fright. There was about a three-foot-long wooden idol wrapped up in red feathers and painted leather in a corner of the shelf. Cut in the rock under the layer of soot were ghost figures, snakes like hoops, lightning drawn as sticks.

"There are parts of this area, this canyon especially, that are set aside for local people so they can carry on their religion," Joe said.

"You mean Indians," Fuchs said.

"Those are the local people," Joe said.

"You mean –" Fuchs began.

"Enough," Roberto said and jabbed the barrel, not savagely, just enough to make Fuchs lean forward tenderly. "He was up here when we got here, Joe."

Joe could imagine the scene. Fuchs discovered by probably a dozen priests, most likely including Ben Reyes. It was unusual for someone from Taos to take part in a Santiago ceremony, but not unknown. A lot of men were in the service. Priests went back and forth between pueblos just to keep the old rituals rolling. The shelf must have stored altars, which Ben and the others had carried away. Ben would be back. Certainly Roberto and Fuchs weren't going anywhere. Joe had to stoop under the low ceiling. If Roberto fired the shotgun anywhere it was going to get messy. Smart of a blind man to choose a weapon with two barrels.

"Why don't we let the lady go back down?" Joe suggested.

"And run for help?" Roberto said.

"May I sit?" Anna Weiss asked.

"Yes." Roberto was pleased. He switched the shotgun from one arm to the other and held out his blanket.

"Thank you." She spread the blanket on the rock and sat.

"You too, Joe," Roberto said.

"Thanks." Joe took the hint.

"Like a picnic." Roberto tilted his face in Anna's direction. He was wearing white shirt and work trousers, the shirt buttoned at the neck and cuffs, barely showing grey body paint inside. His closed eyes were slightly sunken, otherwise he made a more handsome man than Joe had first supposed. Joe's .45

106

was in a snap holster. He wondered how good Roberto's hearing was.

"Warm." Joe noticed that the safety on the shotgun was off.

"Going to be a dry summer," Roberto agreed.

"I still have a share in a bean field down in the pueblo. How do you think beans will do?"

"Bad year for rain," Roberto said. "Good year for lightning."

"He's blind," Fuchs whispered.

"What's that got to do with the weather?" Joe asked. Through his glasses Fuchs' pale eyes were fixed on the gun on Joe's belt. Joe reached for cigarettes. "Smoke? I owe you one."

Roberto nodded.

"He's a madman," Fuchs hissed.

"He's a spy," Roberto told Joe.

Joe tapped the last cigarettes from his pack.

"Sorry, only three," he told Fuchs. He lit all three at once and passed two to Anna, she passed one to Roberto's lips.

Roberto inhaled and smiled. "I can tell she's pretty. There's a feeling around pretty women."

"He doesn't sound crazy," Anna told Fuchs.

"It's not funny." Fuchs looked at the muzzle between his legs.

"You're German, too?" Roberto asked Anna. "I like your accent."

"I'd rather lose it," she said.

"Study Billie Holiday. Get her records," Joe told her. He told Fuchs, "A little Fats Waller would do you a world of good. You were spying?"

"He tried," Roberto said.

"I wasn't spying, I just happened to be here."

"Did you apologize?" Joe asked.

Fuchs snorted.

Most of the priests were old men and they would have to spirit away altars, prayer sticks, stones, fetishes, a lot to carry off a cliff. Joe put in some silence for respect before saying,

"Well, this is a very ignorant person, Roberto. What do you want to do with him?"

"Shoot him."

"Dear God," Fuchs muttered.

"That's an idea," Joe granted.

"Dear God," Fuchs muttered again.

"Are you religious?" Roberto asked him.

"His father is a minister," Anna answered.

"Mormon?" Roberto asked. "We have a lot of Mormons here."

"Lutheran," Fuchs said.

"That's interesting. Don't you think that's interesting, Roberto?" Joe inquired.

"If he's a missionary, that's worse," Roberto said.

"That's right," Joe conceded.

"I am a scientist," Fuchs pleaded. "I don't believe in God."

"You'll have to admit there is some contradiction in what you say one moment and what you say the next," Joe told Fuchs. "It's too bad that you don't believe in God, because there is another way out, aside from being shot. You could become a member."

"A member?" Fuchs asked.

"That's how a lot of priests join," Joe said. "If they happen to stumble on a ceremony, they have to join. That way they never reveal the secrets."

"Like the Communist Party," Anna said.

"The Party cannot be compared to Indian medicine men howling on a cliff," Fuchs answered.

"Where does the Party howl?" Joe asked.

"It is not relevant."

"Touchy, touchy."

"Why spy on Indians?" Anna asked.

"Why are you siding with these ignorants? Why are you with the Indians? Why are you all against me?" Fuchs demanded. Spittle jumped from him to Roberto. "You stupid, little blind man, you wouldn't dare pull that trigger."

Joe had for some time assumed that Roberto wouldn't pull

the trigger, so he was caught flat on his seat when Roberto's finger squeezed the shotgun trigger shut. The spurred hammer rose and snapped, sending a metallic click the length of the empty barrel and into Fuchs. The physicist's face went green and puttyish and his next breath came as a moan.

"Fascinating," Anna said.

Fuchs moaned more deeply, like a cello. Roberto broke the shotgun open. The first barrel was empty, but in the second barrel was the brass eye of an unfired shell. Roberto pulled the shell out, fumbled for Fuchs' shirt and dropped the shell inside it.

"Roberto." Joe shook his head.

"This will make him more religious or more polite, I think," Roberto said.

Joe considered throwing the shotgun down off the shelf, but a new one would cost its owner twelve, thirteen dollars from Wards.

"Got any more shells?" he asked Roberto.

"No."

"They coming back for you?"

"Sure." Roberto was cheerful, as if he were hosting a social event. "You better be going before they get here."

"Yeah."

"It was good meeting you," Roberto told Anna. "I'll see you and Joe again."

"Anything seems to be possible."

"Good." Roberto pointed in Fuchs' general direction. "But don't bring him."

Joe had to carry Fuchs fireman-style off the canyon wall. When they finally got to the floor, Fuchs sped behind the pines, wrenching his belt open while he ran. Anna watched Fuchs disappear.

"This is another planet."

"New Mexico." Joe felt for cigarettes and remembered he'd smoked the last on the shelf.

"If he'd pulled the other trigger, he would have killed Klaus."

"If he wanted to kill Klaus, he would have done it before we got there."

"I thought so, then . . ." She smiled. "Was Roberto crazy or not? Were we humouring him or was he humouring us?"

"Roberto knows what he's doing." Joe took a deep breath and looked straight up at the far-off, converging tips of the ponderosas. Up in the sky, a squirrel swayed on the highest tip. Maybe he was blind. Maybe the other squirrels were coming back.

"They say you are so violent, Joe. You don't seem so."

He liked the way she ran her words together; the accent was sinuous in her mouth, alive and warm under the cool surface. It was the first time she'd said his name. He liked the explosion of the "J".

"I don't shoot blind men."

"Your aura of violence must attract some women, though."

"Yeah, first I fuck them, then I scalp them." He sighed. "Sometimes, the other way round."

She clapped her hands together and laughed.

"Wild, wild, Joe!"

Juniper boughs nodded under mistletoe. Fuchs, shirt stained and reeking, lagged far behind.

"Oppy studied under my father in Göttingen. In Germany," Anna said. "He seemed to live in our house. We thought he would marry my older sister, Emma. My father was very worried because everyone believed Oppy would leave physics for poetry. He was very German in Germany, except when he talked about New Mexico."

"About New Mexico in Germany?" Joe was surprised.

"With my father, he discussed physics. With Emma, he discussed poetry, philosophy, psychology. With me, he talked about wild Indians. I think I had the best bargain."

"Oppy loves to talk."

"Roberto is a medicine man?"

"A priest."

"You believe in Indian medicine?"

"Crazy stuff like that? No, I believe Christ died and rose again in three days and ascended like a B-19. But Indian stuff is all around here. Like Roberto today, like the kiva I told you about."

"I used to believe that if I ate a shrimp, I was an unclean girl and a shame in God's eyes. Once I ate a lobster and was positive that I would die in the night."

He couldn't imagine Anna scared. He had been scared with Roberto; she wasn't.

"What do you suppose Oppy believes in?" she asked.

"Well, he's not a very orthodox Jew. He sort of gets around the whole religious issue by going Hindu. What he really believes in, I think, is science. He thinks science can save the world. If every scientist were as good a man as Oppy, I might agree."

"How good is that?"

"The best."

They had reached the head of the ski slope that looked over Los Alamos. Dark spruce bordered a steep meadow of aspen that ran down the side of the mountain like a shaft of light.

"Enough Indians, enough guides." Fuchs caught up. "What I want to know, Sergeant, is what you're going to do about the madman who tried to kill me."

"Who threatened you, you mean."

"Tried to kill me while you did nothing." Fuchs rose to his toes, levitating on anger and humiliation.

"There's no reason to stir things up with the pueblo. Why don't we just forget about it?"

"Forget about it? I want him reported. You know who he was, you said his name. And he knew you."

"If you report him –" Joe began.

"No. You report him, Sergeant," Fuchs said. "You."

Joe had decided not to report Anna Weiss and to avoid Augustino as long as he could. Now, he had to see Augustino about a medicine man?

"Would you?" Anna Weiss said.

"If Dr Fuchs insists, I have to report the incident."

111

"And put your friend in jail?" she asked.

"That's not up to me." Joe felt like he was backing into a corner. Roberto wasn't his friend; he hadn't known him until two days ago.

"Who is it up to?" she asked.

"The officer in charge of security."

"Captain Augustino?" she asked.

"Yes."

"Ah." Fuchs re-set his glasses. "After all your talk, we see what kind of Indian you really are."

"It's Army business as soon as I see Augustino," Joe tried to explain to her. "I'm a sergeant, I don't have a choice, I don't have the power to make that decision."

"I told you," Fuchs turned to Anna Weiss. "I warned you he was Captain Augustino's man. Good, Sergeant, you do as you're told." Fuchs backed away and then started downhill, stumbling through the dry grass.

"I was hoping for irrationality." Anna Weiss squinted as if she were trying to see something in the distance, on the other side of the mountains. Grey eyes with black edges, as if charred. "The world is full of people who take orders. For a moment, I thought you might be different."

"It's an Army post, it's as simple as that."

"You're right. I was foolish to think anything else."

"And I'm a sergeant on it."

"Captain Augustino's man. And Mrs Augustino's man. Many things, but not very Indian." She looked up at Joe. "The answer to your question is, no, I'm not interested."

She went after Fuchs. Watching her descend, a white figure swinging from aspen to aspen, Joe wanted to call, as if words could reach out and stop her. But he had no words on his mountaintop, he was as dumb as a yearning brute.

Augustino wasn't at headquarters or the Tech Area. In the commissary, Joe heard the captain had been seen driving on Bathtub Row.

Bathtub Row had nothing but long afternoon shadows. No

maids hanging clothes or walking babies. There were no sounds except for jays and drifting shouts of a softball game on the playing field. Walking past Fermi's cottage and Jaworski's stone house, he remembered that *Snow White and the Seven Dwarfs* was the early movie. Everyone with kids, even Kitty Oppenheimer, was at *Snow White*.

At the end of Bathtub Row a garden of poplars and spruces lent privacy to the Oppenheimer cottage. Augustino was coming out of the kitchen door and there was something about the way he moved that made Joe silently stop and watch. Augustino carried a small reel of white wire finer than the electrical wire used on the Hill. He let himself out of the back garden gate and slipped into the trees.

The boy's scooter still sat in the flower bed. It looked rusted to the spot and the flowers lay flat and dead. Joe knocked softly at the door. It was unlocked. The living room's casement windows afforded sunlight that reflected off a hardwood floor and whitewashed stone walls. The furniture was Spanish rustic and rattan, an easy chair with a laurel pattern, stand-up ash-trays, serapes on the sofa, bookcases, Santiago pottery on the mantelpiece. Nothing apparently out of the ordinary.

Kitty didn't like maids re-ordering the bedroom. A four-poster stood over ashtrays, open books, loose butts, water glasses. There was a Picasso lithograph on the wall, a dishevelled bookcase. No white wires along the skirting board.

The study had a Spanish fireplace in the corner, a desk of spreading papers, two ashtrays of cigarette butts and a third ashtray with two pipes, a meerschaum and a briar. Hanging pictures of Krishna and a sailboat off a beach.

The nursery had been a sun porch and still had the yellow light of the porch. A crib at one end and a bed at the other. Teddy bears on a scatter rug. A case of children's books with a top row of German novels. Kitty employed a German nurse.

Joe returned to the living room, moving round the periphery and lifting chairs, tables, sofa. As he moved the bookcase, he saw the white wire that emerged from the edge of the floor, rose almost invisibly up the whitewashed wall and led into the back of the case. He searched through the records on the bottom shelf: Bach, Beethoven, Fauré. He spilled out the books above: Austen, Unamuno, *Jeune Fille Violane, Thermodynamique, Upanishads, The Interpretation of Dreams*. Behind Freud was the microphone, a wire-mesh button no larger than a dime. He snapped it off.

Tracking the wire to the boiler room in the basement, he found a new electrical connection off the junction box and a radio hidden behind a bin of soft New Mexican coal. He took the radio, went back to the living room and neatened up the books. By the time he left there was no sign of his visit or the captain's, nothing but resonance, a fading disturbance like two trails in a cloud chamber.

13

Utah sky was different. Scrubbed clean. Saline. Instead of vultures, gulls.

Fort Douglas, Salt Lake City, was different from Los Alamos because Douglas was so quiet. No booms from a mesa. No Indians. No women. Just the olive drab lethargy of the rearmost echelon of the United States Army.

The motor pool was a Quonset hut with open wings of galvanized steel over shadows and the glow of welders. Joe and Ray Stingo waited at the pumps. A noon sun lifted the reek of petrol off the tarmac. Ray's pompadour, usually sculptured with Wildroot, hung like crêpe.

"Chief, you should've fought."

"They asked for you and me."

"Why?"

Joe walked to the other side of the petrol pumps rather than argue. He and Ray had flown in from Santa Fe the night before and all the way Ray had asked the same question: why?

"The Texas kid killed Shapiro," Ray said.

"That's what I heard."

Ray followed Joe round an oil can.

"Captain Augustino can't have wanted you here."

"The captain never said anything to me about it." Joe hadn't spoken to Augustino since Oppy's cocktail party the week before. "Look, while Oppy's still in Washington, I'm available for this."

"But what about me?"

"You'll be okay."

A convoy rolled towards the pumps. Army sedan, truck, ambulance and tail sedan had started out the day before in Hanford, Washington, and had come 550 miles. Fort Douglas was where the teams switched.

"Too late," Ray moaned.

The schedule was strict. As soon as the lead sedan was at the first pump, four CID lieutenants jumped out and a fresh quartet took their place. Mechanics swung wearily out of the repair truck, a slope-fendered Dodge 6x6. The two men Joe and Ray were replacing both pulled the ambulance handbrake and jumped out. Joe and Ray climbed in, Joe behind the wheel. The rear of the ambulance was green Army. No white cross. No cots, no stretchers, no medicine. Only two fold-down seats and, farther back and taking up most of the space, an open steel square, four feet to a side, bolted to the floor and braced to the walls. Restraining straps of 1,000 lb-test nylon reached in from the eight corners of the square and hooked on to a 50 lb spun steel canister suspended at the centre. The canister was lined with graphite and lead, and bore, inside a hollow of moderating water, a ten-gram, lead-coated, stainless steel capsule of jelly-like plutonium nitrate that drivers called the slug.

The two sergeants from Hanford had bright eyes and stubble and the air of men returned from the dead.

"Want some bennies?" One came over to Ray's window and offered a handful of white pills. Ray took three and swallowed them. "You better take this, too." He handed in the Tommy gun that the co-driver was supposed to carry.

"Secure the convoy!" the lieutenants shouted at each other. They were boys right out of college and straight into Intelligence and would never see war. As they ran around with .45s and submachine-guns they reminded Joe of the sort of kids who brought baseball gloves to big league games. Mechanics clambered into the truck. Its back was stuffed with ambulance, car and truck spare parts in case there was a breakdown on the way. The orders were – as always, from Groves – no stopping.

"Let's for Chrissake go." Ray clutched the Tommy gun. Hair clung to the sweat on his forehead. His face had closed down to a bleak and dangerous glare. He refused to look back at the suspended, eight-armed canister riding in the rear of the ambulance.

"Wait a second, men."

A white-haired man in a tweed jacket and carrying a clipboard bounded out of the garage towards the ambulance.

"Santa!" Joe said.

"I'll kill him," Ray said.

Santa was the Hill psychiatrist. He'd always seemed to be part of the furniture at the lodge, an amiable headshrinker on hand to offer security-cleared emotional assurance to any longhair with the blues. Joe couldn't figure what Santa was doing at Fort Douglas. He expected the lieutenants to block Santa's way because no one outside convoy personnel was allowed near the ambulance, but the officers waved Santa on.

"Permission to come aboard?" Santa took a letter from the clipboard and handed it through Ray's window to Joe. The letter was a pass for Dr Delmore Bonney to accompany the drivers of Army ambulance YO3 from Fort Douglas to Site Y (Los Alamos), and the order was signed by both Oppy and Groves.

"I think you'd be more comfortable in one of the cars." Joe gave the letter back.

Santa shrugged happily.

"Orders are orders. Sometimes even civilians have to suffer."

"Sergeant Stingo isn't feeling too good. It could be infectious," Joe warned.

Santa raised white eyebrows.

"It could be psychosomatic."

Joe pushed open Ray's door. Ray leaned woodenly to one side so Santa could slip through to a fold-down seat. Already the lead sedan and truck, then ambulance and tail sedan were turning round the petrol pumps for the remaining 450 miles to New Mexico and the Hill.

"Nose wipes, boys." Santa handed up cotton swabs. "All part of the routine."

Joe and Ray stuck the swabs up their noses, then handed

them back to Santa who dropped them into separate envelopes.

"It isn't routine for us to make this run," Joe said. "It isn't routine for you to be on it."

"We're bodyguards," Ray said through his teeth. "We're not guinea pigs. They got enough crazy truckers for this run."

"Why do you think they chose you, Sergeant Stingo?" Santa hunched over Ray's shoulder.

"Because they hate me."

"If they hated you they wouldn't have asked me to bring the nose wipes. That's to help check any respiratory radioactivity. When we arrive, they'll take a blood sample and perhaps burn your clothes. Would they take those precautions if they didn't care about you?"

"True," Ray relented.

"You just need a ride from Salt Lake City?" Joe asked as Santa moved to his shoulder. "Why are you here?"

"I'll tell you why they hate me," Ray interrupted. The amphetamines fuelled his paranoia and turned the whites of his eyes pink. "For the first time in my life I'm ahead of the game. My father runs a garbage truck, my three brothers run garbage trucks, and they make $50 a week. I got $10,000 in poker money. I'm getting out of this fucking war with both legs and both arms. When I go back to Jersey I can buy a liquor store. I'll get my own fighters, maybe I'll manage. Get a boat at the shore, get married, have kids. They don't want me to have that."

"Why didn't you mention your mother?" Santa moved back to Ray's shoulder.

"What about my mother?" Ray whipped round. Because he still held the Tommy gun, its barrel pointed at Santa.

"Don't ask a man about his mother," Joe told Santa and pushed the barrel up.

"Why do you think Sergeant Stingo is nervous?"

"Because the Army hates enlisted men, which you are not."

"So why are you here?" Ray asked.

Santa smiled patiently. Fine skin crinkled around his pale

118

blue eyes. His nose and cheeks had the rosy hue of a lifetime of long walks and of the San Francisco Bay and the mellow sun. His Harris tweed jacket smelled like a potpourri of pipe tobacco and bay rum. His hair sprung in white spirals, thin on top, thick at the sides, wisps from the ears. Everyone on the Hill had naturally nicknamed him "Santa". Everyone but Harvey. Harvey called him "Bugs Bonney".

"I'm deeply enthused about the time we're going to be sharing," Santa said. "I understand we'll be driving through some spectacular scenery. In fact, in the garage I heard one of the officers refer to these shipments of –" Santa cleared his throat to indicate the plutonium hanging in the canister behind him – "as the Razzle-Dazzle Express."

"See any officers in here?" Ray muttered. "It's the fucking, glow-in-the-dark Asshole Express."

The Mormon temple swung to the north and shrank to the size of a claim stake under the immense Utah afternoon. The mountains started huge and grew. As the convoy gathered speed through the wide Jordan Valley, Ray looked as though he were entering a black tunnel.

The square and straps were designed to protect the suspended canister from shocks, but it didn't protect the drivers from the sight of the canister. It trembled in mid-air when the ambulance rolled over a cattle guard. It swayed as the road turned. For all its sleekness, the canister had a pregnant quality. The slug deep inside it seemed, in Joe's mind, alive. It was an interesting concept, metal that was alive. Not simply a mineral capable of some sort of chemical reaction, but so alive with alpha activity that the water around the slug was warmed to 100 degrees.

"Magnificent, the sun and these Wasatch mountains." Santa twisted this way and that for better views. "You boys must love this run."

"*Machine-Gun Joe was a rough and ready redskin,*" Joe sang softly, "*He'll never let plutonium touch the ground. And he always will remember the seventh of December, With his be-bop-a-rebop and he'll blow 'em down. I'll tell you what we'd* be doing if we weren't doing this run," Joe said to Ray, not to Santa. "We'd be somewhere in the South Pacific digging mass graves in a coral reef. We'd be burying bodies that were six months old, and pieces of bodies, with one dull shovel for the two of us."

"The South Pacific, you think?" Santa asked.

"Somewhere where no one would find us until the war was one year over," Joe told Ray. "We could play poker for seashells."

The whites of Ray's eyes were turning from pink to acid red.

"Why us?" he demanded.

Santa was atypically silent. The convoy gained altitude at the Mormon hamlets of Orem, Provo and Helper, touched down the Colorado River at Moab and then rose again up La Sals. Ray's blood went on pooling in his eyes. He pointed out every dead rabbit carcass on the road with his Tommy gun and laughed uproariously.

The amphetamines made Ray worse, but not much worse, than the first run he and Joe had made, when Ray sobbed all the way. Ray was a primitive Sicilian, afraid of nothing in the world until he came to the Hill and underwent the safety course on radiation. With his poker winnings he could afford to pay other enlisted men to pull his hazardous duties. Ray was never within a hundred yards of radioactive material, except when he and Joe were ordered to run the slug. The convoy had stopped in Moab to eat, but Ray did not eat, drink, piss or shit and he would not until the trip was over. At least, Joe thought, the night would cool Ray's sweat and the dark would hide the canister that danced at their backs.

Darkness fell at Cortez, Colorado, on the edge of the San Juan Mountains, where the stone climbed over itself like worn steps to the waning moon. Here, the mountain building was recent and ongoing, rubbing and fraying the road to dust. Clouds swept by like steam from the engines of the earth and winds heaved stones downhill, chasing tyres and rattling on the ambulance roof. Joe followed the repair truck ahead. Its red tail-lights would disappear round a wall of stone or wink desperately as it fought a downgrade. On one side of the road was granite, on the other the unforgiving dark of an abyss. Sometimes the road lay on a ridge with a black void on either side, and there ice had chipped away at the tarmac, leaving just enough room for the truck to inch through. The wind rose with them, out of the depths below, sounding like it was pushing boulders uphill.

"Let me confide in you, men, and tell you why you're here," Santa broke the quiet, "why you were ordered to make this run again, although it's not part of your ordinary duties. You were chosen because you have higher clearances than the other drivers and you have some inkling as to the actual nature of the project and of tonight's cargo. As we approach a test shot, more and more men, enlisted men on the Hill and at the Trinity test site, will get some inkling of the nature of the project. There'll be wild stories. You may hear, for example, that Dr Teller once tried to have the project stopped because his calculations showed that one such device would set the atmosphere on fire."

"Did he?" Joe asked.

"Yes, but later calculations showed that such a danger doesn't exist."

"Hardly exists?"

"Hardly. You see, then, how these stories get started. In fact," Santa chuckled, "Dr Teller wants a bomb one hundred times bigger, so he's not afraid."

"What'd he say?" Ray came out of a reverie.

"Teller's not afraid," Joe said.

"Afraid of what?" Ray winced as Joe dodged a pothole.

"All the same, there may be apprehension among the enlisted men as more of them come into contact with this sort of cargo."

"You think so?" Joe asked.

"There's the possibility," Santa said.

"Doesn't radiation cause tissue cancer, blood cancer, bone cancer and immediate or lingering death?" Joe asked.

"Theoretically," Santa granted. "Plutonium's got a clean bill of health so far."

"It's only been on earth five months," Joe pointed out. "Ray and I made the first run."

"In the fucking snow," Ray said.

Ahead, the repair truck fishtailed from side to side over loose rocks.

"But in three weeks," Santa said, "there'll be hundreds of GIs at Trinity and they'll all be wondering why they're there and what they're doing, and they'll be talking to MPs who will overhear scientists talking, that's human nature, and there will be some anxiety, because GIs are not scientists, about being in proximity to a nuclear explosion. You see, there won't be a radiation problem, but there may be a psychological problem. Even though they know the Army would not put soldiers in a situation that was not entirely safe. After all, here's a bomb that's supposed to blow up a city with just a few pounds of refined ore. I was wondering how you two feel about that."

"The city part's okay," Ray said.

"Don't ask us," Joe said.

"But you might feel anxiety," Santa suggested. "You two are the ones transporting that refined ore. Even though you know you're surrounded and protected by dedicated officers, you might feel anxiety."

"You don't feel any anxiety?" Joe asked.

"None," Santa assured Joe. "Not a bit."

Joe glanced back. Behind Santa, the canister floated securely in the web of straps and steel frame.

"No dedicated officers in this fucking wagon that I notice," Ray said.

"Then you, Sergeant Stingo, do admit to ambivalence."

"It was an ambulance," Ray said, "now they made it into this wagon."

"No, I mean ambivalence."

"It was. It's not now."

Ray stirred. All the paranoia that had been floating free up till now was starting to come together, to find its target after

122

200 miles, although it hadn't coalesced yet, hadn't absolutely fixed. He twisted in his seat the better to regard Santa.

"Ambivalence, Sergeant. Wanting two things at the same time."

"Yeah," Ray muttered. "Two ambulances. We could bring twice as much."

"Anyway," Santa persevered, seeing no warning sign in the red eyes staring at him, "I asked myself, how can I treat a problem when I know nothing about it? How can we prepare for the possible mass emotional crises of the test site without seeing at least some enlisted men now in close proximity to hazardous radioactive material?"

"That's why we're here?" Ray asked.

"Because only you and Sergeant Peña actually know what the cargo is. The regular drivers and even the security officers only know that it's vital to the war effort."

"We're here because of you?" Ray asked.

"That's what I was just saying."

"We're here because of you?" Ray wanted to be sure.

"That's what I said I said."

"You?" Ray's eyes jerked back to the road when Joe hit a rabbit. His fingers twisted the handgrip of the Tommy gun.

"Because of me," Santa said with good-humoured firmness. Joe could tell that Ray intended to turn and kill Santa as soon as he dared take his eyes from the road, but the tarmac now deteriorated to raw dirt. Last summer a Colorado Highways truck had spread oil on the road as a thin binder, but a winter in the Rockies had passed and the little oil that remained had become patches of dark slick between the long stretches of ice slick on a route that plunged at twenty degrees down the mountain side. Staying on the road would demand all of Ray's concentration even as a passenger. Even if Joe wanted to stop and take the gun from Ray, the sedan behind would hit them and pitch them over the edge of the road into the darkness that lay like a sea around them.

Santa seemed totally unconscious of the road, the mountains, the dark, as if danger and natural phenomena lay in Joe's area of expertise. Occasionally he commented on the effect of moonlight on a snowy peak, or the glint of a river a thousand feet below. Otherwise he behaved as if Joe had chosen a mildly diverting route.

"You!"

Ray tried to snatch his eyes from the road and kill Santa, but erosion had carved away the outer lane and the brake lights ahead blinked frantically, demanding his attention.

"Please take my word for it, Sergeant." There was movement behind Joe and the tang of pipe tobacco. "Mind if I smoke, men?" A flame glowed for a moment. Joe thought if he looked back there might be a blanket and a dog on Santa's lap. "The three of us are like Helios, bearing the sun across the sky. A new sun, of course. Just as we call the moon when we can't see it a new moon. There is an enormous synchronicity building towards Trinity, a psychic tension. You men feel it, I can sense it."

"You want to sense something?"

Ray started to turn the Tommy gun, but a rock slide had poured over a hairpin bend in the road and Joe had to brake and turn without locking wheels.

"That's why I expect our problems at Trinity will be largely psychological." There was a rustle of paper. "Do you mind if I ask a few questions?"

Joe downshifted. The ambulance slid over stones to the edge of the road. Larger rocks bounced in front and rang off the crankcase underneath.

"Sergeant Stingo, if you heard that you were in close proximity to radioactive material, would you feel comfortable, concerned, a little anxious, very anxious?"

"Shit," Joe said.

The red tail-lights of the truck in front swung wildly.

"Boulder," Joe said.

It was the size of a doghouse and in the middle of the road. The truck cleared it on the right and slammed into the rock wall, scraping sparks off granite. Joe headed for the same space, skidding, holding the wheel steady. Ray and Tommy

124

gun were pressed against the windshield. As the ambulance slipped past the boulder, Joe saw the truck ahead hit the wall again. Wrenches, jacks, tyres spilled from under the tarpaulin, bounced in the ambulance's headlights. As the truck stopped, nose into the wall, the ambulance slid through between the truck's tailboard and the road edge. The lead car had halted in the middle of the road. Joe swung in, braked and pulled the emergency brake at the same time, coming to rest against the car bumper only a second before the tail sedan rammed into the rear of the ambulance. A tyre wobbled out of the dark and past the headlights. Security officers ran up and down waving flashlights and Tommy guns. Even Ray was distracted.

A scream that was both feminine and unhuman erupted by Joe's ear, followed by a powerful, bell-like gong as Santa flew out of his seat head first and hit the ambulance roof. He seemed still to be suspended in mid-air when Joe looked past him to the rear of the ambulance and saw the empty steel square and eight slack straps. The plutonium canister had broken loose and rolled forward, glinting and warm, to nudge Santa's loafers and Argyle socks. The plutonium couldn't explode. Joe would have been happy to explain that to Santa, to reduce his psychic tension, given the chance. Santa dropped to the ambulance floor.

"Gee," said Ray.

"Orders are we don't stop for anything," the lieutenant in charge said when Joe pointed out the slumped figure of the analyst. "He's already in the ambulance, we'll leave him there."

"He's out cold, sir. He probably has concussion."

"Look, Sergeant, we're lucky no one in the truck was killed."

"What about this?" Joe pointed to the canister. "The strap hooks are broken."

"God, we can't have that thing rolling around. Somebody's going to have to hold it. We're losing time. Choose up, one of you has to take it. Or wedge it with something."

The truck, fender crumpled, was already weaving round the ambulance as the lieutenant ran off to the lead sedan. The convoy was re-assembling itself.

"I'll wedge it." Ray's eyes were red but unwavering.

As Joe let out the clutch Ray slipped over his seat to the rear of the ambulance. Cautiously, the vehicles moved down the mountain. Clouds scattered over the stars. There was a scuff of cloth and scrape of metal over the ambulance floor. Joe looked back and saw Ray tucking Santa into a corner. He couldn't see the canister.

Ray was panting when he returned to his seat.

"It was hot, Chief. Like a can of soup."

It shouldn't have broken the hooks, Joe knew. Eight steel hooks shouldn't have snapped. It was as if the canister had leapt forward at the first opportunity. I'll tell Oppy about Augustino, he thought. If they ship me off the Hill, I've got nothing to lose except a phosphorescent glow.

"Like a tin can of hot soup, Chief. Like it was alive."

Down the rest of the mountain curves to Durango and all the way to the hills of Tierra Amarilla, New Mexico, there came from the back the sound of Santa rocking heavily as the ambulance careened like a hearse.

JULY

14

Six clowns wore white paint with black horizontal stripes around their arms, legs, torso. Black circles around their eyes and mouths. Black and white cotton caps twisted into horns. Short black scarves around the neck, knee and wrists. Long black loincloths trailing behind. Rattles of deer hooves tied to the waist. Moccasins.

Together, they joked and prodded the dancers into a great circle in the middle of the plaza. The men wore clean work trousers and handkerchiefs tied into headbands. The women were in dresses. Man, woman, man, woman, each holding an ear of corn in one hand and a yellow zigzag of wood, a lightning wand, in the other. Elders, singers and a drummer with a big Cochiti drum stood along the north side. Plaza and cottonwood framed the sky.

A new touch were the patriotic blue armbands with gold Vs for victory on all the dancers. One man had also come out wearing sunglasses. A clown stole the glasses, slipped them on another clown as the drumming started; deep voices lifted and the dancers began turning counter-clockwise like a wheel.

"We don't need Captain Augustino and his security apparatus," Oppy told Anna Weiss. "Los Alamos has a much better defence. The Hill isn't a place, it's a time warp. We are the future surrounded by a land and a people that haven't changed in a thousand years. Around us is an invisible moat of time. Anyone from the present, any mere spy, can only reach us by crossing the past. We're protected by the fourth dimension."

They and Joe and the rest of the tourists watched from the

broad shadow of the cottonwood on the south side of the plaza. Back from Washington that morning, Oppy had changed to his Western gear: jeans, boots, silver buckle, hat at an angle. Anna wore her jumpsuit and a man's fedora.

"It's perfectly animistic," Oppy said, "an ancient Greek fertility rite, that's what so wonderful about it. The ears of corn, of course, are phallic symbols."

The word from Washington was that Truman's military advisers claimed Trinity was a waste of time, that the bomb was a scientific boondoggle, a hoax, a dud. Oppy put on a brave front.

"You're not going to dance?" Anna asked Joe. So far, she was no more than civil to him, as if they'd hardly met.

"No."

"Joe's different," Oppy said. "He's a progressive Indian. A bebop Indian." Oppy turned to Joe and lowered his voice. "By the way, when we get to Trinity, Groves wants you to patrol for Apaches. That incident in the snow seems to have lodged in his brain. He thinks it takes an Indian to stop an Indian."

It wasn't a major ceremony, not a saint's day or a basket dance, just a dance for late planting, open to the public but unannounced. Maids had told people on the Hill that "something would be happening". Among the hundred or so spectators, Joe saw Fermi and Teller. Foote sported British Army shorts and a sombrero.

The dancers moved with a step. Half-hop. Turn. There were few young men; most of them were in the service. Grandparents and girls moved happily to the sonorous beat, gently stirring up dust. Hop. Shuffle. The monotony used to drive Joe crazy. A placid merry-go-round of tame Indians and corn. Shuffle. Turn.

"Who are the painted ones?" Anna asked Joe.

"Clowns."

"What do they represent to you?"

"Ancient Greeks."

The clowns were performing feeble antics inside the dancers' circle. Joe remembered when they were fierce mimics who imitated Navajos, tourists, Catholic priests, when clowns were at least the heat in the pueblo milk.

Cottonwood leaves rustled; on the hottest day, a cottonwood could sound like rain. Ladies from Santa Fe, veteran watchers, opened folding chairs. Oppy murmured something that made Anna laugh, and Joe excused himself to take a walk.

Behind a low stone wall and a small graveyard at the west end of the plaza sat the mission of Santiago. The walls were adobe seven feet thick at the base; the church looked like a monolith thirty feet high. A fort, actually, from the days when the Apaches used to raid the Rio Grande Valley. On the roof was a graceful iron cross and a bell, both cast in Spain. The door was always shut during dances.

The graveyard had marked and unmarked mounds, and a scattering of new white crosses for soldiers. Their backs to the plaza, two cowboys sat on tombstones and smoked. They were wiry men in sweat-stained hats. The older was about sixty, with calloused hands and a chickentrack neck. The younger had long blonde hair and wore a vanity shirt like the kind Roy Rogers sang in. The satin had turned to a muddy iridescence and strips of curlicue piping had fallen off.

"Sergeant Joe Peña," Joe said and stuck out his hand. "I never saw cowboys at an Indian dance before."

"I'm Al." The old man gave Joe the briefest possible shake. "This is Billy."

Billy cocked his head, as if that reduced Joe in size. His nose twisted when he smiled.

"Fuck off."

"You can see better over in the plaza," Joe said.

"We've seen Indians before," Billy said. The shirt was shabby, but painfully romantic. No one would wear it unless he'd considered the possibility of an Indian maiden eyeing him in it. Joe wanted to give him every chance.

"Indian Service?" he asked.

"Who says?" Al looked up, pushed back his hat, revealing stringy hairs stuck to damp, untanned forehead.

"You're Service riders," Joe said.

Billy dropped his cigarette and stepped on it. "No one said that."

"It's not hard," Joe said. "Cowboys. Here. But not for the dance and you don't care for Indians. And you smell like sheep shit. That's right, you've been out shooting those Navajo sheep. With that?" He looked at the gun on Al's belt, a rust-speckled Colt ·45. "Doing your bit to win the war?"

"Because they let you in the Army –" Billy began.

"But this isn't the Navajo reservation," Joe said. "No Navajos here. You're lost."

"Peña." Al stored the name away aloud. "You work on that magic mountain the Army's got."

"I'll show you the road out," Joe offered.

Billy stood up. "You don't –"

"By the way, that shirt," Joe said and shook his head. "That shirt looks like shit and spaghetti on a plate."

"I told him," Al said. He slid off the tombstone, stretched and started for the graveyard gate. "Catch you later, Sergeant."

Though Billy looked bewildered and reluctant to leave, he followed the older man. Halfway to the gate he turned to say, "We got those Navajos, every one."

The tombstone Al had been using for a seat was a weathered slab of marble that said "Miguel Peña, 1895–1935". Dolores had bought the whitest stone in Santa Fe and it shone while she was alive. Billy had been sitting on a smaller, rose marble marker that said "Dolores Reyes Peña, 1899–1944". She bought it along with Mike's in anticipation; there was nothing more exotic to Dolores than a rose. Only lately had Joe started to realize how young his parents were. He picked up the butt Billy had thrown down, field-stripped it and blew the tobacco away.

There was a certain definition, an edge to the dance when Joe returned. One black and white clown had a camera and was taking a picture of Foote. Then aimed it like a gun. The clown in sunglasses pretended to be blind and stumbled with a stick along the front line of the tourists, pinching a skirt here, feeling a blouse there. In the dancers' line, women giggled Slide. Half-toe. Turn.

A third clown slipped out of the circle. One pillow was tied to the back of his loincloth and another was strapped to his belly. A fur moustache was stuck to his lip, gold stars to his shoulders, and on his head he wore an Army officer's cap with a paper star. Ponderously he walked clockwise to the dancers, so that they passed in review for him. When he added a twitch to the pillow on his ass, the impersonation of General Groves was complete. The other clowns bowed and salaamed. Anna Weiss laughed, but Oppy looked pained.

A Buick four-door drew up in front of the mission. Fuchs was at the wheel and Augustino was with him. Cars weren't allowed that close. When a tribal policeman went to the car and waved it on, a rear window rolled down and Joe saw the Indian Service rider called Al. The car stayed.

The clown in sunglasses produced a small firecracker. Another clown took it, another clown blessed it and a fourth clown put it on the ground and pretended to light it while the clown-Groves raised binoculars to his circled eyes to watch. All the other clowns except the one in sunglasses put their fingers to their ears.

Nothing.

A second match was tried. A third. A fourth.

A dud.

One after another, clowns inspected the firecracker and passed it on until it was with the clown-Groves, who studied it through his binoculars and gave it to the clown in sunglasses, who turned and presented the firecracker to Oppy. The crowd closed in to see. The dancers had never stopped and the singers hadn't ceased their chant, but their eyes were on Oppy, too. Joe had never seen Oppy blush before. The clown in the sunglasses got on his knees and begged.

"Go ahead, Oppy!" Foote shouted. "Be a sport!"

In the car, Augustino pointed to the clown in glasses.

Anna handed Oppy a cigarette lighter. The other clowns fell to their knees to plead. Oppy rescued a smile and lit the fuse

133

and threw the firecracker into the air, where it exploded with a puff and a bang. Whether the firecracker happened to come at the end of the morning dance or was the signal for it to stop, the circle of dancers abruptly broke and dispersed for lunch. The clowns went off in single file, holding on to the long black tails of each other's loincloths, through an alley on the north side of the plaza which was out of bounds to tourists.

Fuchs' Buick was gone.

"You should be proud," Jaworski said and shook Oppy's hand. "They're dancing for our victory and success."

"Wasn't there some element of menace?" Teller suggested.

"Nonsense," Foote said. "Oppy, you played your part beautifully, even modestly."

Oppy returned Anna's lighter.

"Anna, I have to leave."

"I'll stay. They're more alive than you said."

Augustino had joined the group. "They certainly are alive. Can we talk, Dr Oppenheimer? You and me and Sergeant Peña?"

The parking lot was an oat field beaten into a cloud of dust. More cars were arriving than leaving. Augustino's jeep was next to the grey Army sedan Joe had brought Oppy in. Joe still couldn't find Fuchs' Buick.

Augustino asked, "The ones in the black and white greasepaint, Sergeant, are they idiots or traitors?"

"The clowns?"

"Whatever," Augustino said, "that was a serious breach of security. They singled out Dr Oppenheimer here in public view and identified him with explosives. Any outsider with a background in physics had to notice him and Teller. The imitation of the general was in the worst possible taste. What is the religious purpose behind that?"

"You'd have to ask them, sir."

"I'd love to. Who are they?"

"I don't know, sir."

"A tribal secret?"

"I guess so, sir."

134

"There's a great deal you're not telling me these days, Sergeant. They dance again?"

"This afternoon, sir."

"Same clowns, same people?"

"Yes, sir."

"Then I think it would be wise for you to drive the Director back to the Hill now, before there's another incident. You do agree, Dr Oppenheimer?"

Oppy stared back at the plaza.

"I thought we had good relations with these people. I thought we were friends."

"What other incident, sir?" Joe asked Augustino.

"Follow me," the captain said after a pause.

All traffic leaving the lot for the highway had to pass over a narrow cattle guard. Joe stopped for incoming cars while Augustino's jeep went ahead. As always when they were alone, Oppy sat up in front with Joe. He tapped on the dashboard impatiently, as if a herd of morons were holding him back. Word of the dance had spread. From Santa Fe open buses dropped off tourists, who hurried on foot across the guard. A short figure with a camera and binoculars round his neck Joe recognized from the bar of La Fonda, the New Yorker named Harry Gold.

Joe dug into his pocket and gave Oppy what looked like a wire-mesh button.

"That's a microphone Augustino put in your house while you were gone. It's time you knew what's going on around you."

Oppy held the microphone up to the light of the windshield as if he were examining some mildly interesting artefact.

"It was hidden," Joe said. "It wasn't put there for your protection. He's watching you, he's after you."

"I know."

Oppy's voice had fallen to a whisper. He turned the tiny microphone over and over.

"Tell General Groves," Joe said. "Tell the general that his head of Intelligence thinks you're a Red spy."

135

"The general knows." Oppy looked at Joe with a clear gaze of resignation and contempt. It was an inner look, a meditation. He put his hand out of the open window and dropped the microphone on to the dirt outside. "You can't help me, Joe."

"You're in charge of the most important lab in the war and you're scared of a captain? They can't do anything without you. You're the goddamn bomb."

"It's . . . a temporary situation."

The cattle guard was clearing. Augustino's jeep waited far up the road.

Joe got out. "Then I'll help Augustino."

Oppy slid behind the wheel and asked, "Help him?"

"He wants to know who those clowns are. It takes an Indian to stop an Indian, right?"

"Joe –" Oppy started to protest. He began again. "Joe, twenty more days. After Trinity, no one can touch us."

Joe made a wide circuit of Santiago on his way back. Fuchs' car was gone, probably halfway to the Hill by now. The Indian Service riders, Billy and Al, were drinking beers in the back of a tribal police car in an alley. All around the plaza Indians ate fried bread on their roofs. Under the plaza cottonwood in an island of shade, tourists ate sandwiches. Waxed paper floated over the ground on waves of heat.

15

Around the shaft of sunlight that came down the ladder to the kiva roof, three clowns repaired their black and white stripes from Mason jars of body paint. Two clowns without caps rested on the wall benches. The last stood in the shadow of the corner to drink a Coke and piss into a pail. All turned to the side door as Joe came in.

He hadn't been in a kiva for almost twenty years. Outside, the kiva of the clowns was a plain adobe house. Inside, though, the walls were painted with shapes that seemed to hover in the dark. Snakes. Swallows. Stepped mountains and red and white clouds. The zigzag lightning slats of a dismantled altar stood between Spanish chests of prayer sticks and dance wands. The floor was beaten earth, and had the traditional hole that led to the centre of the earth. The clowns themselves seemed dislocated, white blocks, bars of black. Even so, Joe saw that one of the clowns without a cap, a clown with loose grey hair, a heavy belly and spindly legs was Ben Reyes.

"*Psoot-bah!*" Ben said; it was an order for a dog to scram. "Get out!"

"There are two Indian Service cowboys out there," Joe told the other clown without a cap. "I think they came to arrest you."

"You pointed him out," Ben said.

"Fuchs pointed you out," Joe told the other clown.

The clown's long brown hair fell to his shoulders, but he still wore sunglasses from the morning dance, despite the dark of the kiva. He tilted his head and smiled at Joe as if sharing a joke.

"You gave the firecracker to Oppenheimer and you didn't try to take it back," Joe said. "When you were pretending to be blind out there, you still bumped into too many people."

"Not bad for a real blind man, though," Roberto said.

"Not bad."

"They'd really dare do it?"

"You pulled a shotgun on the wrong Kraut. He's our Kraut and there's a war on. I don't know how he knew you would dance, but he knew and the captain in charge of security on the Hill knew and they pointed you out to a pair of Indian Service riders. Don't worry, Fuchs and the captain fingered you and ran. The cowboys watched the dance for five seconds and they saw you from a distance. Bring in someone else to dance. You'll have all afternoon to get back to Taos."

"Coke?" Roberto asked. "You thirsty?"

"No, thanks."

"Hot out there, isn't it?"

"If you're going to get someone, you better do it now."

Roberto removed the dark glasses and laid them on the bench. His eyes looked not only shrunken but painted out.

"Well, it's not as simple as that, Joe. No one is allowed in while clowns are here. I don't think anyone but you would break the rules."

"If six clowns don't come out of here, the riders will come in for you."

"You dance," Roberto said.

"Him?" Ben asked.

"There's no one else," Roberto said.

"It would be a joke," Ben said.

"You show him what to do," Roberto said.

The three clowns by the ladder squatted and talked among themselves. It would be a great disgrace to include someone as ignorant as Joe Peña in a ceremony. On the other hand, it would be a great disgrace to have an elder from another pueblo arrested in Santiago.

"No," Joe spoke up. "For once, Ben is right. I only came to warn you."

Roberto acted genuinely puzzled. "What good is a warning if you won't help?" he asked. "That's a fake warning."

"From a fake Indian," Ben said.

"Fair warning." Joe held up his hand and made it a wave as he moved to the door. "From here on, I don't even know you."

"He went away an Indian and came back a black man," Ben said. "He went into the Army and became a white man. Maybe there's no one there at all any more. Now, his brother was an Indian."

"Ben," Joe said and shook his head.

"Best thing that happened to his mother was she died before today," Ben said.

Joe returned from the door. "Ben, Ben, Ben. Don't say another word."

"I need your help," Roberto said.

The paint was greasy and thick, and he felt as if his whole body were a mask. His hair was tucked up into the striped cap, which was tied by a black thong under his chin. The other clowns painted black outlines around his eyes and mouth, and knotted black scarves around his neck, wrists and ankles. I can't believe this, Joe thought, this is happening to someone else; he felt like he was standing apart and watching himself be prepared, as if he were lending just his body. The tail of the long black loincloth trailed on the floor. No moccasins were found big enough, so he was going barefoot, and Roberto suggested that Joe stay within the circle of dancers as much as he could. Everyone gathered at the ladder and shared a last cigarette. Roberto wore his white Taos blanket, ready for a separate exit. One of the other clowns had the dark glasses now. Ben tucked a bullwhip under his arm. The sun had moved west, making the light from the roof dimmer, the angle sharper, and Joe had the sensation that the kiva was sealing over him. Finally, the clowns climbed the ladder one by one, Joe last.

They burst off the roof and down an alley, dogs and boys

running at their side. Although Joe tried to hang back, sheer length of stride brought him to the front. There was a tunnel of shade, then the brilliant, droning heat of the plaza and a bigger crowd than before. All the northern roofs were crowded. The tourists had spread across the whole southern side of the plaza. Only the watching priests and elders were the same, as if they hadn't moved since morning. Joe expected at any moment someone would shout, "That's not a real clown, that's Joe Peña!" He chased an old lady and a girl into the dancing line.

The plaza seemed to wheel round him. His paint seemed already washed with sweat. He saw Foote. Jaworski and Harvey had come. The drumming started. At the east end of the plaza, among the very last tourists, he saw the Service rider named Al. At the west end was Billy.

Just long enough for Roberto to get away from the kiva, Joe told himself. As the circle of dancers began to turn, he slipped through it and used it as a screen. The steps weren't that hard to pick up, a slow 4–4 beat. Hop, slide, half-turn. Without warning, the singers and drummer went to a fast 3–4, then back to the slow 4–4. Joe stumbled, but it was taken as a joke, because, after all, he was a clown.

The whole idea was that everyone did precisely the same step in the same way without embellishment or conspicuousness. The circle was a cosmic gear moving in clouds, calling in game, drawing up corn. Any individuality was a loose screw.

"Cloud flowers lie over the mountains, cloud flowers are blooming now over the mountains. First the lightning flashes in the north, then the thunder rumbles, then the rain falls, because flowers are blooming," the singers sang.

Though there wasn't a cloud in the sky, the dancers bounced happily, hop, turn, a cob in one hand, a lightning wand in the other. Their worn, clean coveralls and crisp, faded dresses made them look like dolls of sober industry. The women and girls didn't raise their knees as high as the men or stamp their heels as hard. But they recognized Joe. He saw their glances stealing towards him and caught their whispers when he as much as turned.

"In the fields you can see melon flowers," the singers sang. *"In the fields you can see corn flowers. In the fields the water bird sings and overhead the black clouds grow."* A hundred dancers softly made the ground tremble.

One more revolution of the circle and he'd quit, Joe told himself. The circle moved so slowly, though. The entire population of Santiago seemed to be present, dancing or on the roofs, surrounding him and waiting for him to do something. So many of the women looked like Dolores. Not just Dolores the famous old potter, but Dolores as a young woman, Dolores as a girl. Half-toe. Turn.

Two of the clowns took folding chairs away from the ladies from Santa Fe and sat, pretending to gossip, put on lipstick, adjust girdles. A third patrolled the edges of the plaza, keeping back the spreading line of tourists. He threatened a spectator who had come halfway to the circle from the east end. It was the younger cowboy trying to get a better look at Joe, and he ignored the tubby, old clown waving him back. When the clown uncoiled a whip and cracked it at Billy's feet, Billy knocked him down.

The entire circle slowed, watching the confrontation. Joe saw the tribal policemen hanging back; they didn't want a hassle with the Indian Service. Without being aware of it, Joe was through the dancers. He seemed to cover the distance to Ben in a few steps. Billy pointed a warning finger.

Joe stepped over Ben, took Billy by the front of his shirt and, with one hand, lifted him high off the ground. The cowboy kicked and swung his fists while Joe carried him to where most of the crowd watched under the cottonwood. Joe intended to set him down gently, but, released, Billy somehow flew over the first two rows of spectators to the base of the tree.

As the crowd retreated, Foote's sombrero rolled forward. Chairs folded with claps. One man laughed. Al worked his way to Billy, laughing the whole time as if his friend had participated in a great joke. Clowns joined in as if Joe were fooling. Foote

141

and the entourage from the Hill, Harry Gold and the tourists from Santa Fe started laughing anxiously, because they wanted to believe it was a set-up performance and the huge clown was nothing to be afraid of. Anna Weiss didn't smile. She hadn't stepped back. She watched Joe as if a giant had stepped out of the blue sky.

The drummer never missed a beat.

The circle went on turning.

Afterward, men who were clowns washed in the river a couple of miles outside Santiago. Since he wasn't really a clown, Joe washed alone where cottonwood logs and sand had stopped up a pool. Thimbleberries with white, papery buds grew thickly down to either shore. Black paint slowly yielded to oatmeal soap and a yucca brush.

The sun was dazzling on the surface of the Rio. It took Joe a while to realize he was not alone, to see Anna Weiss watching from the smooth flank of a log that rose out of the sand.

16

In Unit 20 at the Cordoba Motel, daylight made a hot, white edge round the window blinds.

She twisted, spread herself, and as she settled into him he put his hands on her hips and helped her down. Widening, her eyes never left his. Despite the drawn blinds, she glowed, as if inner-lit. Yet her eyes were luminously dark, her hair was dark, the tips of her white breasts were dark. Deep inside her, he still rose. As if he had stepped off a high building a long time ago and only now was hitting ground. Falling and rising at the same time.

"I've never made love with a giant before."

He turned her on her back and drove deeper. Perspiration shone between her breasts. As she wrapped her legs round him, the bed groaned. Anna pulled him in with her hands until he was lifting her high with each stroke.

Her shoes and fedora were by the door where she'd dropped them as soon as she came in. Her jumpsuit was sprawled, empty, across the middle of the floor. His uniform lay over a chair.

Outside, the afternoon dimmed. Inside a pearly greyness crept along the walls. The room was decorated with photographs of the Alhambra. The pictures trembled as he held her against a wall so that only her toes, barely, touched the floor. The whole wall trembled, like a vertical sheet.

She was weightless and strong. She seemed to ride him, to be on all sides of him, to swallow him and be swallowed at the same time.

When they moved away the wall bore the damp imprint of her back and his hands.

Her body had both a blue paleness and a sheen of life. His belly looked black against hers.

As he lifted her, the bed, the entire room seemed to rise. The more and deeper he had her, the further he went the next time, until he felt himself dissolving.

The radio in the room, the Capehart console, looked like an old trombone player napping in a chair.

The walls could be paper pages now, ready to burn, tear or fold back and drop him into space.

"You're crazy to do this," he said.

"Oh, yes, I've been certified."

"Certified?"

"Officially," she said and smiled.

It was the dual moment of knowledge. The learning of legs, hands, skin, sweat, when the body is the whole terrain and obsessive scope of attention. Every word echoes on and on and becomes the colour of action. Breath synchronizes and the sheets twist.

They sat cross-legged on the bed, the ashtray and haze of smoke between them. Although the heat of the day had faded, their sweat shone.

"I was in love," she said and lit a cigarette for him and put it between his lips. "I loved a French boy. He was very poetic. I loved a German boy. He was very depressed. It was fun to be in love. What I liked was the element of irrationality. This isn't love at all; this is pure irrationality."

He inhaled, filled his lungs and let the smoke escape so his breath filled the room. Of one thing he was certain. "You've never been in love before," he said.

Her grey eyes watched as if from a cat's distance. Until they closed and she arched. With her hair back, her forehead seemed higher, the lofty brow of genius, so the black hair was the giveaway, swaying, a flag whipping the dark above him. Until he pulled her head down and opened her mouth with his, and she gathered his hair in her fingers and would not let the kiss go.

She asked, "You've been in love?"

"It was a flight to the moon, a night in June. Icy fingers up and down my spine, that same old witchcraft when your eyes meet mine."

She rested the tip of her finger between his eyes.

"Tonight is the last night in June."

"I knew one of them was right."

In total dark, he took her from behind, the deepest, final fit, the groove of her back against his chest. So deep it seemed he flowed into her for ever. So still, they both shook to the pounding of her heart.

The car was a Plymouth two-door she had borrowed from Teller at the dance. Joe had found jazz on the radio. Stars lit the road. Wind whipped Anna's hair around her face.

"I loved King Kong," she said. "I would have traded places with that girl. King Kong was very popular in Germany. And, you can play the piano."

"Great."

"And a boxer. I asked all about you."

"Was a boxer."

"You were good?"

"Not bad. I got interested in other things."

"Music?"

"I love the piano. I love the weight, the shape. Something about a concert grand, playing a high E in an empty house."

"And women? Is it the same, the high E in an empty house?"

"Well, a little. How did you get involved in neutrons?"

She thought for a moment, but Joe could already hear her voice. Most important for him was that a woman should have her own voice, and he'd never heard anyone like Anna.

"I could always see numbers. It's like having your own world, or a world you only share with a few others. Prime numbers.

Positive numbers and negative numbers in patterns like physics. I did a paper on reaction multiplication when I was sixteen to amuse myself. I was in a sanatorium."

"Why?"

"Hysteria. Anaemia. Pregnancy. It depended on which doctor you talked to. I was lucky to be in the sanatorium at all because they weren't supposed to take Jews, but my father, although he had lost his professorship at the university, was so respected I was allowed in. The sanatorium had once been a monastery with gardens and orchards, even lemon trees, that ran in terraces to the river, the Elbe. In one garden was a bower of honeysuckle that stirred with bees. I retreated there. I tried to think of things so small and insignificant that they would be almost pure mathematics, that they would have nothing to do with the larger, real world. I watched the bees move from flower to flower. This was just after the Meitner-Frisch article on fission, you remember that?"

"I think I was fighting in Chicago that day. I must have missed it."

"Bees and neutrons are, a little, the same. The paper was only a few pages and it couldn't be published because I was a Jew." For a moment Anna looked into the canyon, and to the mountains beyond, to distant lightning collecting at a peak. "You didn't tell anyone, did you, about Harvey? You didn't report your friend Roberto either, did you?"

"That doesn't mean I agree with Roberto."

"Or with Harvey and me."

"Two more weeks to Trinity and then it will all be over. Maybe it will fail." He could feel her disappointment. "I hate arguments. I'm a coward. True arguments are full of words and each person is sure he's the only one who knows what the words mean. Each word is a basket of eels so far as I'm concerned. Everybody gets to grab just one eel and that's his interpretation and he'll fight to the death for it. Roberto's from Taos, which he thinks gives him the right to say 'up' is 'down'. Harvey's from Texas, which makes it strange he and I agree on a goddamn thing. As for you and me?"

146

"Yes?"

"Which is why I love music. You hit a C and that's a C and that's all it is. Like speaking clearly for the first time. Like being intelligent. Like understanding. A Mozart or an Art Tatum sits at the piano and picks out the undeniable truth."

"You're going to hear about me," Anna said slowly. "That I'm insane and a tramp. I don't care what people say, but I want you to know that only one is true."

"Which one?"

"Which one is important to you?"

Joe hesitated, and during that long moment they neared the first checkpoint. Joe kept the MPs supplied with cigarettes and ration coupons; he'd expected to be waved through as usual. Tonight, the checkpoint was a Western scene, the sort of painting daubed for tourists: the amber light of a shed reaching out to men on horseback, the riders slouched and weary, horses steaming in the night air. But also jeeps with their headlights on, blocking the road on each side of the checkpoint shed. He stopped fifty feet before the shed and left the Plymouth's lights on.

"Stay here," he told Anna as he got out. "If anyone asks, we were driving around, you don't know where."

The horses were lathered bright in the headlights. Among the riders was Sergeant Shapiro. Corporal Gruber had one arm in a sling.

Shapiro laughed.

"Fell off his horse, Chief. Broke his fucking arm."

As Joe pushed into the shed, Captain Augustino looked up from the map he was sharing with Billy and Al. The captain was sleek in an Eisenhower jacket. The two cowboys were crusty from a day's riding. Al's little eyes and mouth were drawn tight and there was a white stubble on his jaw line. Billy's hair hung lank, dirty and yellow.

"Speak of the devil." Augustino looked delighted, as if some deserved amusement had come his way at the end of a weary day. "Come in, come in, Sergeant Peña. You know our friends

147

Al and Billy from the Indian Service. Billy's the one you tossed like a sack of manure at the dance."

The shed was small for four men and a pot-bellied stove. The light was a hanging bulb. On the walls were a clock, map, telephone, a yellowed silhouette guide to German planes, clipboards with old orders of the day, licence lists, sign-in and sign-out sheets. Joe suspected that the only names signed out and not back in were his and Anna's.

Augustino paused to let the general discomfort grow. "You missed the excitement, Sergeant."

"Yes, sir?"

"Absolutely, Sergeant. Why, we had a regular posse out, a dragnet looking for an Indian friend of yours. You know, your friend who assaulted one of our guests with a shotgun. The same friend whose place you took at the dance. Weren't you supposed to be driving the Director?"

"He wanted to know the identities of the dancers, sir. So I joined the dance."

"Just like that. Did you determine any identities?"

"No, sir. They didn't take off their paint around me."

Al snorted. "You didn't know the dancer whose place you took was about to be arrested?"

"How would I know that?"

"Excellent question, Sergeant," Augustino said. "That's just so excellent it's what we've been asking all day. These gentlemen suspect some kind of informer, but it's my belief that they're dumb and you're smart. Who's right, do you think?"

"I wouldn't know that either, sir."

"Well, I have an intimate and high regard for you, Sergeant, I do." He smoothed the map with his hands. "Now, we have spent a vigorous day on every highway in northern New Mexico and riding up every dirt road and arroyo around Santiago pueblo. We did find some rattlesnakes. I think it was Corporal Gruber who had a nasty spill. Your friend, however, seems to have vanished."

"He must be pretty fast, sir."

"And blind at that, Sergeant. Both shocking and remarkable. And how was your day, Sergeant? Was it a full one?"

"Yes, sir, I was still trying to carry out the Director's request. Unfortunately, I was not successful."

"Wherever he was, that's where we'll find his blind friend," Billy told Augustino, "and we won't have to scramble into every pisshole Indian ruin again."

"Were you alone, Sergeant?" Augustino looked out at the Plymouth. "Alone on this quest?" The captain took the sign-out sheet off its hook, "Don't answer. Don't do anything until I'm back."

Then Augustino was out of the door and striding eagerly to the Plymouth's headlights. Joe could make out Anna's silhouette inside the car.

"Tossed me like a sack of shit, huh?" Billy asked.

"It was the captain's expression," Joe murmured and watched Augustino lean through the Plymouth's window.

"Now, Billy acted like a genuine asshole today, interfering in a ceremonial, and I'd like to apologize." Al had a wheezy, singsong voice. "In exchange, I want you to tell me who tipped you we were going to pick up your blind pal. Someone did, because you didn't figure that out on your own. Please, I've been kicking Indian ass for twenty years, I know Indians. Turn round, please, when I'm talking to you."

In Al's hand was his rust-spotted, short-barrelled Colt, an old-fashioned model called "The Shopkeeper's Friend". Al was a small man – cowboys tended to get worn down like fence posts – but the gun made him a little larger, as if he were levitating. Billy leaned back.

"This is Indian country," Al said. "The Indian Service is the only thing that keeps it running in any civilized manner. Abuse the Indian Service and you undermine the system that keeps you people alive."

Joe looked out of the window. From his gestures, Augustino was asking Anna to step out of the car.

"At the very heart of the system is respect. Billy and I spend weeks surrounded by Indians, enforcing the laws. Laws about sheep, about booze, about proper schooling. All that keeps us safe from all the drunken bucks is respect. Hell, otherwise they'd have to send the cavalry in with us every time, wouldn't they? Look at me."

Al's eyes were screwed up with the earnestness of communication. His hat had moved back, showing hair stuck flat as feathers on the white and shining upper half of his forehead.

"That's why what you did today to Billy was so dangerous, because it undermined our professional respect. Even if it was nothing but Pueblos who saw. Thank God it was Pueblos, not Navajos or Apaches. So, Billy apologizes."

"I apologize," Billy said quickly, as one word.

"Now," Al said, "you tell us who tipped you and you tell us where your blind friend is."

Through the window, Joe saw Augustino stepping back as if Anna were getting out of the car.

"Son of a bitch, you look at me!" Al raised the gun to Joe's waist. "Listen, you're just one more buck to me, one more bar-room hero. You come back with your stories as if this was the only war in history. You bucks came back from the First War the same way and I trimmed you down fast. You don't want to talk, then watch while I blow your balls off. Because you're a fucking Indian and I'm the Indian Service and you're not acting right."

Al's hand was steady, broad, calloused at the web from handling rope. He moved the ploughshare hammer back.

"No," Joe said. "No, this is a United States Army post. I'm a staff sergeant carrying out the orders of the Director of an Army project. You're a shitkicker and a sheepfucker and you won't do anything."

Al paused, snorted, lowered the Colt and eased the hammer forward. The door opened behind Joe and Augustino returned, alone.

"You were right," Al told Augustino, "it's going to take a while after this war to get things back to normal."

Augustino looked at the gun.

"Out," he told Al.

150

"I was just –"

"Out, both of you."

While the cowboys slipped past Joe and through the door, Augustino sat on the map. He took a cigarette from a case, lit up, sighed.

"Fun and games, fun and games, Sergeant. Not to be taken seriously. A pair of drifters like that, if they weren't employed by the government they'd be in a soup line. At least they can stay on a horse, which is more than we can say for the Military Police. Sometimes I think we have the 'Dead End Kids' in uniform." Augustino's gaze shifted to the door and the car waiting outside. "She says she asked you to drive her around. She says you were a courteous chauffeur all day and all night. Dr Oppenheimer says he sent you back to check on the dancers. Everyone's covering for you, Sergeant."

"Yes, sir."

The captain removed his cap, setting a tone of informality. In the light of the bulb, his eyes were deep-set and hidden. His narrow cheeks had a faint blue sheen. Hair crept from his cuffs to the back of his hands.

"You know, Sergeant, the incident between Fuchs and your medicine man sounds to me like a classic misunderstanding between races. Now you're Dr Oppenheimer's unofficial liaison with the pueblo. I can understand how you wanted to settle the problem quietly. But I hear that the Sunday after you left Fuchs, you were looking for me. Did you find me?"

"No, sir."

"You were told I was up on Bathtub Row. You looked for me there?"

"Yes, sir."

"Who did you see there?"

"No one was home, sir."

"And after that, you didn't look for me any more?"

"Slipped my mind, sir."

Augustino shook his head like an overburdened confessor.

"Sergeant, I think you've gone over the edge. You allow Fuchs to be assaulted with a gun. You couldn't have over-

151

powered a blind man? But you do attack an officer of the Indian Service? You in an Indian dance? You! I'll tell you, Sergeant, you were already back in the hole at Leavenworth, you were buried deeper than ever until you drove up in that car."

Joe followed the captain's eyes to the Plymouth.

"Sir?"

"Racing up and down the highways today, I went through Esperanza and I saw that coupé in a motel courtyard. I know all the cars on the Hill. And I made a note of the licence and the time."

"We may have stopped there for coffee, sir."

"I went by the motel tonight. The coupé was still there. And now it's here and I see you have been following my instructions after all."

"It's not like that, sir."

"I don't want the sordid details of how you do it, but I do badly want every personal and intimate detail of Dr Weiss' life, her connections with the Party and her connections with Dr Oppenheimer."

"She won't tell me that stuff."

"She will. I think you have a talent with women, Sergeant. By the time you're done, I bet she tells you everything."

The lighted road seemed to shift like snow as Joe walked from the shed. He swung into the car, put it into gear and closed the door. He didn't dare look at Anna.

Horses coughed and shuffled as the Plymouth moved forward. MPs twisted in the saddle, staring. Al and Billy stood, one on each side of the car, as it rolled past the shed.

"You never gave me an answer," Anna said. "Which do you think I am, insane or a tramp?"

"Do you want to see me again?" Joe asked.

"Yes."

"Then you must be insane."

17

In the Explosive Assembly Building on Two Mile Mesa, Joe held a twenty-inch model of the Trinity bomb steady on a wrestling mat. It was a sphere of pentagonal steel plates bolted together at the edges. Foote and a private named Eberly were adding the last lenses of high explosive. The temperature inside the green Sheetrock building was about 120 degrees and all three men were stripped to the waist and wore a second, fluid skin of sweat. Foote was a baronet, and one of the more eccentric scientists on the Hill. In the sun he always wore a Mexican sombrero. In the Assembly Building he always wore a chain rattling with religious medals. Eberly was a graduate student who had first come to the Hill as a civilian scientist, then been drafted and sent right back at a quarter of his previous pay. He was gawky, with as much neck as head, and an Adam's apple that pumped with incessant outrage.

The lenses were cast wedges of Baratol and Composition B, both TNT-based explosives but with different speeds of detonation. Just as glass lenses bent and focused light, so did the sooty-grey lenses of high explosive focus their shock waves from the outer circumference of the bomb towards the centre, creating not an explosion, but an implosion. Of course, this was merely a model to be detonated on the mesa, so in place of a plutonium core was a croquet ball.

Other wrestling mats were covered with other models of the bomb in different stages of assembly, non-sparking brass tools, Radio Flyer wagons, tubs of water and bottles of warm milk. The walls bore blueprint diagrams, ghostly X-ray negatives, a portrait of the Virgin of Guadalupe, a prized picture of Hedy Lamarr in the nude and, every twenty feet, a fire extinguisher and a bucket of sand. The last two items were purely ornamental because it was understood that if there were any fire in the Assembly Building, everyone in it would be at stratocirrus level.

Foote prepared each lens, a little Kleenex into this hole, Scotch tape over that crack. After he slid each one into place, Eberly took over with a brass wrench, bolting a steel plate over the lens, pentagonal plate interlocking with plate like a puzzle being slowly solved, building up the walls of the sphere. Joe simply kept the ball from rolling.

"I hate the Army," Eberly said.

"The Army wants you to hate it," Joe said. "It's the Army system. It's what binds us into a fighting unit."

"No, it's an individual thing," Eberly insisted. "You know the new security campaign? Lesbians! Why, of all the WACs here, does Security pick out my girl and ask if she's a lesbian?"

"Joe, I do really appreciate your helping out," Foote delicately changed the subject and slid another heavy lens into place, its smaller, concave tip resting against the croquet ball. "Oppy keeps sending my boys down to Trinity. It's a hell of a place, they tell me. *Jornada del Muerto*, Dead Man's Journey, it used to be called by the Old Spanish. Scorpions, desert, snakes, stinging ants, hostile Indians. I keep asking how that distinguishes it from the rest of New Mexico. Saw you dance, by the way. Very impressive."

"Anything for the tourists."

"What does a man like you do after the war? Obviously, you're too old and too intelligent to be a boxer any more. You're the least likely sergeant I've ever seen."

"Groves is going to be the Atomic General. Maybe I'll be the Atomic Sergeant."

The surface of the next-to-last lens was pitted; the Baratol had cooled too fast after casting. Foote stuffed the holes with tiny wads of Kleenex.

"I didn't even know women *could* be homosexuals," Eberly said.

"To crush a solid ball of plutonium into a denser, super-critical mass is theoretically conceivable," Foote told Joe, "if the ball is crushed by a perfectly symmetrical shock wave, which is possible if every one of these lenses is detonated in the same millionth of a second."

" 'Critical', 'symmetrical'. It's just another bomb, right? When I took Oppy and Groves down to Trinity at Christmas, they were talking about a blast equal to about 500 tons of TNT. That's big, but that's not fantastic."

"Been upgraded. The estimate is now 5,000 tons. Another difference is that your normal, ordinary bomb will generate temperatures of a few thousand degrees. A nuclear explosion can be ten million degrees. Different animal altogether."

Foote dusted the final lens with baby talc. As he lowered it into the last hole, he steered the descending tip with a shoe-horn.

"If she's a lesbian," Eberly said, "what does that make me?"

The lens stuck with an inch to go. Foote laid the last plate over the lens and picked up a rawhide-covered mallet. Sweat dripped from the end of his nose. Like a diamond cutter tapping a stone, he had to hit the obstinate lens hard enough to move it, but not so hard as to shatter the goods. In fact, considering the expense of the project, the lens was at least as valuable as a diamond. And a diamond cutter didn't have to worry about sparks.

Foote licked his lips.

"Lesbians, indeed."

He rapped the plate. The explosive lens underneath seemed to shrug and then slide into place. Eberly aligned the plate and began bolting it down.

"I think I could use the poisonous fumes of a good cigarette," Joe said and rose limply from the mat.

"Go ahead. We'll finish."

No smoking was allowed inside or within fifty feet of the

building, but everyone took nervous cigarette breaks over a sand bucket at the far wall where Hedy Lamarr floated on her back. Joe lit up. To one side of the bucket were the X-ray negatives. There were five of them, tacked up in sequence next to someone's scribbled note that they had been taken a millionth of a second apart by an X-ray bunker at the Hanging Garden.

On the first dark film were twelve lights like a ring of flares. Detonation. The X-rays had turned shock waves into pure light.

On the second film, the lights had expanded and joined to form a flower shape, a daisy. The outermost edge of a burning flower.

By the third film, the delicate trim was gone and the lights concentrated into twelve lines reaching for the centre.

In the centre of the fourth film, the lights outlined a dark disc, a metal core. Some of the lights rebounded, a corona.

On the last film, the core was crushed to half its size. the rays swirling. A collapse not into darkness but into light.

Joe looked back at the bomb on the wrestling mat. Completed, it was a two-foot, quarter-ton sphere of steel plates. Maybe a puzzle ball. Or a dull metal spore. Nothing that the X-rays showed, which was, at its birth, a small sun.

That evening everyone crowded into Theatre 2 to see a film that had just arrived from Washington. Robert P. Patterson, the Undersecretary of War, his desk and his flag filled the screen. He had a pug face, a nap of grey hair and big hands folded between an array of pens and telephones. The film was grainy and the sound uneven, adding to the sense of urgency.

"The importance of this project will not pass away with the collapse of Germany." The Undersecretary leaned forward. "You know the kind of war we are up against in the Pacific. We have begun to repay the Japanese for their brutalities and their mass murders of helpless civilians and prisoners of war." Patterson shook his head with resolution. "We will not quit until they are completely crushed." He turned his hands into fists. "You have an important part to play in their defeat. There must be no let-up."

The evening films were *Back to Bataan* and *Bugs Bunny Nips the Nips*. By then, Joe and Anna had slipped out.

18

In the glow of the flame the room seemed to vibrate. Anna looked around at the crucifix and saints on the adobe walls, the low ceiling *vigas*, the striped blanket on the cot, Joe standing piñon logs in an inverted V over the burning kindling in the corner fireplace. Through the shutters came the evening sounds of distant children, a screen door slamming, a dog being chased, *"Psoot-bah!"*

"I wanted to get away from the Hill," he said. "Didn't you?"

As he laid Anna down on the rough blanket, he kissed her open mouth, her neck, the small, dark tips of her breasts. He slid his hand over the pale sheen of her belly to her legs and to the essential mystery, a twist of copper over a soft, white anvil.

"Welcome to Santiago."

A breast as still as marble. Then a sudden heart-stir.

"It's raining," she said.

Joe watched flashes picking at the door jamb and around the shutters.

"Just thunder. A strange summer. No rain, just lightning."

"I'm afraid of you."

What did she suspect? he wondered.

"Maybe that's just your way of saying you love me."

"Why do you say that?"

"I love you. I love the way you taste like piñon smoke, the way you feel, and I could make love with you until this bed breaks."

"You can't!"

"I can try."

More slowly, he entered her as if he were leading her, lifting her to the very heart of herself. She rode him in the narrow, yellow light of the fireplace. As beads of sweat dampened her, she glowed like a respondent flame, her hair bright as fire.

Sleeping with his arms round Anna, Joe dreamt of Augustino. The captain was following him with a rifle as Joe climbed a steep, snow-covered hill towards Anna. Both Joe and Anna were naked, while Augustino was dressed like an Apache with a corduroy coat and a high-crowned Boss hat. The snow turned to ashes. Anna disappeared and over the crest of the hill came horses, a herd of mustangs shrouded in steam and the radiance of a phosphorus bomb.

Thunder sounded like a far-off cracking of the earth. The fireplace had the dull, subsided glow of embers. Anna wasn't in bed. Her clothes weren't on the chair. The shutters were open to a full moon. It was after midnight and Joe didn't know where Anna could have gone unless she was visiting the outhouse, but her side of the bed was cold and he had the sense that she had been gone for some time. He put on trousers and shirt and went out.

The pueblo was blue. Blue adobe, blue fence, blue trees. He held up his hand. Blue. Lightning played over the Jemez, but the rest of the sky was clear, the stars dim only because of the brightness of the moonlight. The ground felt like ice.

The jeep was still by the pump. Joe ran past the Reyes' house to the outhouses. Anna wasn't there and it was on his way back that he noticed a free-standing shadow in the night, a pillar of smoke braided with embers rising from the Reyes' yard. Sitting on chairs on either side of a fire were Anna and Sophie Reyes, talking in voices too low to carry.

Sophie was so shy as to be practically a family secret. Except for the pots her nieces sold under the portal in Santa Fe, Joe doubted that anyone outside Santiago would ever have known she existed. She had cropped grey hair streaked with black and white, and a soft, hesitant face. She wore a smudged apron outside the traditional one-shoulder dress and cotton shirt. The fire was the smothered variety, cowpats heaped on burning wood to turn the pots in the centre of the fire a carbon-rich black. Joe didn't know what was more unlikely, that Sophie would be firing pots in the middle of the night or that she would speak to Anna. The two women watched Joe let himself in through the gate.

"I couldn't sleep," Anna whispered.

The women each held blackened sticks, as if they'd been tending the fire during their conversation. Pots already fired were stacked on charred racks to one side of the yard. Raw pots of different shapes lined the other side. Ears of corn, strings of chillies and dried camomile hung in the striped moon-shadows of the open porch at the back of the house. By the chairs were tin pails of temper and shards, and fresh clay in twists of newspaper.

"What are you doing?" Joe asked.

"You can see what I'm doing." Sophie leaned back in her chair the better to regard Joe. He didn't remember his aunt's gaze as being quite so direct.

"In the dark?"

"It's light enough. I was lonely. It's good she came by. She talks quietly. That's nice. We don't wake anyone up."

"It's cold."

"Then go back to bed," Sophie said.

Joe ignored the suggestion. Besides, it was warm around the smothered, nearly invisible fire.

"You have a good woman," Sophie said. "She thinks up numbers."

"She's a mathematician."

"That's what I said. Like Thinking Woman."

"Thinking Woman?" Anna asked.

"Thinking Woman thought up the world," Joe said. "Her thoughts became land, water, animals, people. Whatever she thought became real."

"Like you." Sophie tapped Anna's stick with her own. "His other women were all sluts."

"Thanks," Joe said.

"That came from leaving here and going to New York and the Army," Sophie told Anna. She looked up at Joe and demanded, "Why did you go into the Army?"

"Yes, Joe," Anna asked. "Why did you?"

This night-blooming conversation was unreal, Joe thought.

"It's complicated."

"You were in the Army at the beginning of the war," Anna said. "You must have enlisted."

"See how smart she is," Sophie said.

"Not exactly enlisted."

"Then you must have been in trouble," Anna said.

"See?" Sophie said.

"Okay. I was with some friends in New York. We decided to give a free concert to soldiers in New Jersey, at Fort Dix, which was for Negro soldiers. We thought we'd give them some jazz, maybe a parade."

"This was arranged with the officers, Joe?"

"No. Our arrival was not expected."

"What time of day was this, Joe?"

"About three in the morning. About this time. A lot of dumb things are done at this time."

"You mean you were drunk, Joe."

"See?" Sophie said.

"There was some damage, Joe?"

"Some of the musical instruments got pretty banged up when we hit the main gate. I vaguely remember a scuffle on the way to the parade ground and a holding action around the bandstand. Then I mostly recall seventy or eighty MPs sitting on me. Anyway, the Army was after men. They offered us a choice, jail or enlistment. We all chose enlistment. I was the only one who passed the physical."

"That is a crazy way to enlist in the Army."

"I didn't say it was well thought out. Anyway, enlisting cold sober in broad daylight is crazier."

161

"Men are so dumb," Sophie told Anna. "My husband should be here where there are things for him to do, but he wants to go hide in the canyons, he wants to be a hero. And I'm the one who has to walk all day to take him food and cigarettes."

"He's with Roberto?" Joe asked.

"Where else would he be?"

Then that was why Sophie was firing pots at night. Things made sense if you just waited long enough.

"The Indian Service has riders from here to Utah looking for Roberto and you stroll by with his bacon and eggs?"

"You walk past them?" Anna asked.

"Yes. They don't pay any attention to an old woman getting clay. They're looking for Joe."

"I'm not involved with Roberto."

"That's not what Roberto says," Sophie told Anna. "He talks about Joe all the time."

"You miss your husband," Anna said.

"Yes. Tonight, the devil went by my window. He had yellow skin and silver horns and a rifle."

Joe said, "Sophie, do me a favour. Next time you see Roberto, tell him I'm not involved. He wants to play cowboys and Indians, I don't. It has nothing to do with me."

In his house, Joe lit a kerosene lamp and poured two glasses of Scotch while she looked at the photographs on the wall.

"No pictures of you."

"They're of my brother Rudy. I don't think he made it off Bataan. Funny, I can picture him better at night than during the day because we used to keep animals out back. I took care of the horses. Rudy had a rabbit hutch. We used to feed them in the evening and I can still see Rudy and those white does in the hutch, that fuzzy whiteness in the dark."

"But no pictures of you?"

"I left home. When I was fifteen I went to El Paso. A circus had its winter quarters down there and I caught on hauling water and hay."

"That must have been exciting."

"Hauling hay for elephants? Mainly, I remember sneezing," he said and gave her a glass. "Well, that was more words from Sophie than I can remember. You like being Thinking Woman?"

"I like the idea that I thought you up, that you're my idea."

"Your idea?"

"My biggest. What else did you do at the circus? I feel responsible."

"There was an old sideshow fighter. Local heroes paid $5 against $50 if they could knock him down. No one ever knocked him down. He showed me the first things about boxing, that's probably why I'm basically a counterpuncher. But the best was the circus band leader. I played a pedal organ a little bit here at the church, but he taught me the piano. He used to describe himself as 'a gentleman of the Negro persuasion', and he drove the Texans crazy because he dressed better and acted finer than any of them. He was a ragtime player. And stride. Name it. He hated me fighting, but that's where the money was; that was the ticket north."

"You must have been a good fighter. I asked you about the pictures twice and you ducked the question each time. You must never have been hit."

Joe studied a photo of Rudy on a horse.

"You know, Sophie's right. Indian men do work on their dignity. They don't talk a lot. As Oppy would say, they're non-verbal. They internalize everything, and to an outsider, which may include women, they may not say a word. They'll drink themselves to death or drive off a cliff, but they do it with a sense of quiet dignity. I'm not that Indian. I've spent half my life away from here. I've got a half-breed brain now. Lost the old natural dignity."

"You have better than that, you have invulnerability."

He was astonished. "Me?"

"You seem to be the giant who has attracted all the men from here up to the Hill."

163

"Look, Santiago is a poor place. This is still the Depression here, it's always the Depression here. For the last twenty years the most dependable income here has been from pottery, and that's made by women. One reason the men work so hard on their dignity is that it's all they've got. Then the Army took over the Hill. The men are happy to work up there, they don't need me as an attraction. There is a price. If the lowest caste on the Hill is the soldiers, lower than them are the Indians."

"Have you ever been hit, or hurt, or touched?"

"Lower than the Indians is me, because I'm not really from either place, I just serve as a go-between. At least the men from Santiago know who they are and have some place to go home to. Who am I? I am a driver, a joker, a mascot. I am the most insignificant person on the Hill. I am a has-been fighter, a so-so musician who's going to be scrambling for jobs in nightclubs for the rest of my life. A giant? That's a joke. I feel like I'm committing a perpetual fraud, a hoax, because inside is a coward. Men are fooled, Oppy and Roberto are fooled, but I don't want you to be. I didn't mean to enlist in the Army, I wasn't a hero on Bataan, I made a deal to get out of the stockade. I'm like the Gestapo, Fuchs was right about that. This is not self-contempt, this is simple honesty. Rudy was fooled. Rudy joined the National Guard because he wanted to be like his big brother. Dolores wasn't fooled. She said Rudy would be safe at home if it wasn't for me. When I ran away I took one son from her. When Rudy left, I took the other. She wrote to me in the hospital in Australia and said as far as she was concerned, I was as dead as Rudy. Not to write and not to come home. That seemed unfair to me, but after a while I saw there was a grain of truth in what she said, because I had tried to cut everything Indian away from me, and maybe Rudy got caught and trampled in the process. See, Dolores cut right through me. So that's why there are no snapshots here of me. When Rudy comes home, that's when my picture goes up."

"You mother's dead. You said your brother's dead. How can it go up?"

"You're Thinking Woman, think of something. Anyway, I have been hit and I have been hurt. And you, you could completely destroy me."

She sat across the table from Joe. The moon in its downward transit no longer entered the house; the lamp flame was the only light.

"I didn't run away from home. My childhood was very quiet and bourgeois compared to yours. I fantasized. I thought I would be an actress like Marlene Dietrich and have wealthy lovers. Then I thought I might be a female aviator who crash-landed and had to live with someone like Tarzan while the rest of the world searched for me. When I was rescued, they would understand that I had been forced to submit. There may have been wild Indians involved."

"In any respectable fantasy."

Anna took a deep breath.

"But from the age of fourteen on, my fantasies turned to fear. Not anxiety. Fear. That everyone wanted to hurt me, kill me. Not my mother or father, of course, or my family, but everyone else. The gardener, the tram conductor, the postman. The police, naturally. I stopped going to school for weeks at a time. Our doctor said I was suffering from unspecified hysteria. An alienist came from Berlin and said I was suffering from female castration complex. Perhaps so, but I thought he wanted to torture me. A crazy child! They took away my pencils, scissors, even my stockings. My father knew Freud. He wrote to him in Vienna. Freud wrote back to say I was suffering from a 'flight motif'. More and more German Jews, he said, were suffering from 'flight motif', but it was his opinion that Nazi brutalities were diminishing and that a young girl should consider how extremely unpleasant it was to be a refugee. I remember he added in a postscript that all he ever wanted to see in America was Niagara Falls. There is some charm in Freud contemplating the great running bath of Niagara Falls. My mother and father were reassured because they were Germans first and Jews second. So I was sent to the sanatorium where sometimes we were given water cures and sometimes sleep cures, and where I hid in my bower full of numbers and bees. At lunch we listened to Herr Goebbels on the radio loudspeaker. Everyone had to. Actually, the doctors were kind. One who was a communist suggested a trip to Sweden. He falsified the documents without telling my parents, but I think they knew he put me down as Aryan. How else would I be allowed to leave? It took a communist to know how to do such things. He was going with me, so it was not all out of good will. It was an odd thing. We docked in Stockholm and suddenly I was not crazy. I do wonder, Joe, why me? Why, out of all my family, good, rational people, uncles, aunts, rabbis, professors, old ladies, babies, why was I the only one to escape? The question is, did God save me or did He just forget me? So, I am ready for a new God. Thinking Woman sounds to me like a great improvement."

"Did you see any more of the doctor who got you out?"

"He seduced me. A lot of men seduced me in the beginning."

"Communists?"

"Who knows? The world is full of communists. In Germany, the only ones who stood up to the Nazis were communists."

"And Oppy?"

"What do you mean?"

"How did you run into Oppy again?"

"In New York. He needed a mathematician. He was rounding up refugees like stray cats. He used to have long brown curls, you know. He cropped his hair, like Joan of Arc, to go to war. Yes, like Joan of Arc! First he asked if I wanted to see my numbers come to life, then he invited me to the project."

"He's a seducer."

"Yes. Do you know what my work is? I turn my equations into programs for an electronic computer. I turn each millionth of a second of an imaginary Trinity into a deck of punchcards so that we can estimate what will happen in the real Trinity. You see, everyone else is working to Trinity. Oppy inspires everyone to work so hard."

"There wouldn't be a bomb without Oppy."

166

Anna refilled his glass and her own.

"There wouldn't be an Oppy without the bomb. There are other physicists here more brilliant by far."

"Come on. Harvey starts a sentence and Oppy finishes it for him."

"He's quick to finish other people's thoughts. But they're still other people's thoughts. What I meant to say, though, is that no one looks ahead to after the bomb is used. Or asks whether the bomb should be used or, at least, demonstrated to the Japanese first. Because they haven't reached the event of Trinity itself, they don't think of the consequences. On the punchcards are not only the fireball, the shock wave, the radiation, but also an imaginary city. So many structures of steel, of wood, of concrete. Houses shatter under shocks of one-tenth to one-fifth of an atmosphere. For steel buildings the duration of the shock is important. If the pulse lasts several vibration seconds, peak pressure is the important quantity. I can stop the blast at any point. I can go backwards or forwards. Nobody else sees it. It's as if they can't imagine a shadow until the sun is up. I see it every day. Every day I kill these thousands and thousands of imaginary people. The only way to do it is to be positive they are purely imaginary, simply numbers. Unfortunately, this reinforces a new fantasy of mine. There are times when I feel as if I am one of those numbers in one of the columns on one of the punchcards flying through the machine. I feel myself fading away."

"To where?"

"To Germany. Freud was right, after all. It is difficult to be a refugee once you think you are dead."

Joe pulled a crate from under the bed and took out a wadded ball of newspaper.

He unwrapped the newspaper at the table and set down by the lamp a small, gleaming black pot with a tiny top hole.

"It's a seed pot. It's the last pot I have of my mother's."

"It's beautiful."

"I was supposed to sell it with the rest, but I couldn't. I wanted to have something of hers."

"It's a work of art."

"Like a little, smooth earth. Nice, huh?" He let Anna admire the pot for a second more, than blew out the lamp flame. He stepped back across the room.

"What are you doing?"

"I'm going to throw you a pot."

"I can't see."

"I can't see you, either. This could be interesting."

"I can't –"

"Catch!"

Joe tossed the pot lightly, underhand. It rolled from his fingertips into the dark. A last, faint nimbus of moonlight clung to the open window. Joe watched the pot tumble past the dim glow and disappear into the darkness on the other side. He waited for an explosion of clay. There was a sharp intake of breath from the other side, no other sound.

He stepped gently across the floor, reached into the dark and found her hands. Anna had caught the pot as it passed her ear and she still held it there tightly, off-balance. When Joe had first pulled out the crate, he hadn't know what he was going to do. An impulse was there, the start of an arc, the opportunity to risk all.

Anna was shaking.

"That was crazy."

"Maybe. But we proved you're here." He moved his hand from hers, down to her necklace and shirt and the weight and heat of her breast, where he felt the accelerated rhythm of her heart. "And alive."

The nimbus at the window became brighter and harder. For a moment Joe thought perhaps the moon had turned back, pulled by the pot's dark flight, a vying gravity. If he could raise the dead, he could raise the mountains and affect celestial bodies. The nimbus became a beam of light gently probing the dim outlines of lamp, table, chair, then a white shaft that poured through the window and filled the room. A car engine idled outside. It must have rolled in neutral on its own momentum all the way from the road behind the Reyes' yard.

"Who is it?" Anna asked.

Joe set the pot on the table. He cracked the door to look out, but the headlights were too bright and whoever was in the car wasn't getting out.

"Can't see," Joe said.

He slipped his ·45 from its holster and tucked the gun into his trousers, then crouched below the light and pulled Anna to the kitchen. Through the shutters over the sink he had a view of his jeep parked by the side of the house, of a corn field, the stalks standing in ranks, and of the Reyes' yard. There was no more smoke in the yard. He remembered Sophie's nightmare and deciphered it. Sophie said she'd seen a devil with yellow skin and a rifle. The silver horns were captain's bars and the devil was Augustino. Joe didn't know why the captain had come, but his own mind was decided. He eased open the casement window.

"Why not wait to find out?" Anna whispered.

"Because I think I know."

Joe went through the window head first, rolling between the jeep and the wall of the house. There were no more cars, no footsteps, but Augustino was capable of coming alone. Joe rose, his back sliding against the corner of the wall. He freed the ·45 from his belt, cocked it, thumbed off the safety. As the night wind brushed over the field, rows of corn dipped and rustled. Dogs were quiet. He heard nothing in the corral, nothing on the roof. Only the deep, powerful count of his heart.

In one long step he swung round the corner of the house and through the headlights, and stuck the ·45 in the face of the driver, a coloured man wearing a tuxedo. The car was a Cadillac.

"Joe?" Pollack asked. His eyes opened so wide and white they seemed to ooze. "Joe, don't you shoot your bestest friend. Don't do it."

Joe let the gun drop and hang.

"What the hell are you doing here at this hour?"

"Leaving you a note." Fountain pen and paper were still

frozen in Pollack's spidery black hands. "How else can I get into communication with you working on the Hill? I can't reach you there. All I can do is leave a note."

"At this hour?"

"I didn't know you'd be here. You were supposed to come by the Casa Mañana last weekend and sign those papers."

It was the night Joe had gone to the hot springs with Anna and Harvey.

"I got sidetracked, sorry. You have the papers, I'll sign them right now, right here."

"I have them," Pollack said, although he made no move to produce them now that he'd regained his composure. "Know what the buyers want to do? They want to tear down the club and build garden apartments. They have the money."

"That's what counts."

Pollack sighed.

"A sad end for the Casa Mañana."

"You'll have a new club in New York."

"But it will be one of many good clubs in New York. There was only one good club in New Mexico. It was the best, right?"

"The best. You've got the papers?"

"The only authentic jazz in New Mexico. Even if I was gone, it would be like a last laugh."

"You want me to sign or not?"

"They're from Fort Worth, the buyers. I heard them talking to each other. Calling me 'Rastus'. 'Tar baby'. Called me 'the dinge' in my own club. Joe, can you get your hands on $50,000? If you can, the Casa Mañana is yours. Club, licence, lot, everything."

Joe carefully slid on the gun's safety and tucked it in his trousers.

"Half price?"

"For you."

"Serious?"

"Have I ever joked about the club?"

"There are laws about Indians drinking liquor, let alone serving it."

170

"There are laws about bootlegging and your father was a bootlegger. Afraid?" Pollack smiled a yellow grin. "You want it or not?"

"I want it," Joe said and knew at the same time. The future was here. The future had come coasting in as a silent Cadillac. "I want it."

"You have the $50,000 now?"

"I need a month."

"A week. Eddie Jr's coming in from Italy and I'm going to be there at the dock."

Joe had, after pocket and black market, a little over $15,000. If he sold all the tyres and nylons he could lay his hands on, he still couldn't raise another $500 in a week. And he'd be leaving for Trinity in ten days.

"Two weeks. If I don't have the money for you then, you can still sell for twice as much and blow the difference on Eddie's welcome home party."

Pollack gave his hand through the window.

"Two weeks, Joe, not one day more. We'll show the white trash what this war was all about."

Joe watched the Cadillac roll away down the road and across the dark plaza. When he turned around, Anna stood in the doorway. He didn't know how long she'd been there or how much she'd heard. Some ghost of the headlights still seemed to play on her and the house. She and the house glowed. Joe Peña's Casa Mañana.

19

Omega was at the bottom of Los Alamos Canyon, a natural trench of basalt and pines deep enough and narrow enough to shield the Tech Area, a mile away, from any explosion. The hangar itself was divided by a cement barrier. One side was occupied by the miniature reactor that Fermi called his "Water Boiler". On the other side was an experiment of Harvey's called "Tickling the Dragon's Tail".

A croquet ball sized round of plutonium coated in glittering nickel was the Dragon, the core of the bomb. It nestled snugly in a twenty-inch paraffin bowl on top of a hydraulic piston. Over it, suspended face-down by a chain, was a second, hollow bowl of paraffin. The idea was to check whether an outer sphere of high explosive "lenses" would, simply by being in place around a nearly critical core, reflect enough neutrons for the plutonium to go critical and explode prematurely and relatively ineffectually. The paraffin was mixed with sooty-grey carbon flour so that it had basically the same atomic make-up as high explosive, without the risk, in case of mishaps, of wiping out the eastern end of the canyon.

Only Harvey, Joe and Oppy were in Omega. Harvey's usual Critical Assembly team was scouting Trinity, and Fermi's team refused to be near the hangar when the Dragon's Tail was being tickled. Harvey had protested that at least two physicists had to be present for the experiment, and Oppy had answered that while General Groves had done his best to turn him, Oppy, into an administrator, he was still a physicist. Oppy had insisted that Joe stay and push the red and green buttons on the wall that raised the lower bowl holding the Dragon up to the hanging hollow bowl.

Drawn up to the Dragon on steel tables were a Geiger counter, a radiation graph that drew a red line on rolling paper, and a neutron scaler that measured radiation with a bank of six red lights. If the Dragon got too hot and Joe didn't react in time, the three counters were wired to drop the hydraulic piston, bottom bowl and core to the floor.

Wearing a long white lab coat, Harvey plotted the curve of criticality with a slide rule and clipboard.

"Raise it ten inches," he said.

Joe pushed the green button as Oppy continued the argument that had gone on all morning.

"You say, Harvey, that the Japanese are all but defeated. By any rational measure, they should be, I agree. You think it would be feasible to set off the bomb in a publicly announced demonstration. An island in Tokyo Bay would be ideal. Somewhere they could bring their best scientists and generals. If we do drop the bomb on them, you want it to be employed against a remote, purely military target, a base as far as possible from civilians. You don't see why women and children should die simply because we want to make a point. You add that there are American POWs in a number of the Japanese cities we may have contemplated attacking. You believe that if we are the first nation to use such a weapon we will be historically tainted. That we will sacrifice the good will of the entire world. Much worse, you fear an armaments race, a building of horrible weapon after horrible weapon, such as mankind has never known and cannot survive. That our actually using such a weapon in war will poison any chance of international agreement on the future control of such apocalyptic devices. Last, we bear the direct and special responsibility of these weapons because we are the men and women who created them. Who should say how and if these weapons are used if not us?"

Those indeed were Harvey's points better than Harvey himself had put them. Abashed, he kept his eyes to the clipboard.

"Eight inches more."

"We all have the same nightmares," Oppy said as he walked, hands in his jacket pockets, toes out, around Harvey, the tables, the Dragon. "These are the years of nightmares and they are not ended yet. If you walked away before Trinity, I would not blame you. I'd envy you." Oppy lifted his gaunt face, evidence of his fatigue. "We'd all envy you."

Joe did figures in his head. By calling in loans and cashing his last gas coupons and travel vouchers, he could bring his bankroll to $20,000. How could he more than double it in two weeks? How much scotch and commissary sugar could a man sell?

Maybe high explosives were the answer. Hilario had mentioned contractors down in Albuquerque. With a couple of mules, he could clean out the magazine bunkers on Two Mile Mesa.

"To go up into the mountains for a year," Oppy said. "Not see a headline or hear a radio. Not come down until the entire, awful thing is over."

Harvey glanced at Joe for psychic support. "Five inches."

Assuming he got the money together, there was the problem of musicians. He could only afford a couple of men from New York or Kansas City. He'd have to use some Mexicans. Horn players. There was a trolley that ran from Juarez to El Paso, and he could slip them over the border that way.

As the two bowls came within a foot of each other the Geiger counter started to concentrate on what was happening, taking a definite interest. The scaler measured fast neutrons by multiplication. One light for two neutrons, two lights for four. Up to six lights for sixty-four escaping particles, then starting over again. The red lights blinked like eyes rousing from a nap.

"It won't be over soon." Oppy's voice took a sharper tone. "The Japanese didn't give up on Iwo Jima or Okinawa. They will fight ten times harder on their own islands. It won't be just kamikaze planes. Army intelligence says they're building kamikaze boats and teaching people to strap dynamite to their chests. The estimate I've seen for the invasion is one million casualties. Japanese and American, soldiers and civilians."

"Four inches," Harvey said.

There was a bar and kitchen to stock. Utilities, water, linen. It might be tricky, getting around the liquor laws on Indians. He might not be allowed to pour a bottle even if he owned the place.

The Dragon shone like ice.

"A demonstration on an island sounds like a good idea," Oppy said. "With a bunker for the Emperor and his generals. But what if a single enormous blast didn't convince the Japanese that it was caused by a single weapon? We can barely convince *our* generals, let alone theirs. And what if the bomb was a dud?"

"Eighty percent critical." Harvey watched the red line on the graph paper, and then for the first time answered Oppy. "The uranium bomb works."

"We have two bombs. The uranium bomb we think will work, and the plutonium bomb we hope will work. We don't have enough refined uranium to make another. The plutonium bomb must be tested at Trinity. We can get more plutonium, though it won't matter if Trinity doesn't work. The point is, we have none to expend on good intentions and mere fireworks." Oppy spoke through a veil of weariness. "God knows, I wish we did. But the invasion will be carried out before bad weather sets in over the Japanese islands. It won't be postponed while we build more bombs or while we negotiate when and where the Emperor should sit for a better view of a peaceful demonstration. Should he come to Trinity? Trinity is in twelve days. Stop time for me, Harvey. Give me more bombs and a cushion for the divine Emperor to sit on and watch."

"Three more inches, Joe. Then at least a base, Oppy, not a city."

"A waste. A waste of the bomb and a waste of the soldiers. The Japanese would censor every report and all that would be left would be a wisp of smoke and rumours. You know the blast effects, Harvey. There wouldn't even be that much to see in a camp—not like a city, not like buildings."

"Not like civilians?"

"A target that will end the war, Harvey."

"Civilians and American POWs?"

"They'll put POWs in every city. And how many more POWs and dead and wounded will there be after the invasion? How many cities will we conventionally bomb off the map? How many American graves?"

"I didn't become a physicist to learn how to vapourize Japanese." Harvey's voice rose.

"None of us did." Oppy's voice became nearly tender. "But you tell a mother of a young soldier who died on the beach of Japan—and there will be many thousands of them—that you had a bomb that could have ended the war and that you chose not to use it. Tell his wife. Tell his children."

The Geiger counter ticked like a speeded-up clock. The scaler lights multiplied rapidly now that the two bowls were only eight inches apart. In the shadow between, the ball still glittered, like a note between two cymbals. A chain reaction of one kilogram of plutonium released as much energy as thirty-four million pounds of TNT, Joe had heard. Some percussion.

"The issue is not the weapon, Harvey, but the war. Ending the war and saving us from the hideous slaughter to come."

The trade-off for that kind of power was an alpha radiation that could destroy first the bone marrow, then the kidney. Everyone knew that the doctors on the Hill refused any responsibility for the Dragon.

"Eighty-eight percent critical at three inches." Harvey scanned the rolling graph. "The issue is the future after the war. Two inches, Joe."

After the war the Army would close its bases in New Mexico, Joe thought. The soldiers would be coming home from Europe and the Pacific, though, and they'd flock to the Casa Mañana.

"Teller had the same fears. I'll tell you what I told him: that if the issue is the world's postwar future—and I agree it is—the only way to demonstrate the implausibility of any more war is to use this bomb, to make all mankind a witness. This, finally, will be the war to end all wars. Edward Teller will be with us at Trinity. In fact, I had hoped that you would do the count-down for the test."

"Eighty-nine," Harvey read.

The Geiger counter sounded like a bow drawn across a bass string. The lights of the scaler flickered, drawing nervous red dashes.

"One more inch, Joe," Harvey said.

"After the war there will have to be international control of all nuclear devices, and international cooperation for the peacetime uses of the atom. A sober, frightened world will do that, Harvey. But we will have to take the moral lead. We will share information with our allies."

"With Russia?" Joe asked.

"Yes, with Russia. Of course," Oppy said.

"Ninety percent. Half an inch, very slowly."

The Geiger counter echoed an accelerating, snapping wave of electrons.

"The future is then," Oppy said. "The war is now. The Japanese would use the bomb if they had it. They wouldn't hesitate. They started this war. Our cause is just. It is written in the Bhagavad Gita that 'There is a war that opens the gates of heaven. Happy are the warriors whose fate it is to fight such a war. Not to fight for righteousness is to abandon duty and honour.' We scientists are soldiers, no more. We are on this mesa by an accident of history, because our nation has been attacked. We have no special competence in political or social or military affairs. We are not the people elected or trained to make those decisions. We are not an elite divinely chosen, simply because we are physicists, to govern mankind."

"Stop."

Closed to within an inch, the Dragon's two bowls nearly made a single gray moon, almost hiding an inner, brighter moon. There was a faint rise in the Geiger's pitch, a touch more hysteria in the red lights.

"Still ninety percent," Harvey said happily. It was just what he had predicted.

"Yes?" Oppy asked.

"I don't know."

"Ask Joe. This is why I wanted Joe along, because he is the only man you know who has actually fought. Speaking for the men who will be on the boats that will hit Japan in a few months' time, Joe, what would you say to Harvey?"

You sly son of a bitch, Joe thought. He took his hand from the button and found his thumb had cramped. He'd listened to the ticking of atomic particles, but what had filled the hangar were words, a web of them spreading and connecting from roof to floor. And all preamble to ensnare Harvey so that Joe could strike the final blow.

"Tell me, Joe," Harvey said.

"Speaking for the boys in the boats," Joe said, "I'd say you were a phoney, I'd say you were lower than a Jap. I'd say you were actually a traitor."

Harvey swallowed. The Geiger amplified electrons at the anode, ions at the cathode. Neutrons danced to the beat of lights.

"On the other hand . . ." Joe moved closer to the Dragon. "Speaking as a friend, I don't think you should care what anyone says." He leaned across the Dragon's near-moon and nearly buried core. "If you really think the bomb is that bad, then –"

Ticking soared into whine. Stylus flew from graph paper. The six scaler lights were solid red, flashing so fast that no intervals could be seen. The hydraulic piston dropped, carrying the bottom bowl with it, shaking the concrete pad of the floor. The silvery core lurched up to the lip of the bowl's hollow, made an indolent circuit, then dropped heavily back into place. The whine plummeted. Red lights flashed again with a slow, regular pulse.

"What the hell was that?" Joe looked at the stylus, still vibrating free. A red line led off the paper. "The Dragon went off all by itself."

"Don't move!" Harvey began sketching on his clipboard.

Joe was close enough to Harvey to see him draw an outline of the room, the position of each man around the Dragon, equations, a curve of criticality. There was a foul greasiness to the air, a smell of melted paraffin.

Joe still wanted to finish what he was going to say, but the moment had gone. Imploded. Oppy knew it; the blue gaze said it. That was the colour of Oppy's eyes, Joe thought: ion-blue.

"You set me up."

"I asked you to tell the truth and you did," Oppy answered.

"I'm not done."

"Yes, you are."

Harvey stared up from his scribbling. "You did it!" he told Joe.

"Me?"

"The core was already near the margin of criticality. The human body is composed mostly of water – hydrogen dioxide – which reflects the neutrons. Oppy and I didn't matter. You're bigger. When you leaned over the Dragon, you triggered the counters."

"You're a more unpredictable factor than I'd thought," Oppy said.

"It doesn't matter," Harvey said, "we got the data."

"Well, are we radioactive now?" Joe asked.

"We're fine," Harvey said. "Nothing really happened."

"Nothing really happened," Oppy agreed.

They looked at Joe with twin scientific detachment, a sudden, palpable line between them and him. He stared back, for the first time his mind fully engaged. It was obvious that Oppy had won. What was interesting was Harvey's surrender, his relief about it.

"You know," Harvey said and turned to Oppy, "it occurs to me that the bomb would probably be flown to Japan. What if the plane crashed? Maybe I should run the Dragon in salt water."

Even his Southwestern tonalities seemed to change subtly, to ape unconsciously Oppy's Eastern croak. His stance shifted, his enthusiasm grew.

The effort of winning Harvey back had taken a toll on Oppy. Each crisis appeared to take an ounce of flesh, and now he looked cadaverous and more determined than ever. He nodded proudly, encouraging the flow of ideas that was purely Harvey, until Harvey asked, "You really wanted me to count down Trinity?"

"I wanted an American physicist to do it," Oppy answered, "and my first thought was you. An American voice."

"Listen." Joe broke the mood.

Oppy snapped, "What?"

"Just listen."

Omega was hidden in tall pines, amid the calls of jays and canyon wrens, the wind tugging at treetops. It took a moment to hear the siren.

"Fire," Harvey said.

They counted the blasts together. Oppy wore an ironic smile, as if disaster were only to be expected.

"Tech Area," said Joe.

In the middle of the Hill, squeezed between the Main Drive and the mesa's southern rim, the Tech Area held twenty-six nondescript buildings. Each structure was labelled with a placard from "A" to "Z", but this was the only sense of order to them. Half were white Army clapboard, half green Army sheetrock. They were at all angles to one another and shared a military style that decreed that every side look like the back.

A transformer was burning. In some ways the fire was well located: at the back of the Tech Area, away from the gas stocks, cyclotron and particle accelerator, near the fire station and close to hydrants. But it had taken time to cut power to the transformer, and by the time Joe and Oppy arrived, power poles, cables, switching equipment and the high wooden fence around the transformer were all throwing flames and creosote-black smoke into the afternoon. Because of the fence, firemen couldn't get their hoses as close to the transformer as they wanted.

Watching the firemen and the fire was the whole population of the Tech Area: physicists from the cyclotron shack, soldiers from the boiler house, doctors from the medical labs, office clerks and, in front, the Indians who swept every building. A truckload of construction workers rolled up to join the spectators.

Oppy stared at the fire. "No, no, no," he insisted.

His prayer was answered. The Texans leapt from the flatbed of the truck. As soon as they were off, the driver honked and moved toward the fire. The truck was an old Reo with a girder for a bumper, and as fire fighters ran from its path, the truck accelerated until it rammed through the burning fence and into the concrete barrier around the transformer. The truck backed up, lurched forward again and crashed into the burning gate of the fence. The driver rammed the fire a final time, taking out the other fence posts and shovelling more rubble into the transformer and around the base of the power poles. He backed into the clear, kicked open the cab door and hopped down like a rider who had just busted a cow in record time. He was big, in a blue work shirt and jeans, the only construction man in a shirt. He was young, with a fair crew cut and the fluid, arrogant grace of an athlete. A hero. He thrust his left fist into the air. A southpaw.

While technicians swarmed around Oppy, as if the truck had been a manifestation of his will, Joe stood aside and was joined by Felix Tafoya. On the Hill, with his khaki work clothes and push broom, Felix was invisible; in Santiago, he was the calf cutter and brander, an honoured figure. His nose had been kicked askew by a hoof years before.

"That *tejano*," he told Joe, "that's Hilario's fighter."

"Seen Hilario lately?"

"I'm cutting tomorrow. Hilario's bringing someone who wants to see a real old-fashioned cutting."

The fire chief led Oppy and Joe around the remains of the transformer. He was a civilian named Daley. Smoke had turned to a film of ash on his face, rubberized coat and boots. He coughed up phlegm dark as tar. Both high-voltage poles were charred and iridescent. Burned cables and wire floated on mud. Joe imagined that Daley was conducting the tour out of professional habit, as if they were stepping through the smoking bricks of a tenement.

"This is really what I wanted to show you and the sergeant." Daley picked out of the mud a carved zigzag, half blistered gold, half blackened wood.

"The dancers had those at the pueblo," Oppy said.

"It's a lightning wand. It's supposed to bring lightning," Joe explained. "Did it?"

"People saw the bolt hit," Daley said.

Oppy looked impatiently in the direction of his office. When he glanced back, he was smiling. "Joe, arson by Indian wand is your department. You handle this. I can walk from here."

"Before you do," Joe said quickly, "I heard some calves are being cut in Santiago tomorrow. I ought to be there in case any of them are hot."

"Cows and wands are definitely your crucial responsibility. Just make sure you're at the La Fonda by eleven. We have visitors coming."

Oppy stepped out of the mire, slapped soot off his hat and headed in the direction of the administration building.

"Arson is what Captain Augustino says," Daley told Joe. "He's got a dozen of these sticks from different fires. Brush fires. He'd be here now, but he's down at Trinity."

"This is not an incendiary device," Joe said and took the wand. "It's a stick. Someone threw it in the fire. You have a lot of Indians up here."

"They really think they can bring lightning?"

"They think they make the world go round."

Joe noticed that the paint that remained on the wooden head had a micaceous glitter, a fancy Taos touch.

"If you say so." Daley spat, grinned and wiped his chin. "Hell, you should know."

20

Three hours of riding brought Joe to the far side of Santiago Canyon. There the foothills between the canyon and the mountains rose in swells of yellow rabbit brush. He had taken Oppy's horse, the tall bay called Crisis. The stallion hadn't been taken out for a month and it ate up the distance with an eager lope.

While Joe dismounted to water Crisis at a tank, he saw the Indian Service riders crossing the rise ahead of him. Al and Billy halted to stand in their stirrups and examine the tank through binoculars, then moved on. Joe waited another minute in the shadow of the tank until a second pair of Service officers riding drag followed. When they were out of sight, he swung up on Crisis and started again towards the Jemez.

Though he rode in warm, glassy sunlight, a rare rain fell in the Jemez, covering the peaks with a grey as faint as waves in a stone. As the trail ascended, it reached ponderosas, cedars, cattle bones, and a new profusion of wild flowers, shooting stars, scarlet gilia. On the last ride of the canyon before it folded into the mountain was a small, battleship mesa. Joe had to kick the horse up a steep path of loose stones to the top.

The mesa was not a mile long and less than a hundred yards across at its widest point. Cedar and juniper huddled over dwarf sage. The cedar was twisted and vigorous, meaning half dead and half alive. The same with the cholla Joe saw, half green stem and half empty lattice. A trick of survival in the high desert was to bloom and die at the same time. Cedar made good firewood. A dead cedar branch could last for years if it didn't touch the ground. He tied Crisis to a live bough and went the rest of the way on foot.

In the middle of the mesa were ruins, a worn grid of stone walls about knee-high. The stones were volcanic ash. Adobe had long since washed away, along with any sense of what was storeroom, what was quarters. All a puzzle now, Joe thought. White nuggets in the stones were timber cinders a million years old. He picked one out and it turned to talcum between his fingers.

The only excavation on the mesa had been performed by animals. Between the walls were gopher mounds of soft earth, richly mixed with shards of pottery that were black, white, reddish brown, and bits of obsidian strewn like jewellery.

Joe sat down for a smoke next to a kiva completely filled in by a gooseberry bush, its boughs as dark as a cherry tree's. The sun dropped over the far side of the Jemez, turning clouds red, rung by rung.

"Hello, Joe." Roberto and Ben Reyes stepped out of the cedars. The men were in blankets and braids.

"Brought you some cigarettes."

"How did you know we were here?" Ben asked.

"The clay. Sophie was seeing you and she was getting her clay. This is the place."

"I knew you would come," Roberto said.

"I came because they're finding your wands on the Hill."

"What kind of cigarettes?" Ben asked.

"At fires on the Hill. Luckies." Joe handed the packet to Ben, who tapped one out suspiciously.

"How'd you know they were mine?" Roberto squatted by Joe.

"Mica in the paint. Typical Taos horseshit."

"Yes." Roberto grinned. Roberto had such a long nose and his hair was so brown, he had to have some French trader or horny Mormon in his background, Joe thought.

"I like Chesterfields." Ben put two in his pocket, one in his mouth and gave the packet back.

"You're welcome. You're a real frightening pair of desperadoes." Joe gave Ben the lighter. "You're supposed to be hiding, not getting into more trouble. Fires are serious business to those people."

"He thinks we're causing the lightning?" Ben lit his cigarette.

"Who?" Joe took the lighter back.

"The doctor?"

"Oppenheimer? He sees that he's supposed to think that."

"That's smart enough." Roberto held up two fingers for a smoke.

"I don't know whether to laugh or cry." Joe lit cigarettes for Roberto and himself. "You said you were going to escape, not take on the US Army. I'm warning you. Right now, you're hiding from the Indian Service. That's one thing. The Army will send a Captain Augustino. Augustino will find you. And Augustino will find out who's been helping you on the Hill, planting a wand every time they see a fire."

"You think that's the way we do it? First the lightning, then the wand?" Roberto asked.

"That would be my first guess."

"They sent you?" Ben asked.

"Nobody sent me. I'm supposed to be on the post right now."

"But they notice the lightning," Roberto asked.

"Yeah."

"Then we're doing a good job." Roberto let out a long, plumed exhale. "Good cigarette."

As the valley went dark, a full moon rose from the Sangres. They made camp on the eastern tip of the mesa, where ancient raincatches rose in worn steps. Ben built a fire in a crack of the rock, using stones to prop cedar twigs and bark. Joe started the bark with his lighter. The fire caught quickly and had the advantage for fugitives of being impossible to see from a distance, but they had to keep feeding it because they were burning no more than tinder. Ben made a stew of chilli and jerky in a can. Looking over the Rio Grande, they could make out lamplights in Santiago and Esperanza, even the village of Truchas high in the Sangres, and the bright, pollenish haze of

Santa Fe at the tail of the Sangres range. Los Alamos they couldn't see at all. They cupped the glow of their cigarettes and waited for the stew to boil.

"I'll get you a pair of Greyhound tickets to Tucson. You don't like Tucson? How about Los Angeles? The two of you haven't lived until you've seen the Pacific Ocean. What have you got against the Hill, anyway?"

"What they're doing there," Ben said.

"You don't know what they're doing there. It's a secret. It's the biggest damn secret of the war."

"I had a dream they were making a gourd filled with ashes," Roberto said.

"A gourd of ashes?"

"I had the dream in Taos. Two Hopi men had the same dream, two elders. A woman in Acoma had the dream."

"Four dreams." Joe nodded, as if the conversation were sane. Ben went on stirring the can, listening. Roberto tilted his head up. "Each time, they take the gourd to the top of a long ladder and break it open. The poison ashes that fall cover the earth."

"That's it?"

"That's it."

"Then let me set your mind at ease. I've seen what they're making. It's not a gourd of ashes. Let me get you those bus tickets."

"There's more."

"I was afraid of that."

"In my dream there was a giant."

"How about train tickets?"

"As soon as I met you, I knew the giant was you."

"Roberto." Joe controlled himself. "Roberto, you're a nice guy, bright, and I'm sure you're sincere. But you're playing medicine man in the middle of a war. Out in the real world, soldiers are dying, cities are burning, women are raped. What they're trying to do on the Hill is end the war. If you and Ben insist on being buckskin loonies, okay, just don't include me."

"Hot!" Ben shoved a tin plate of stew at Joe.

"But the ashes will poison the clouds and the water and the ground and everything that lives on it. All the dreams are the same about that," Roberto said.

"Sounds like scientific proof." There were no forks. Joe picked up steaming, grey-green strips of beef with his fingers.

"They will erect a great ladder in the sky. Then, in my dream, a giant climbs the ladder."

"Not bad," Joe told Ben. "Starving helps. Just in your dreams?" he added to Roberto.

"It's not that I dream better, it's that I can concentrate on dreams. Being blind helps. To me there's not the same difference between day and night, awake and asleep. One leads to the other."

"Dreams and reality?"

"Two sides of the same thing. Don't you agree?"

"I would have said the major difference in the world right now is not being awake or being asleep, but being alive or being dead. And one doesn't lead to the other like a hand to a glove. More like a stump to a glove." Joe put down his plate. "So, don't dream about a giant on a ladder. Dream about Japan. Dream yourself a hundred thousand dead men bobbing in the water. Dream red beaches, banzai charges, kamikazes, paper cities and B-29s. Put a meter on your dream. One million dead, two million, three. See, I don't mind you dreaming; I just mind easy dreams."

Well, I'm a bad guest, Joe thought. A pall had fallen over the dinner party. Ben looked like he was choking. Either he was choking or he was angry.

"I have to catch a cutting in Santiago." Joe rose to his feet. "That was your last warning. Good luck."

Roberto lifted his sunken eyes.

"All the same, you were in my dream," he said.

Joe rode back on a moonlit ridge between canyons. Around him was a seascape of ridges, a foam-brightness on the rocks and junipers. There was so much beauty at night that no one saw. He still heard himself speaking, and Oppy's words coming out— invasion casualties, kamikazes. It was the way he felt, but the words sounded like a formula. To give Roberto credit, he really didn't talk about the war at all. He just cared about his precious pueblos and the rest of the world could go to hell. In return, Oppy appreciated Indians, as people from a time warp. Sophie was right, Joe thought, he didn't seem to have his own words. Music, maybe, but not the kind of words and formulas that announced and explained actions. As if there were no words for where he was, which was in between. In a no-world, on a high ridge, in the sweet light of the moon.

He came down off the ridge near an irrigation ditch where alfalfa fields, flowered blue, rolled in the night breeze. After putting Crisis in the pasture, he carried saddle and tack to the Hill stable. There was still time to sign out a jeep and get down to Santiago to catch Felix cutting. He'd take a Geiger counter and check some cows as an excuse for the trip.

In the tackroom, the saddlebags opened and spilled. Horses coughed in the stalls. He used his lighter. On the floor were boxes of horseshoe nails, bent snaffles, broken reins and two yellow zigzags. Lightning wands. Roberto must have put them in the saddlebags.

His first instinct was to burn them, but he was in a hurry. He stuffed them in his shirt and slipped out of the stable door.

Between the stable and the Hill, a nine-hole golf course had been hacked out of the scrub. The greens were sand and a rake was provided at each hole. Joe intended to dump the wands, but he was out in the moonlight in the clear and if there were any MPs awake, the flash of the sticks would catch their eye. He still had the wands when he reached the motor pool. Keys were kept in the ignitions. In the back of a jeep he put a Geiger counter. Under the seat he stowed the wands where he could reach them easily and throw them away on the road to Santiago.

21

Men sat on the top rail of the corral and shouted encouragement to boys in batwing chaps who chased calves in the dark. The cutting and branding was done at this hour because the work bus to the Hill left at dawn.

Two fires were going, one outside the corral for coffee, one inside for Felix Tafoya. The men at the coffee fire juggled mugs and shakers of salt to take Joe's hand softly and say good morning. Inside, running after a calf, the boys gave Joe a quick glance. He noticed that the largest boy wore a homemade chevron sewn to his sleeve and tucked his bandanna in like an Army tie. Everyone in Santiago had a son or a nephew in the service and Joe knew he was not only a hero to them, he was the possibility of coming home alive from the Army.

The calves were Herefords with cotton-white flashes on their heads. The boys lassoed, tackled and dragged them one by one to the fire. Wearing a leather apron over the coveralls that were his Hill uniform, Felix knelt by the coals, chose a knife with a double-wrapped rawhide handle and honed the blade on his apron. Arms and hooves converged. The heat and glow of the fire seemed to invest Felix with a magisterial glow. *"Coont-da, hitos!"* While the boys held the calf still, Felix squeezed the testes to the bottom of the sac, sliced and flung them into the coals, then doused the wound with kerosene. The glowing orange dogleg of a running iron dug into the calf's flank, and the smell of burning hair joined the standing odours of coffee and cow manure.

In his white suit and hat, Hilario Reyes came down the fence as nimbly as a lizard.

"The Chief himself. See my boy yesterday? I hear he put out a fire and saved the whole hill."

"He looked good."

"You mean great. What are you doing here?"

"The Army sends me to look over the cows. What's the lieutenant-governor of the state of New Mexico doing here?"

"I have great respect for the old-fashioned ways and traditions of the people here. You know, I've never missed a dance in Santiago. Most of all, I love the taste of balls."

Hilario gave a grin of open, energetic venality before going to talk to the men gathered around the coffee fire. To check out the statement about the Army and the cows, Joe assumed. Hilario liked being the fisherman, not the fish.

Joe leaned against the rail and watched the boy with the rope try a *peal*, a fancy throw designed to catch a calf's hind feet. He caught the calf by the head instead and almost flew out of his shoes and laces as the calf kept running, until two more boys tackled it.

Felix came to the fence to offer Joe a stick that skewered what looked like two burned chestnuts.

"Joe, if you're talking to Hilario, you need all the *guevos* you can get."

Someone on the top rail threw a shaker of salt. Joe snatched it out of the dark.

"Coont-da!"

"Hilario's friend didn't stick around long," Felix said. "He went to look at the old cows in the pen."

Joe peeled back the blackened skin and liberally salted the pearly insides. It was an odd ceremony, the cutting of the calves and the redistribution of their bullhood around the corral. A secret male ceremony all the more effective for the early morning hour, something basic and shameful and powerful. The roasted balls had the texture of oysters and the flavour of nuts.

"Heroes will soon be a drug on the market." Hilario returned. He wasn't so much a lizard, Joe thought, as an incorrigibly evil elf. Even the white outfit had the bright aura of a bad fairy. "You won't be able to swing a cane for heroes.

190

All with their scars and ribbons and stories. See, I'm already gearing for the veteran's vote. I'm going to be the vet's friend. First, I'm going to be your friend."

Felix laughed and went back to the branding fire, where the boys were wrestling with another calf.

"How are you going to do that?" Joe asked.

"Teach you how to measure your grip on reality. Profit is the only fair measure of reality. Market value, Chief. The value of a has-been is not high, but I'm going to help you cash it in. I'm speaking of $2,000 in your hand right now."

The ground around the branding fire was pulverized and dry. Boys and calf struggled in explosions of dust.

$2,000? That wouldn't buy Bar Top and tablecloths for the Casa Mañana.

"Why?"

"There's not a loyal native New Mexican who wouldn't put his last dollar on you in the ring. Formerly eighth-ranked heavyweight in the world. A big night at the gym in Santa Fe, crowds of friends and well-wishers, lots of priests, they always tone up a fight. I can't think of a better way to celebrate the imminent end of the war than Chief Joe Peña's farewell appearance."

"I'm retired."

"This is the Texas boy I'm talking about."

"I look forward to improved relations between Texas and New Mexico."

"Then let me ask you a question." Hilario raised his voice so everyone in the corral could hear. "Out of sheer curiosity. Could you beat him if you did fight him? Out of curiosity."

Joe shrugged. Along the rail the men leaned forward, salt shakers and cigarettes in hand. Holding a knife, Felix looked up. Even the calf seemed to lie still.

"Because I think he'd kill you," Hilario said. "Southpaw, ten years younger, ten years faster. You look soft and tired. You should be scared of the boy, it's no fun getting beat up in public."

"How does all this make you my friend?"

"I wouldn't want you to get hurt without being properly paid."

"You mean, without you getting properly paid."

"That, too."

Joe shook out a cigarette and lit it. How washed up did he look? he wondered. He wished he'd paid more attention when the kid beat Ray. He remembered the figure walking away from the truck at D Building, rolling the wide shoulders, fist high. Joe wished he'd seen the face again. The face always said a lot more.

"Give me a straight answer," Hilario said. "See, that is what I mean by testing reality. Could you win?"

"Really?"

"That's what we're talking about."

Joe still hesitated.

Hilario said, "$5,000, Joe. Side bets are up to you."

"$10,000, winner take all."

"You're crazy. We are talking about reality."

"Uncle, the reality is that war is over and the soldiers are going home. You're an ant in the desert watching a picnic pack up. Does the kid think he can beat me?"

"He knows he can."

"Then winner take all is fine with him."

"Then the rest of the rules are mine. No priests. No gloves, no ring, no referee. Strictly a sporting event for interested parties. Anyway, you know how to use a ring, you'd just tie a faster man up in the ropes. A referee just gets in the way. I can keep time for rounds."

"How many rounds?"

"As long as it goes."

"In a week," Joe said.

"Impossible."

"We fight in a week. You said before you could put the fight together in two days.

"I need Texas money, from El Paso, from Lubbock. That's a long way to come."

"I'll make it easy for them. We'll meet in the middle, south of Socorro at the Owl Café. The night of the 15th. Behind the café. Yes or no?"

At the last moment, Joe thought Hilario would back out.

"You *came* here to deal, you big son of a bitch. You came looking for me."

"Looking towards peacetime, Hilario, same as you."

"Okay." Hilario nodded to Joe and added a public nod for the other men at the corral. "Okay, you place your bets, Joe. I think you'll be surprised at the good odds you'll be able to get on the famous Chief Joe Peña."

Feet trussed, the calf tried to swim on the ground. Felix squeezed the sac, clearing the way for the sizzling edge of the knife. It was okay. Hilario would put it together. It wasn't a matter of face, it was a matter of action, of money willing to ride on the only two fighters in the state. The calf's eyes grew.

Joe walked into the cottonwoods to relieve himself. He was going to have to start taking better care of his kidneys. One more fight. And get some sleep. A blue morning star lay over the river. Jupiter? Venus? What if there were no moon? Men walked around bound by the gravity of the earth, but also lifted by the floating mass of the moon. What if there were no moon, no lift, only the heavy and monotonous chain of the earth? No better light at night than stars that said "We are cold and far away". What if he lost?

For his alibi's sake, he got the Geiger counter from the jeep and found the pen on the far side. Even in the semi-dark Joe saw the cows were Felix's oldest mavericks from the highest, driest canyons. The man at the pen was just as unlikely, a short figure in a suit. His back was to Joe because he was patting the steers through the fence, wisely, because the animals were wild enough to stomp him if he went into the pen. Not patting, Joe thought. Combing, and dropping the combed, loose hairs into an envelope.

The man looked around, surprised. "Chief! Oh! Chief!" He had a swarthy, heart-shaped face, a full lower lip and black hair that was so wavy it was almost marcelled. When he turned, the comb and envelope had vanished. With his double-breasted suit he wore cowboy boots. He took a wobbly step forward and gave Joe a pudgy hand to shake. "I didn't hear you coming. We met at the La Fonda, in the bar. Harry Gold."

"From New York."

"I came with Happy."

"With Hilario. What's going on?"

A giggle escaped Harry Gold.

"I lost my new hat."

Joe peered into the pen. There were five cows, black and brown, a mix of Angus and Hereford, a group of scarred and wary veterans. The meanest-looking cow was standing on a crushed stetson.

"You wanted to buy a steer?"

"I was thinking of having a barbecue."

"Felix is cutting calves right now. Take one of them."

"Good idea," Gold agreed.

"He'll slaughter it and dress it for you. Better than a butcher."

"These cows looked a little old."

Not just old. As the light improved, Joe saw that two or three of the animals were mottled around the stomach and flank. Usually a cow greyed at the muzzle first. As he opened the gate, the nearest steer lowered a set of mossy horns a yard wide at the tips and retreated. Joe pushed his way into the middle of the cows and peeled back some of the milky hair. The skin underneath was black. Like the cow he'd killed before.

"Your hat." Joe came out of the pen with a twisted brim of felt.

"Thanks," Gold said and backed up into a cowpat. He looked down. "New boots, too."

"Soak them and leave them on," Joe suggested.

"I'll try it. *Adios*."

"Absolutely."

The whole time, Joe had been holding the Geiger counter. Someone who didn't know what it was would have asked, Joe thought.

Harry Gold knew.

22

By the time Joe got to Santa Fe, Indian women were spreading their blankets on the *portal*, the porch of the old Governor's Palace on the north side of the plaza. FBI agents in plain-clothes and snapbrim hats were taking their places on benches under the plaza cottonwoods.

The agents followed scientists from the Hill whenever they came to shop, waiting in the plaza because the Army bus from the Hill let the shoppers off just half a block away on Palace Avenue and all the shops were around the plaza. At the end of the shopping everyone always headed to La Fonda for cocktails.

Joe relieved Ray Stingo, who was so excited to hear the fight was on he didn't want to leave for the airport to meet the VIPs arriving for the Trinity test. Only small planes could land at Santa Fe and the ride over the mountains was so rough it was commonly called the "Vomit Comet". Oppy was at the La Fonda with some psychiatrists who had arrived on the morning train at Lamy.

Instead of shooting and burning the cows, Joe had chased them up Santiago Creek and hoped they'd find their way back up the canyon. Sweaty, dirty and tired, he strolled to the shadow of the obelisk in the centre of the plaza, where he could watch La Fonda. He took out a cigarette. Put it back in the packet. No more smoking. He'd thought he hated boxing. Even exhausted, though, he felt his body lift at the prospect of a fight, as if he'd deprived it of worthy adversaries. The first few tourists were up, making their way to the *portal*. No soldiers yet. Joe saw Hilario drop Harry Gold in front of La Fonda.

Hilario drove on and Gold went into the hotel. In the plaza, the "creeps" concentrated on their newspapers; the morning headline was that Truman had arrived in Berlin.

A spy? After all this time, a real spy? It took more evidence than a few hairs from a hot cow.

A man with an aureole of silver hair approached the obelisk. It took Joe a moment to recognize Santa because the Hill psychiatrist was covered with white blisters and his hands were in cotton gloves.

"Hives," he explained to Joe. "Purely psychosomatic, nothing contagious. Ever since we took that ride through the mountains with the you-know-what."

"Yes." Joe whispered, "I'm supposed to be with Oppy right now briefing our teams. We have some excellent men. Jungians, alienists, some strict Freudians. General Groves has written some press releases and we're going over them for psychological impact. Of course, if the bomb is a dud, there won't be any release. If the bomb makes a big bang, then we'll report that an ammunition dump exploded without loss of life. If we blow up the desert and everyone in it, then we have to come up with a different story. The main thing is to avoid panic. And send our teams, most of which will be stationed well away from the blast, to those cities that will be most affected by runaway fallout. I feel I can confide in you."

"Yes?"

"In that instance, a press release would choose an alternative, assimilable emergency. 'Epidemic', 'tainted water', 'chemical warfare'. I say we ought to say 'chemical warfare' right at the start because people are never going to believe 'epidemic'. The Freudians want 'tainted water', naturally."

Gold walked out of La Fonda in shoes instead of boots, wearing a fedora in place of his late stetson, smoking a cigar and holding a newspaper folded under one arm. He crossed the street to the smaller pseudo-adobe building on the opposite corner, the ticket office of the Santa Fe Railroad.

"You're wondering," Santa said, "if all this is going on inside, why am I out here?"

"Yes?" Joe mumbled, distracted.

"They're picking volunteers for the team for Trinity. Do you think I'm cowardly?"

"What do you think?"

Santa laughed in a whisper.

"I knew you'd say that."

Gold emerged from the ticket office, stood at the corner, looked at his wristwatch and looked at the public clock, a giant pocketwatch on a column outside a jewellery store on the south side of the plaza. He started back across the street to La Fonda, changed his mind and continued to the south side, past the curio shop, the jeweller's, a haberdasher's and into Woolworth's, and sat at the counter.

"But it's good to have someone to talk to," Santa said.

"Excuse me." When Joe saw a waitress bring Gold a coffee, he left the obelisk for the ticket office. The clerk was a grandmotherly Spanish woman who told Joe he had just missed the friend he described, but she could sell him a ticket on the same train going to Kansas City and New York on the 17th. Joe said he didn't know if he could go then, but not to tell his friend if he returned to the office because Joe wanted it to be a surprise.

As Joe went back to the plaza, he saw Santa vanishing in the opposite direction, moving stiffly like a man in a body cast. In Woolworth's, Gold was still nursing his cup. Although he had a newspaper, the *New Mexican* judging by the eagle on the masthead, Gold didn't bother reading it. He sat looking at plaster sundaes, his lower lip pendulous with thought. He tapped the crystal of his watch, dropped change on the counter and came out.

The plaza was coming to life, tourists not so much wandering in as suddenly appearing as skirts on the *portal*, as kids with pistols running around the bandstand. The bank on the east side of the plaza opened its doors. Mail trucks rolled from the post office, a block away and across from the cathedral. There were no traffic lights; cars and trucks ran counter-clockwise round the plaza and sorted themselves out at the corners.

Gold stood on the kerb, poised to dash through the traffic

directly across the plaza and towards the obelisk and Joe. A milk truck went by. A carload of Navajos. Now Gold was walking up the streets, under the pocketwatch, past the Indian drums in the curio shop windows and, again, to the ticket office on the far corner. Then he appeared to make a decision to take his time. He strolled past the office, past Thunderbird Curios and the bank's Ionic columns to a Territorial style building that housed Guarantee Shoes, crossed Palace Avenue and made a detour down a sidestreet to Maytag's. Joe didn't know why he was following Gold. Curiosity? A sense that everything about Gold was wrong? He seemed carried by the wake of the fat little man. Maytag's sold washing machines on one side of the store and music on the other. Gold scrutinized the Hit Parade list taped to the inside of the window. At last, he came back up the street to the plaza and Santa Fe's central attraction, the Indians on the *portal*.

The *portal* was a shaded arcade. Women from the pueblos of the Rio Grande valley sat against the cool adobe wall. In front of each was a blanket or rug displaying red San Juan pots, black pots from Santiago, or Santa Clara's double-necked wedding pots, turquoise jewellery from Santa Domingo, or Navajo beaten-silver concho belts. A few women wore the single-shoulder dress; most wore cotton dresses, aprons and sweaters. They yawned or read movie magazines or gossiped, paying cursory attention to the Anglos who stooped or knelt to fondle or disparage the wares exhibited. This being a holiday event, the would-be buyers dressed like dudes and browsed with intensity. Gold joined a trio of sergeants who were studying a blanket of earrings, bracelets and hairpins. The crown of Gold's fedora came to the shoulders of the soldiers. One sergeant admired a hairpin with a peacock tail of silver and jet. Joe slipped between the cars parked diagonally along the kerb of the *portal*. The adobe overhang was supported by massive posts of ponderosa pine worn smooth by generations of tourists, and Joe could look at an angle through the colonnade without being seen himself. Some of the women selling pots he recognized. Almost in front of him was a sleek and chubby girl with black bangs, a teenage cousin of his named Polly, for Paulina. She'd put down a copy of *Modern Screen* to show one of Sophie Reyes' smooth, obsidian-dark pots to a kneeling man in a panama. Gold moved closer, his eyes jumping from blanket to blanket. He stopped to pick up and examine a silver cigar holder. He seemed genuinely to want it, and he replaced it on the blanket with regret. He joined two nuns in the examination of silver crucifixes, falling into the spirit of friendly reverence. Gold seemed to suffer from boosterism, enthusiastically entering into whatever mood he encountered. Good-naturedly he let himself be talked into trying a clip on his tie. The clip looked like a silver bomber. His tie had hand-painted palm trees. He gave the clip back and bent over the next blanket, Polly's.

"For fruit?" Gold lifted a bowl with an embossed serpent around the rim.

Polly shrugged, but the man in the panama said, "Would you put fruit on a Rubens? That's a bowl by Sophie Reyes."

"She's famous?" Gold was impressed.

"To collectors."

"You collect these?" Gold turned the bowl round.

"I collect Dolores. She's dead and her pieces are very hard to find."

"Like art?"

"It is art." The man in the panama looked up as he took the bowl from Gold and Joe saw that the collector was Captain Augustino in civvies. "The pots are an expression of the native concept of the earth, and man's emergence from the earth, each pot both earth and womb. A beautiful, powerful concept."

"The decoration –"

"There is no decoration," Augustino cut Gold off. "There is representation. The snake is the never-ending cycle of the world. It's a representation of lightning. Lightning brings rain. Rain brings corn. You see the contradictions of violence and fruitfulness married in this symbol. The bowl is a vision of primitive harmony. Although not quite as fine as a Dolores."

"That's the one you collect?"

"I can show the collection to you, if you'd like."

"Thanks, but I'm in Santa Fe for only a day . . ."

Harry Gold worked his way past the last blankets and out of the *portal* to the corner, where he checked his wristwatch again. An open tour bus was at the corner and the guide was saying something unintelligible through a megaphone. Cameras leaned out of the bus. If Gold took the tour, there was no way Joe could stay near without being seen. At the same time, Joe was wondering about Augustino. The captain was supposed to be 200 miles south at Trinity.

The tour bus pulled away without Gold. Gold was walking fast, trousers flapping around short legs. Joe looked back. Augustino had disappeared from the *portal*. Joe had to trot across the plaza flagstones to see Gold head toward Woolworth's, where he'd started out, then make a right past Rexall Drugs, left on Don Gaspar Street, which wasn't much larger than an alley, and hurry past the bars and the pawn shops. Joe stayed a block behind, but Gold seemed unconscious of the possibility that he might be followed. Two blocks from the plaza, along the avenue called the Alameda, the Santa Fe river resembled either a dried-up open sewer or a creek. Rocks, brambles and rusted cans filled the bed, although cottonwoods grew luxuriantly on the near bank, tapping the dampness below. A concrete span called the Castillo Bridge led to an opposite bank of poplars and, beyond, the white dome and cupola of the state capitol building in the distance. In the middle of the bridge's walkway, Klàus Fuchs smoked a cigarette and contemplated a scooter abandoned or carried away by some past flood. The tyres were gone, perhaps gathered in one of the war's rubber drives. Fuchs rested his foot on the middle of the three iron pipes that served as guardrails. A folded newspaper was tucked under an arm. Joe stopped in the shadows of the cottonwoods to watch.

As Gold walked on to the bridge, he began feeling his jacket pockets, trouser pockets, shirt. A cigarette dangled from his mouth. He reached Fuchs. Fuchs fumbled through his own pockets, found a match and lit Gold's cigarette. He didn't wait for a thank you before leaving, a grim kewpie doll marching off the bridge and up the Alameda. Gold assumed the same stance Fuchs had had on the bridge, foot on the rail, gazing at the scooter on the dry rocks underneath the span. Up the Alameda, Fuchs got into his Buick. He hadn't come in the bus. He'd avoided the plaza completely. No more than two words could have been said on the bridge, Joe thought. Gold pondered the river, the branches overhead, and through the screen of poplars the faraway cupola on the state dome. He smiled at two girls on bikes. The tour bus rolled by, heads swivelling, leaving a trail of muffled facts and dates. Gold snapped a look over his shoulder in Joe's direction, but out of fleeting caution and not because he'd seen Joe move. Gold relaxed and finished his cigarette, stifled a gaping yawn that closed into a smile of relief, flipped the butt and left the bridge.

Gold walked down the Alameda, turned on Guadalupe and again on San Francisco, making a loop back towards the plaza. The Lensic Theatre had stucco walls and Moorish trim. Gold stopped to read a playbill for *Here Come the Co-eds* with Abbott and Costello. He saw his reflection and rubbed the blueness of his cheek. Passing a moment later, Joe saw his own reflection, a sergeant in a rumpled uniform, hair lank, face ominous. The plaza was busier now. Tourists spilled out of Woolworth's to stop Indians and ask them to pose. Like a man breasting waves, Cleto, the necklace vendor from Santo Domingo, stood in the middle of the pavement, arms of turquoise necklaces outstretched. Cleto's grey braid had come undone, the belly of his shirt was spotted with chilli, and still he maintained an expression of majestic contempt. Gold sidestepped the crowd around Cleto and then had to wait for Army trucks to pass. Across the street, at La Fonda's loading station, porters in *mariachi* vests shuffled suitcases. Joe slipped by Cleto. Once in the hotel, Gold would be out of reach. Something had happened on the bridge, though Joe didn't know what. Gold stepped up on the kerb, newspaper held tightly under his arm. It was the *Albuquerque Journal*. Gold had had the *New Mexican* when he went to the bridge. In his mind, Joe watched again as Gold, cigarette stuck to his lips,

201

feeling his pockets for a match, walked to the centre of the bridge and joined Klaus Fuchs, who handed his folded newspaper to Gold the better to, without a word, find a match in his jacket, brusquely light a stranger's cigarette, take back his newspaper and leave Gold to a solitary view of the Santa Fe river. Not *his* newspaper, though. Gold's paper.

At the loading station, Joe grabbed Gold, who gave an involuntary hop of surprise.

"I was hoping I'd see you again," Joe said.

The blood rushed so quickly from Gold's face, Joe thought the man was going to swoon.

"You were?"

More cars were parking, more suitcases were being unloaded. Joe encircled Gold with an arm and started to lead him out of the way.

"I was thinking how you lost your stetson. A friend of mine has a shop around the corner. Come on, we'll pick you a new hat."

"I don't want to trouble you."

"No trouble."

Gold struggled discreetly. Keeping a grip on him as porters pushed past was like squeezing a beachball.

"I have a call to make."

"Right round the corner. Just take a second."

"Joe! Over here!"

It was Anna's voice. She stood on the far kerb, wearing the turquoise necklace he had given her. In her hair was the silver hairpin he'd seen on the *portal* and in her hands was the black pot that Augustino had been admiring. With her Hawaiian shirt, she achieved a Pueblo-Hebrew-Polynesian beauty. She also had a Maytag's bag. It was the weekend, why wouldn't Anna be in town shopping? She crossed the street behind a tour bus as it pulled in front of the hotel. The FBI agent behind her waited to cross; she wouldn't be hard to follow.

"Why should there be traffic signals?" Anna showed the contented smile people wear when they suddenly take possession of a new town, when they've decided they will stay a while and, against all odds, are comfortable. She paid no attention to Gold or to the porters or to the people hopping down from the bus. "How boring it would be with traffic signals."

"Go to the bar," Joe told her. "I'll be right there."

"See what else." She carefully put the bowl into the bag and took out a record. Billie Holiday. *Lover Man*. "What shall I do first, make a pot or sing the blues?"

Gold freed one hand and gave it to Anna.

"Harry Gold."

Joe was trying to steer Anna towards La Fonda when Oppy came out of the hotel and took in the trio on the curb with a strained grin. His eyes looked out from wells of exhaustion.

"Where the hell have you been, Joe? I've been waiting for half an hour."

"Harry Gold," Gold said and offered Oppy his hand.

"Am I interrupting your private business and affairs?" Oppy asked. He disregarded Anna and ignored Gold's hand. "Santa told me you were out here. You went for a walk, a drink, a little spree?"

"Can you wait a minute?" Joe asked.

Cleto inserted himself in front of Gold and presented an arm draped with necklaces.

"Two dollars."

Tourists from the bus gathered around Cleto and pushed Gold aside.

"I have to make an appointment with a sergeant?" Oppy asked. "With my own driver? And where were you last night? I went by your room and you weren't there."

"I went out for a second."

"I came by twice," Oppy said. "I looked all over and couldn't find you. In the Army isn't that called AWOL?"

"Ask me where he was," Anna said and Oppy flushed as if she'd slapped him across the face.

The tour bus pulled away. Cleto moved on.

"Please ask me," Anna insisted.

Oppy lowered his head like a man on a cross.

"No?" she said. "Well, if you do think of any questions, I will be at the bar having a very early, not-so-perfect martini. I will be returning to the Hill later with Klaus. I know how you want to be sure where everyone is at all times."

Oppy didn't raise his head until she was gone, and then he blinked as if he were trying to will away a scene.

"Joe, where were you?"

Gold was already gone. Joe saw him trotting up the street past a camera shop and as the tour bus rolled by, Gold skipped off the kerb and jumped on to the running board, his newspaper clutched under his arm.

"I met a spy," Joe said.

Together, Joe and Oppy walked a block to the old Spanish courtyards on Palace Avenue. This was the Hill bus stop and Joe's jeep was parked outside, but Oppy opened a wrought-iron door to the smallest courtyard, a narrow passageway of carved beams and squash blossoms around a browning lawn. The screen door at the inner end of the courtyard was the Hill's anonymous parcel drop and reception centre in Santa Fe.

"You mean Gold," Oppy said in a low voice although there was no one else in the courtyard. "Augustino told me about him. Augustino is handling it. I don't see how you're involved."

"Gold was in Santiago this morning."

"Augustino is handling everything. What you can do is stay out of Captain Augustino's way. Let's hope you haven't scared Gold off. You know, Joe, we are fast approaching the climax of this enormous endeavour. I don't have the time or the patience to deal with you and your different adventures any more, not when the effort of thousands of people and the lives of many, many thousands of soldiers are in the balance. You are the smallest possible factor in Trinity. Please don't fuck it up. Stay out of my way, stay out of Captain Augustino's way and, if you want to do Anna Weiss a great favour, stay out of her way, too."

23

How high the MOON? the horns asked. Tables sat on circular tiers around the dance floor and bandstand, each table set with red cloths and candles, some with sweating pails of champagne. *HOW high the moon?* trombones wondered. Waiters in red jackets balanced steaks on trays. Wrought-iron sconces lit the curved adobe-like wall. Out on the hardwood, a generation of young officers danced with women in full skirts and puffed shoulders, blondes coiffed like Ginger Rogers, brunettes like Lamour. The club comfortably held two hundred diners and dancers, and another forty at the bar. *How HIGH the moon?* The lead sax stood to pursue the matter with a stutter of riffs. When the clarinet argued in falsetto, Joe thought of Harvey. The bass man thumped at the musical question, passed it to the drummer, who tapped it in the top cymbal, let it slip out on to the snare drum and when it bounced from there, socked it into the bass drum. *How high THE moon?* In front of a red plush curtain the band wore white Eton jackets, the music stands were white with glittering clefs and the piano as white as a tooth, although the pianist was in khaki. Joe caught the tune in his right hand way up the keyboard, as if everything had been delicate introduction. He went at the tune like Basie, like a chick pecking at a diamond, until he turned the hand to boogie woogie, paused for a horn reprise, and at the horn's last brassy gasp came down the keys in slowly assembling minor chords.

"Remember how I enlisted, the parade at midnight?" Joe had asked Anna. The interesting thing was not that he was

205

willing to bribe Shapiro and leave the Hill and drive to Albuquerque five days before Trinity, but that Anna was willing to go with him. For the occasion, she wore her hairpin and a long green velvet Navajo skirt. Pollack had given her a gardenia for her hair and she sat with the owner of the Casa Mañana at his table near the rear by the bar. In his tux, Pollack looked more like an African ambassador than a nightclub owner. He poured champagne for her and drank seltzer himself.

"One more time!" the sax section shouted.

And this time, Joe played "Moon" with little quotes from "Blues in the Night", "Swingin' the Blues", "Blowin' the Blues Away", sliding across the luminous melody. He could feel everyone moving with him, as if a lid had been taken off the club to unveil a starry, cerulean night, because these people were ready for the impossible. Better than a moon in June was a moon in July. They'd been at war for five years and now the war was over, the war was almost over. "Blue Skies Smilin' at Me", Joe injected, and the entire club seemed to rise. If blue skies were going to explode on them, they were ready, so he made the melody . . . *bluebirds singin' a song* even as he brought the "Moon" down a chromatic descent, a chord at a time. The tunes merged and split again, accelerating until keyboard and crowd swung between flight and plunge. Joe cued the horns, who stood and hit the Charlie Parker riffs that settled the argument by demanding *How High the Moon? How High the Moon?* as if it were the sun.

"Is this the Casa Mañana?" Pollack asked Joe when he joined the table. "Is this not a wonderful club?"

"No, thanks," Joe said and waved off a drink.

"You said you were partners with Joe's father." Anna played with her new hairpin, which she had taken out for the gardenia.

"With Mike Peña," Pollack said.

"Doing what?"

Pollack glanced at Joe. "Distribution, mainly."

"A dangerous business," Joe said. "Mike was distributing a load of booze up from Mexico one night when a tyre blew or he hit a cow or someone drove alongside and shot him in the head. The truck crashed and the gas and alcohol blew like a Molotov cocktail."

"It wasn't clear whether a bullet was found," Pollack said.

"The investigation was led by a Judge Hilario Reyes," Joe explained. "It was very inconclusive."

"I sent Joe down to El Paso before he could get himself into trouble," Pollack told Anna. "I had a brother working in the circus. I thought Joe was going to feed the elephants, but he caught on to music real fast. Of course, he used to play the organ in the pueblo even before that. He was a choirboy and everything."

"Did Mike like your music?" Anna asked.

"No." Joe had to laugh. "He hated it."

He took her on to the floor and they danced to "Flamingo", the Ellington version.

"Are there clubs like this in Chicago?" she asked.

"Great clubs up there."

"Would you go to Chicago to play?"

"No. When I get out of the Army, I'm not going to take orders from anyone. I'm going to have my own club. For the first time in my life I know what I want."

"What is that?"

"This." He took in the seraphic row of white music stands against the red velvet, the warm languor of the women in their long hair and short dresses, the waiters gliding under trays of iced drinks, and the music curling within the circular Hollywood-adobe walls, eddying and overlapping into echoes that asked for a sharp piano riff, the stab of a minor chord.

"It must be wonderful to know what you want," she said.

"One fight will pay for it."

"Then the Casa Mañana will make you rich?"

"It's the music, not the money. Sooner or later, a great club loses money the way a beautiful balloon loses air. You mind my fighting?"

"It sounds like a bad movie. We had such movies in

Germany. The man who fights one last time to pay for an operation for his sister so her sight can be miraculously saved. Naturally, he loses his."

"I'm going to win. And I won't go blind or break my hands."

"If this is what you truly want –"

"It is."

"Then I don't think anyone in the world could stop you."

It was midnight when they came out of the club into the parking lot, half a block of cars surrounded by a low adobe barrier.

This part of Albuquerque's Central Avenue was called "Old Town", as if the Old West were lined with curio stoves and pawn shops with steel shutters. At night, except for the Casa Mañana, the street was deserted. Black, except for the tents of light around streetlamps. As Anna got into the jeep, she touched her hair.

"My new pin. I left it on the table."

Joe returned for the pin and when he came out of the club again he took a shortcut through the kitchen and out the back. There were fewer cars there, the jalopies of waiters and kitchen help. Among them, he heard voices and laughs and then something hitting the ground.

Between a pair of Fords, a tiny beam of light played from a horizontal face to a shirt, to a double-breasted jacket and a hand in the jacket pocket. As Joe approached, the beam slid back up to the face, which was round as a plate, subcutaneous blue on the upper lip and chin, eyes closed and mouth slack. Spread on the man's chest were licence, business cards, post-cards, money. Kneeling over him was Captain Augustino, still in civvies.

"Harry Gold." Augustino read the cards under the light. "Harry Gold of the Philadelphia Sugar Company. Harry Gold, licensed driver of the Commonwealth of Pennsylvania. Street map of Santa Fe, $1,250 in cash. Harry Gold on vacation."

An empty champagne bottle rolled away from the captain's knee and came to rest against a tyre. Joe assumed Augustino had used the bottle against the back of Gold's head.

"You know about him," Joe said.

"Heinrich Golodnitsky, to be exact, Sergeant." Augustino flicked the light back to the plump face and crumpled hat. "Heinrich Golodnitsky of Russian-Jewish lineage. Golodnitsky, who came at the age of three to an America of sugar-sweet opportunity, not only to find gold on the streets but to be Gold. Golodnitsky, Gold. Heinrich, Harry." Augustino pointed the beam at Joe and some of the light escaped to touch his own lean, passionate face. "See, you always thought I was crazy, Sergeant. Yet, here he is. It's like catching a real devil. A small devil, but a devil all the same. We were at the bar. You played well. Dr Weiss looked lovely."

"I thought you were at Trinity, sir."

Augustino opened the back door of the nearer Ford. "I thought you were on the Hill. Help me get him into the car."

The band could be heard faintly in the lot. He could make out the beat, but not the tune. Two-four time. A whisper of horns.

He gathered Harry Gold in his arms and laid him on the back seat of the car. "What are you going to tell Gold when he wakes up?"

"The concussion will eliminate any short-term memory. I'll tell him he got drunk, fell down and hit his head. He *was* drunk."

"He won't believe it. He'll go right to the Russians."

"Of course he won't believe me. But, apart from treason, Harry Gold is a two-bit chemist, a nothing, a zero. The luckiest day of his life was when he became a spy. You think he wants to lose his only interesting quality? Also, even if he realizes I knocked him out, he'll know he's already caught and on the cross. Hope springs eternal even in the breast of pathological scum. He's not going to tell the Russians anything. Tonight never happened."

"Like us, sir. I never saw you, you never saw me."

"Would I stand in the way of romance, Sergeant? When we're on the same team at last?"

*

On the way back to the Hill they stopped to swim in the Rio where it cut a deep curve in the sandbanks above Santiago. Berry petals passed on the dark surface of the water. There were five days left until Trinity. Minutes seemed to hurry by, as if rushing to a deeper, quicker channel of time.

"A choirboy? I can't believe it," she said.

"We'll go to Harlem an' we'll go struttin'," he sang to her, "an' there'll be nothin' too good for you."

She was cool and weightless to the touch and she slipped away from his hand. Something was wrong, although he didn't know what.

"Sometimes I wonder what my father's dreams for me must have been," she said. "A lecturer's chair at the Mathematical Institute. Learned arguments with other professors as we watched Göttingen slip into the dusk."

"Sounds like a travelogue."

"The memory of a refugee *is* a travelogue. Anyway, a proper husband, also a professor, two children and a villa on the Wilhelm-Weber-Strasse with windowboxes of clematis. I don't believe my father ever dreamed of the Rio Grande or you. I will miss it."

"Miss it? What do you mean?"

"I will miss this place."

"You're leaving?"

"Everyone will be leaving soon after Trinity. I'm leaving before. I've only told Oppy and you."

"That doesn't mean you have to leave New Mexico."

"Yes, it does."

"What about us?"

"Us? This is your home, and now you have your music here, too. It's not my home, and I don't have my work here."

Though he was floating, he had the sensation he was about to fall through the water.

"You came tonight to say goodbye?"

"Yes."

"No. You asked me to come to Chicago. That's what you were getting at when we were dancing."

"Joe, we've only known each other a month – really, two weeks. This is not the end of a long affair. We were just getting to know each other. I've never seen you happier than you were tonight."

"I thought you were happy, too."

"Not like you. It must be wonderful to be so in love with music."

"You're leaving to make some sort of ethical statement about Trinity, right? You feel forced to go?"

"You could say that."

"Then come back."

"And do what? Sell cigarettes in a nightclub?"

"You wouldn't have to do anything."

"But I *do* do something. I'm a mathematician, and I work at a certain level. Besides the Hill, there is no such place here for me to work. Could I work with you? You wouldn't know what I was saying. This is not insulting. I'm not asking you to leave your music, to live in Chicago and erase blackboards for me."

"Then the hell with the club. I'll go with you, once I'm out of the Army."

"Now that I know that the club is what you want most in life? Oh no."

"I love you. There'll always be another Casa Mañana."

"I don't think so. I think this is your chance. For you to give it up and follow me, that would be a small version of Joe Peña. You know, the first time I saw you at the Christmas dance, Klaus Fuchs pointed to you and said, 'There is the Chief, stupid and dangerous and larger than life.' You aren't stupid, but you are the other two and I don't want you to change. I don't want you any smaller than Chief Joe Peña."

"It's beginning to sound as if I've been some sort of conquest for you. Entertainment. Part of your tour of Indian country."

"That's not true."

"It's simple. I love you and I'm willing to go. If you loved me, you'd stay."

She reached out for him. "I do love you. We can make love right now."

He wanted to. The water was getting colder and colder. She hovered in it like a flame.

"Then stay." He could only stand her silence so long before he turned. "Then go. Let's get you out of here. Let's get you packed and gone."

She followed him out of the water, so he was the first to see two figures squatting on the sand.

"Hello, Joe."

24

In the quarter-moon, Roberto and Ben Reyes showed the fatigue of a chase. Their hair was loose, their necks limp. Sophie Reyes hung back behind a log.

Joe picked up Anna's skirt for her.

"One's blind. The other's so old it doesn't matter."

"They need your help," Sophie said.

"Do they?" Joe asked. He stepped into his trousers. "Well, the lady's in a big hurry. So, excuse us, but we're going."

"It was the Indian Service. They came at sunset," Roberto said. "It was lucky they came from the east. Ben saw them."

"A buckle shone," Ben said.

Joe snatched his shirt from the ground.

"Really? And you desperadoes slipped away? How many were there?"

"Just two," Ben said. "Those Service riders."

"No one riding drag? You sure are lucky. Two cowboys came straight into the sun. You flush and nobody follows. You came back here to your house?"

"Your house," Roberto said. "We thought they might be watching Ben's."

"Naturally. You could have kept on going."

Anna buttoned her shirt.

"Joe," she said, "he's blind."

"Blind and crazy."

"Have you climbed the ladder in my dream yet?" Roberto asked Joe.

"See what I mean?" Joe asked Anna.

"The Service came by with a Federal warrant," Sophie said. "They were talking about sabotage and the FBI. They said they were watching the bus terminals, so Ben and Roberto should give themselves up."

"You saw the warrant?" Joe asked.

"I can read," Sophie said stiffly.

"They need your help, Joe," Anna said.

"To what? I already gave them two chances to escape, but they wanted to play cowboys and Indians, only now it's getting a little rough. I told them there was a war on, they didn't believe me. What do you care? A minute ago you couldn't get out of here fast enough. Come on, I'll take you back. You're shivering."

"I gathered some sticks there," Sophie said. "We could be warm if you have a match."

"You have to help them, Joe," Anna said.

"I don't *have* to do a damn thing. I'm not responsible for them. Don't tell me what to do. I made a fool of myself for you, but that's over, right? Over, and you're going. I don't want to hear any more about ethical choices from you. All I want is you in the jeep, you on the train and gone."

"Joe," Sophie said. "Please."

In a depression in the sand was driftwood that looked like antlers. He knelt and lit the shavings underneath with his lighter; yellow flames branched from stick to stick. In the glow, Ben's face was dusty and scraped from a fall. Roberto's hands were wrapped in bloody bandages. Joe looked up. Was the entire universe Indian, or were there scattered craters of sanity?

Roberto's eyes turned to the heat.

"That spy on the cliff. Whatever happened to him?"

"He means Fuchs," Joe told Anna. "So far, Roberto, he seems to be getting away, which is more than I can say for you. A Federal warrant? That means another country, at least until this thing blows over."

"Smokes?" Ben asked.

Joe gave him his Luckies.

"Keep the pack."

214

"I prefer Chesterfields," Ben said, but pocketed the cigarettes. "What do you mean, 'another country'?"

"Mexico's the nearest one. You can be another Pancho Villa, Uncle."

"I don't like Mexico. They do something funny to their beans."

"Yeah, they mash them into shit and pour flies over them. That's why they have such good beer. Uncle, are you listening? Mexico's your only chance. The war'll be over soon, people will calm down and then you can come back here."

"You'll take them?" Anna asked.

"Well, this really has nothing to do with you, does it?" Joe said. "You'll be in Chicago or somewhere. We will be a fond memory. You'll look at your pot or your silver pin and you'll always think of us. And, Lord knows, you'll always be grateful for your short but fascinating sojourn in Santiago."

"Stop it, Joe," she said.

"The Indian mysteries revealed, the firing of the clay."

"Please stop."

"The exotic nights with an authentic chief."

"I'm sorry."

"Joe, will you take them?" Sophie asked.

"Yeah. Okay, okay. It's not that hard. It means going to El Paso and taking the trolley into Juarez. We'll put some sunglasses on Roberto and a serape on Ben. Easy. But I won't be able to take them through until Sunday night."

"That's the night of the test," Anna said carefully. "That's the night you're fighting."

"Test of what?" Roberto asked.

"The weapon," Joe said.

"The gourd of ashes?"

"That's the one."

"And the ladder? You're going to climb it to the gourd?"

"I'm not climbing anything. I'm not even going to be there for the blast. The general wants me to drive around and make sure no wild Apaches wander on to the test range. That's why I can get away and fight. After the fight, we'll go down to the border. The trick is for you to hide out until then. And for you to get to the fight with a car."

"A serape?" Ben muttered. He already had the manner of an emperor going into exile. "Where are you going to fight?"

"Below Socorro is a little town called Antonio. There's just one cross-street. Make a left and go half a mile to the Owl Café. At the back of the café is a motel. The fight will start in the motel courtyard at 8 pm. By nine it should be over and the cars cleared out. That's when you show up."

"What if you can't go?" Anna asked. "What if there's a problem?"

Joe talked to Ben and Roberto.

"Park in the courtyard and put out your lights. Wait five minutes, no more. There'll be MPs all over the place. If I can't join you in five minutes, that means there's a real problem. There won't be, don't worry, but in case there is, tell the driver to just go back to the highway and turn south to El Paso and then put you on the trolley car. When you find a place in Juarez, call the Casa Mañana in Albuquerque and leave a message where you're staying. If there's a change in plan before then, I'll tell Felix Tafoya, who seems to be just as good being a clown or tossing lightning wands as he is pushing a broom."

"Good." Roberto grinned. "You figured that out."

"Yeah. And Ben, your former brother Hilario told me the other day he'd never missed a dance in Santiago. I didn't see him at the dance when they came for Roberto, but let's assume Hilario was absent-mindedly telling the truth about his perfect attendance. He fingered Roberto and left. He'll be at the fight, so keep your head down."

Sophie came out of the dark, taking off the blanket she wore as a shawl. Joe thought she was finally joining the circle at the fire, but she threw the blanket over the flames, smothering them as she stomped on the blanket.

"Indian Service," Joe told Anna.

"You're sure I can keep the cigarettes?" Ben asked.

"Yes. Get out of here," Joe said.

"That's good of you," Ben said in Tewa. "You're a good boy."

All the dogs on the east side of the pueblo were, by now, barking the alarm. Sophie and Ben led Roberto up the riverbank and around a screen of thimbleberries. Joe and Anna climbed to the jeep and pulled on their shoes.

"This is, you know, much more interesting than a walk round Göttingen," she said.

"Very few cowboys in Göttingen," Joe said.

He started the jeep. Headlights out, they rolled past cottonwoods and watertanks and on to a dirty road between the pueblo and fields of barley and sorghum. Over peach trees was a glimpse of the church's low brow. The air stirred the smell of roasted chillies. Joe drove along an irrigation ditch towards the wooden planks that bridged a cross-ditch. The planks coughed as the jeep passed over.

"There!" Anna said.

Fifty yards ahead, the two Service riders were on horseback. Al, the older one, waved both arms for Joe to stop. Billy seemed to have acquired a handgun with a long, bright barrel.

Joe turned behind a windbreak of sunflowers. If he was stopped, he was AWOL. Anna was breaking security. At the same time, he could see what the riders were up to. Sophie, Ben and Roberto had taken to the ditch and Billy and Al were waiting for them to come up. The fields were a maze of ditches, all fed by the mother ditch at the north end, along the highway. If the fugitives reached the corn fields, where the rows of stalks were shoulder-high, the riders would never catch them.

Joe eased through the sorghum, the grass beating against the wheels. The riders paid no attention. The jeep rolled into the corn, mowing a row as it went. The stalks bent, broke. Red corn, blue corn, black corn, beaded corn, Indian corn. At the end of the row, he stopped.

To his right, about twenty yards down the dirt road, Al was shouting, "Open her up, Billy."

To Joe's left, thirty yards up the road, Billy was leaning out of his saddle to turn the wheel that would raise the wooden gate of the ditch. Roberto, Sophie and Ben were neatly trapped. The flood of water would drown them or drive them back to Al.

"Get out," Joe told Anna. "I'll come back for you."

"I want to go with you," she said.

"I don't want you with me and I don't have time to argue. I want you waiting here until I come back and drive you nice and slowly to the Hill, so you don't miss your train in the morning."

Anna clutched the back of the seat.

"No."

"Okay," Joe said.

He slipped the jeep on to the road, turned and stood on the accelerator. Billy was still leaning from his horse and yanking the gate wheel when he heard the engine approach. Twenty feet from Billy, Joe hit his headlights. The cowboy wore a gold sateen shirt and an expression of astonishment. His horse reared and toppled backwards out of the glare. Joe heard man and mount hit the water of the mother ditch, then the jeep was across the planks of the ditch and on to the highway, heading north.

A hundred yards up the highway, Joe spun around because he had to come back down the highway and along the mother ditch to get to the Hill. Billy was screaming he couldn't swim. Al had ridden up to the ditch and in the wan moonlight sat patiently on his horse, aiming his gun with both hands. A speckled Colt, Joe remembered. There was no way the cowboy would really shoot, he thought. Not an Army jeep.

As he passed in front of Al, Joe changed his mind, turned off his headlights, slammed on the brakes. The gun flashed, bobbed, flashed again. He floored the accelerator. The third shot was over-corrected, rushed, behind the jeep. The shots after that sounded like a tin pail being futilely kicked.

For miles, Joe and Anna drove without lights and without saying a word, as if the dark and quiet sustained the moment of escape and delayed the saying of goodbye. He and she were so different, he thought, that any words divided them. It proved how strange the Hill was that they'd met at all. Let the last little triumph roll as long as possible, for ever if possible.

He had to turn the lights on when they hit the switchbacks. As the jeep climbed, Anna acted busy by cleaning bits of corn stalk from the floor. She found two items that had shaken loose from under the seat, two zigzags of carved wood.

"What are these?" she asked, without directly meeting Joe's eyes. This is how it ends, he thought. Without real words, without even looks.

"Roberto's crazy wands."

"What are you supposed to do with them?"

"Call down lightning. Water your fields. Bring back the buffalo. Stop the bomb."

"You can do that?"

Joe took the wands from her and threw them sideways from the jeep. They spun, glittered and then plunged into the dark of the canyon.

"Not any more," he said.

FRIDAY

25

Orders were no stopping en route, but as Joe went through Antonio, he slowed by the Owl Bar and Café enough to see Army engineers and MPs stationed in the motel courtyard. He gained speed again, leading a convoy of two jeeps, two CID sedans, a carry-all truck of spare parts and a covered truck bearing Jaworski and the sphere of steel and high explosive that was the implosive shell of the bomb.

"The MPs are there to evacuate the town in case of, you know . . ." Ray Stingo rode in the lead jeep with Joe.

"What's it like down here?" Joe asked. Ray had been in and out of Trinity for a week.

"Typical Army fuck-ups. We got some scientists, some of the million-dollar whiz kids, laying some wires out in the bushes and a B-29 comes over shooting some antelope. Fifty-calibre machine-guns. Scientists are running, diving, trying to fly. You see, the rest of the Army doesn't know about this." They were already out of Antonio. Ray took a long, swivelled view of a far-off, flat horizon of buffalo grass, grey sage, yucca spears. "Fucking place for a test. You gotta shake your shoes every morning to get out the scorpions. You gotta bang a wrench on the jeep to chase the rattlers. There's gypsum in the water to fuck up your plumbing. Every five minutes you gotta run into the bushes and then it's you and the shit and rattler all over again." There was alkali in the water, too. Ray's black spit curl was plaster-hard. "It may be a new weapon, but it's the same Army."

"The odds?" Joe asked.

223

"Two to one. Odds on the fight are so good they scare me. I was thinking, I could be real set up on the Hill. I'd just piss away the money back in Jersey. I think I'll stay."

"There won't be any Hill after the war."

"Chief, I got one smart idea my whole life, okay? We didn't build this bomb for the Japs, we built it for the Reds. And we didn't even fight them yet."

Besides the convoy, Joe had seen no other Army traffic on the road. Stallion Gate was little changed. New barbed wire, new fence posts. A checkpoint that consisted of a tarpaulin-covered lean-to that provided a miserly wedge of shade. The MPs had been issued with pith helmets. Before leaving the Hill, each man in the convoy had been given a pink pass with a T for Trinity, which they exchanged at the gate for round white badges.

"Foreign Legion, Chief." Corporal Gruber was one of the MPs at the gate. His arm was still in a sling. His eyes were red from alkali dust. "A hundred degrees every day for two weeks. Fucking badges? Security? There must be fifty guys every night who walk off the desert for a beer. Single file between the snakes." He wrote Joe's name under the proper date and time on his clipboard. "Friday the 13th. Some day to bring down the bomb. Feeling good, Chief?"

"Good enough."

Gruber licked dry lips. "It's a question of confidence, right?"

"To a point."

Gruber waved him through. "One more fight, that's all we ask."

The ranch access road that Joe remembered as a faint trail in the snow was newly graded and topped with *colichi*, a sand-and-clay compound that had quickly disintegrated into fine white powder. Clouds of dust followed another convoy far ahead. Jaworski joined Joe and Ray in the lead jeep. He had a portable FM receiver and around his neck he wore the Polaroid all-purpose red goggles issued for the test. With his dark moustaches, he looked like a touring grandee.

"We're supposed to monitor the receivers at all times here,

in case of an accident," Jaworski said. "Keys are supposed to be kept in ignitions at all times, in case of evacuation. That's why the roads are so wide. Myself, I wonder what you're supposed to do if there is an accident and you're not near a road and you don't have a real field radio you can actually transmit on."

Some static-ridden communications were erupting from the FM. Mainly, there was music. Carmen Miranda.

"Don't ask me how," Ray said. "The Army spent months finding a special channel just for us? It's the same channel as the Voice of America. The Latin edition. Orders are, ignore the *sambas* and the bombers."

"Well, what do you do if you're stuck out in the open and the bomb, accidentally, goes off?"

"The flash, the burst of gamma rays and neutrons would kill anything within a mile and a half of the tower. If you could get a couple of miles away and find a depression, a stream –"

"A stream in the *Jornada del Muerto*? That sounds like planning. There couldn't really be an accident, though, could there?"

"Yesterday, Joe, they were testing the firing circuits on a dummy bomb in the tower. Out of the blue, a lightning bolt. Imagine if the real bomb had been there. By the way, Anna Weiss asked me to tell you goodbye. She left early this morning for Chicago. She borrowed Teller's car to drive there, otherwise I suppose you would have driven her to the train station."

"I suppose so."

There were a couple of hundred men at Trinity, but they were so spread out over hundreds of acres that only a few could be seen at a time. Still, the closer the convoy got to Ground Zero, the more evidence of activity there was. A cable strung on a seemingly infinite line of stakes. The first blast-wave gauge, a box designed to bounce in the springs of a hoop. Photographic bunkers grey as shells on a beach, periscope stalks aimed south at a tower seven miles off in the clear, trembling air. Ground Zero. Six miles from the tower, the convoy reached the North 10,000-metre shelter, a timber bunker that sank into a protective slope of raw earth. Bulldozers browsed on the slope, tamping it. From North-10,000, a fresh tarmac road ran straight to the shot tower. Single cables multiplied into racks of wires. Planted in dead sage was an unmanned instrument bunker, a concrete block with portholes for cameras.

"Skyshine hole." Jaworski pointed to the single socket aimed away from the tower. "To monitor the general neutron scatter."

Skyshine? It sounded pretty, like the glitter of sequins shot in the air.

"Nervous?" Joe asked.

"Things have changed," Jaworski said. "We used to detonate shells using a long string. No one had a gauge. A charge worked or it didn't. No oscillographs or ionization chambers. What hasn't changed is that there will only be a handful of men who actually assemble the bomb. There'll be a hundred others screaming that this seismograph is vital or that pressure gauge must be repaired, but the only thing that counts is the weapon, right? Of course, in the war against the Kaiser we dropped nothing much greater than grenades from planes, and there was no background neutron scatter."

The tower at Ground Zero looked like an oil rig without the pipes, a spindly structure of steel beams and tie braces that rose 100 feet to a platform and galvanized-iron shed perched in the sky. One tower leg had steel steps with landings every twenty feet. A wooden ladder reached from the bottom landing to the ground. Foote was waiting on the ground in his sombrero and British Army shorts. His high explosives team of half a dozen draftees sat in undershirts, bathing shorts and handkerchiefs worn on the head pirate-style. As the convoy wound around and stopped at the tower base, CID officers jumped from the two security sedans and formed a skirmish line, pointing submachine-guns at cactus and rabbitbrush.

Foote ambled at their backs.

"They seek him here, they seek him there, those Frenchies

seek him everywhere. Is he in Heaven, is he in Hell, that demmed elusive Pimpernel? Joe, you brought my goods?"

The truck drove directly under the wide callipers of a chain and pulley that was suspended down the centre of the tower. When the truck's tarpaulin was removed, Joe and Ray bolted the callipers to the bomb. Steel cable groaned as it turned through the pulley sheave. The truck rolled out from under and the dangling bomb was lowered to a knee-high steel cradle, where it resembled a globe on a stand, a matt-grey moon four and a half feet wide, with two rims and patches where the detonator ports were taped. As soon as Ray disengaged the callipers and the pulley was lifted free, Foote's men set a canvas tent over the bomb and the security cars drove off.

"Want to join the pool?" Foote asked Joe. "A dollar apiece."

"For what?"

"The bang, what else. The new official anticipated yield is 5,000 to 10,000 tons of TNT. Jaworski and I have both bet on 10,000. I think it's the first time we agreed on anything. Teller bet on 40,000 tons. He's always an optimist."

"Oppy?" Joe was supposed to find him, now he was at Trinity.

"Oppy predicts 300 tons. Three hundred tons is a dud. We're a little worried about Oppy."

Harvey and the plutonium core had arrived earlier that morning at a ranch house a mile south of the shot.

The rancher had been bought off and pushed out, but, except for Harvey's Plymouth and the four jeeps parked with their backs to the house and their motors running, the place still looked from the outside like any ordinary spread: barn and corral, a windmill to pump water and a cistern to hold it, a one-storey house within a low stone wall. Inside, the parlour walls were blue with a genteel white band below the ceiling line. The oak floor had been vacuumed and the windows sealed with plastic sheets and masking tape. All the furniture had been removed except the table, which was covered with brown paper. Working at Trinity, Harvey had already joined the two silver-plated plutonium hemispheres into one 11 lb sphere the

227

size of a grapefruit. Dressed in a white surgical coat, rubber gloves on his hands, he was now filling holes on the sphere's shining surface with tiny wads of Kleenex, the fill-all of Trinity. Geiger counters conversed on the floor. Six silent men in lab coats monitored the counters, gave Harvey one tool and then another. The only person without a task was Oppy. A man six feet tall began to look strange when his weight got down to seven stone. Oppy's head seemed gaunt and swollen at the same time, too large for the neck that stuck out of the lab coat. His hands wrung a cold briar. Somebody had hammered a nail in the wall for him to hang his porkpie hat from, the same as in his office on the Hill. The hat was there, but Oppy seemed oddly out of place and miserable, not triumphant at all.

"Remember the Dragon," Harvey said although he hadn't looked up from the core when Joe came in.

Joe stayed back by the wall, which was a foot thick, making the room relatively cool, maybe ninety degrees. The plastic-covered window faced the idling cars, poised for flight in case of a mishap, in case of a slip of Harvey's hands. Joe's mission orders now that he was at Trinity were to stay with Oppy at all times and make sure the project Director survived any accident.

Harvey gave the core a final polish with an emery cloth.

"I gave away my clarinet."

"Too bad. You had great potential," Joe said.

Harvey's Critical Assembly team followed his every move with the intensity of chicks watching their mother turn an egg. One of them put on the table long brass tweezers and a small, shockproof case studded with plugs. He unlocked the case and raised the lid. On a bed of foam rubber lay a pearl, a one-inch ball of platinum-coated polonium. This was the core within the core, an "initiator" which would emit a burst of neutrons in the first millionth of a second of detonation.

"I think I'll stick to what I'm good at," Harvey said.

He re-opened the larger core, propping the top hemisphere with his finger. With his free hand he picked up the brass tweezers and used it to lift the tiny ball. He had to place the "initiator" in its nest in the centre of the core, and the insertion had to be done in slow motion while the building radiation was monitored. Harvey blinked through his sweat, but his hands didn't falter. His finger prodded open the core a little more, a little more as the ball and tweezer advanced. The ticking of the Geiger counters rose like the pulse of excited hearts. Oppy looked like he was going to sway and drop.

"Those icy atoms up and down my spine," Harvey sang softly. *"The blue of ions when your eyes meet mine. A strange new tingle that I feel inside, and then that radiation starts its ride."*

Oppy's pipe hit the floor and spun across the boards. Harvey froze, fingers in the maw of the two hemispheres. "Joe, will you please take Oppy for a walk?"

Outside in the hot, dry air, Joe found his shirt had soaked through with sweat. Oppy sat on the low stone wall, hat on his knee.

"I suspect that before his flight, Icarus was throwing up. I wish we could just go into the mountains again, Joe, go riding again like we used to. I've ridden that horse of mine just once this year. I know they don't need me in there, but it's my test, Joe." He looked up at Joe. While the rest of Oppy had been worn down to bones and clothes, the blue eyes had the intensity of a man enduring pain. "I asked Groves for another week or just another four days. When this is over, we'll go riding."

"Sure."

Harvey called Joe inside. The core was closed and complete and sat in a lead-lined wooden box.

"He's been like this since he got here. Maybe he should go back to the Hill."

"It's his test," Joe said.

They carried the box on a litter out to Harvey's car and put it on the back seat. Joe took Oppy in the jeep and slowly led the way to the tower. The breeze of late afternoon was picking up. Dust devils whipped around the tower base.

Inside the tent, Foote and Jaworski had removed the polar cap at the top of the bomb and taken out a brass plug so that the plutonium core could be inserted. Harvey opened his box and attached the core to a vacuum cup. He tested the seal, then hooked the chain of a manual hoist on to the cup's eye. He pulled off his lab coat and kicked it away. Tested the seal again. Harvey looked like a plump and innocent boy, the sweat coursing off his belly, his fine blonde hair standing as if magnetized. Foote cranked the core up from its box. From a corner of the tent, Oppy and Joe watched Jaworski steady the core with a pencil as Foote swung it over the waiting bomb. Wind beat on the tent.

"One proper dust devil and a few grains of sand and we can put our symmetrical implosion into a pisspot," Foote said.

He lowered the core. One moment it hovered over the bomb like a moon above a larger body, the next it was descending by its chain into the bomb's interior.

And stuck.

Jaworski waved his hand up. His moustaches had started to sag. Foote cranked up the core and lowered it into the bomb again.

It stuck.

Foote cranked the core halfway out of the bomb, slipped the hoist's ratchet and painstakingly let out the chain again. The core made its slow downward passage, nudging lenses of high explosive as it descended.

And stuck. By a millimetre or so, the plutonium core was simply too big, or the hollow inside the bomb was too small.

"I don't believe this," Oppy said and stared first at the bomb and then at Foote. "It isn't possible. You measured wrong?"

The tent walls shook. Measured wrong? Wouldn't fit? Like a pair of tight jeans? Joe pictured anyone telling that to General Groves, and he could see every man was imagining the same scene.

Harvey laughed.

"It's the desert heat. The plutonium's hot, expanded. Grade school physics. Leave the core where it is, it'll cool."

It took five minutes, but the temperature of the plutonium and high explosive equalized and the core slipped meekly into place. Jaworski unsealed the vacuum cup, and as Foote raised the chain Harvey inserted a three-foot-long manganese wire down to the resting core to check its neutron count. Connected to a Geiger counter, the wire detected a cascade of ions, a noise like a hive.

"I'm done." Harvey withdrew the needle. He paused at the hole as if he couldn't trust the moment, then slipped quickly out of the tent flap.

At once, Foote and Jaworski began replacing high explosive. Lenses that appeared loose they made snug with Scotch tape. As the work went on into the evening, lamps were brought in. Thunder could be heard walking across the valley.

"Italy has just declared war on Japan." Harvey returned to the tent.

"Hell, this war *is* almost over," Joe said.

SATURDAY

26

Joe ran in the early morning; he did roadwork whenever he had the chance now. Punching the air, ducking, slipping punches right, left. Cool sweat ran down his chest.

As he ran, he played music in his head. He worked on a "Fugue for Night". He thought it could be bebop, but it became a double waltz for minor chords, constantly changing, rising and falling because there were so many kinds of night. Mountain night. Desert night. Even the deep, fungal night of the Philippines had variations. Then there was the interior void without moon or heart that was life without Anna. Sometimes the physical reaction came before the thought itself. A burning in the throat, a hollowness in the chest, and then memory. If she was driving to Chicago, she was still on the road. It was as if his body were actively betraying him. Sometimes his eyes told him they actually saw her in the dark, as if hope could gather shadows and take on human form. Then the shadows would fade and he was alone again on the flat void, and he knew how much he preferred even illusions.

Sometimes, with sweat and concentration, he didn't think of her at all.

He brought down the moon on flatted fifths.

The sweat poured.

At eight in the morning, Foote struck the tent at the base of the tower and Joe hooked a pulley cable to the rim of the bomb. It had to rise 100 feet to the trap door in the shed on the tower platform, a long way to lift 5,000 lbs of steel and

235

explosive and 11 lbs of plutonium. The sky was a paralyzing blue, blue as a burst of water; not a ragtail hawk up yet, only the dots of weather balloons basking in the sun.

When Foote waved up to the platform, the two-cycle engine of the pulley motor started overhead. As the cable went taut and the sphere and its cradle cleared the ground enough to stir, Foote's team began throwing GI mattresses down from the back of a truck. The bomb rose cautiously an inch at a time, while Joe and Foote slipped mattresses under the ascending sphere.

"This is the greatest scientific programme in the history of mankind?" Joe asked.

"Absolutely," Foote said.

"If the cable snaps, you're going to catch a 2½-ton bomb with mattresses?"

"I concede we may have reached a certain point of intellectual exhaustion." Foote blithely watched the bomb rise. "Reminds me of the late Queen Victoria being lifted on board a ship. A feeling somewhere between the religious and the ridiculous."

Much of the exhaustion was located next to the tower, in the jeep where Oppy was talking to Jaworski. Oppy's eyes were red from the alkali dust.

The bomb rose smoothly as a plumb, stabilizing side ropes stretched to skates that jerked up the rails within two opposite tower legs. Joe and Foote could stack mattresses up to ten feet, but no higher. The bomb, rocking gently in the air, rose to twenty feet, to fifty feet. After all the security back at the Hill, it occurred to Joe that he was looking at the easiest potshot of the war; if a saboteur wanted a chance, this was it.

"Where is Captain Augustino?" Joe asked as Oppy approached the pile of mattresses.

"The people back on the Hill tested a dummy of the detonators last night," Oppy told Foote, ignoring Joe. "There was no symmetrical shock. I am informed as of five minutes ago that we have a dud."

236

"It'll work." Foote tipped the brim of his sombrero the better to keep his eyes on the bomb.

"Two billion dollars." Oppy laughed. The laugh became a cough that sounded like his lungs were ripping. While he bent over, he lit a cigarette. "No, Joe, to answer a question of immaculate irrelevance, I haven't seen Captain Augustino. Please get it through your skull that I don't care about Captain Augustino. Captain Augustino does not concern me."

"I suppose he concerns Joe." Foote craned his neck. "From rumours I've heard, I supposed he'd like to nail Joe's cock to the ground and shoot him through the head."

"The captain is after bigger game than that," Joe said.

The bomb shook. A skate rattled down a track, its rope whipping the air until the skate dug itself into the dirt at the tower base. Forty feet overhead, the bomb slowly yawed from side to side, still attached to the other skate and twisting with a new inertia.

"Fucking Mother of God," someone said.

"Dear me," said Foote.

The bones in Oppy's face seemed to sag.

"The cable's stuck!" the man on the platform shouted. "Coming off the wheel. I'll have to free the other skate."

It was Private Eberly. A soldier in shorts. Crew cut. Gawky as a crane, but he came down the tower's steel rungs like a hero, taking each flight of steps Navy-style. The second landing put him on a level with the skewed bomb, but one tower leg away. He'd have to walk across a narrow, open horizontal brace of the scaffolding fifty feet above the ground. Diagonal braces would support him most of the way, but in the middle where the braces rose out of reach, Eberly would have to be a tightrope walker. Why not? After the most powerful weapon in the world left the hands of geniuses like Oppy and Harvey and Foote, why shouldn't its fate hang on the nerve of an ordinary soldier? Let him be the man of the day.

Jaworski ran from the jeep.

"Don't try it!"

"Try it," Oppy whispered.

Eberly clung to the rising brace as long as he could, then spread his arms for balance. The steel was about four inches across, and Eberly moved on anxious, splayed feet. Don't stop, Joe thought. The soldier tilted, regained his equilibrium and stood motionless in the centre of the horizontal brace. Don't look down, Joe thought. Eyes level, Eberly started again towards the far tower leg. He misstepped. He pulled his foot back on to the steel. His arms waggled like duck wings. He looked down and dived.

Eberly turned in the air and landed on his back in the middle of the mattresses. He slid off the stack to the ground and to his knees, winded but unhurt.

"Joe?" Oppy said.

Joe was already propping the ladder against the tower. He climbed to the steel steps of the tower leg and climbed those to the second landing, where Eberly had been standing a minute before.

Because Joe was taller, he could hang on to the diagonal strut longer. The breeze was stronger at forty feet than he'd expected. The steel ball slowly rolled and although Joe knew he was being watched from below he felt oddly alone with the bomb, as if it had been waiting only for him. He spread his arms wide, catching the wind, and walked with a quick, steady pace across the beam to the descending diagonal brace and to the tower leg.

The skate was jammed. Joe called down for a hammer and caught it as it spun up. He hit the skate and freed it, and the bomb gently swung to the centre of the tower. Joe tucked the hammer into his belt and walked, arms out, back across the beam.

Joe was vaguely aware of someone saying "Bravo" down on the ground. He continued up the tower steps, rising to the second and third landings and on to the platform at the top. Most of the platform was taken up by the eight-by-twelve shed of corrugated sheet iron. Outside was the engine and hoist. Joe started the engine. As the pulley wheel turned, the cable slipped back into its groove. Joe could see the bomb inching up the scaffolding again. He kept his heel on the engine switch, ready to stop it in case the skate jammed a second time.

West, he had a distant view of volcanic cones. South was more interesting. A blast smudge showed on the desert floor where a practice blast, a mere 100 tons of TNT spiced with isotopes, had been set off on V-E Day. Fire-breaks had been ploughed around the blast, giving it the look of a bullseye. Farther on was the ranch house where Harvey had assembled the core the day before. There were random scars of tyre tracks and a tarmac road that ended in the middle distance at South-10,000, the control bunker six miles away that would fire the bomb. Joe could just make out the slap-up buildings and the windmill of the Base Camp ten miles away. Behind the camp was a dry sea of brush and dust that lapped against the Oscura Mountains. The name meant "dark". And, low and broken, the Oscura seemed to lie in the shadow of larger, invisible mountains. It was a region of illusion. On the other side of the Oscura were snowy dunes called White Sands. Joe noticed that tarmac roads also ran west and north from the tower, new roads virtually without traffic, in place purely for disaster.

"The fact is, I'm scared of heights." Eberly climbed back on to the platform.

"Heights are about the last thing you need to be afraid of around here," Joe said.

As the bomb eased up through the platform, Eberly removed the trap door from the shed roof. When the bomb was halted at the pinnacle of the hoist, Joe and Eberly gently swung the hoist 180 degrees, so that the sphere hung over the open roof. Then Eberly lowered the bomb and Joe bolted the cradle to its new home on the shed's floor of solid oak planks.

Oppy, Jaworski and Foote arrived up the steps while Eberly and Joe swung the hoist again to bring up the heavy detonator gear. The Explosive Assembly team carried up electrical leads and coaxial cable. Harvey climbed to the shed to open the bomb's polar cap and re-check the neutron count with the manganese wire.

239

"Forty-two hours," Foote muttered to Joe.

"You'll make it."

"Oh, I know the bomb will. I mean him."

Oppy leaned against the shed wall, eyes intent on the bomb. His shirt sleeves were rolled up and showed wrists like straws. His entire body seemed to maintain a faint existence only to carry the painfully brooding skull.

Joe ran at night and on the road met what he first thought was Einstein, but was Santa, stumbling along, his white hair drooping, mouth gnawing distractedly on his moustache, wearing a jacket and long scarf.

"How are the hives?" Joe asked.

"Much better. Really under control. Up to my chin. A walking bandage of skin salve."

"I thought you weren't going to volunteer for Trinity."

"I wasn't in the La Fonda," he told Joe, "so someone else volunteered me, naturally. They gave me a hut down at the Base Camp. Already getting some interesting cases, GIs who hear the scientists talking and, as a result, focus their anxieties on the end of the world."

"That's what you predicted."

"Thank you. So, in fact, it's worked out. It's really an opportunity to be here. If you think about our psychological history really being built on anxieties. Of a sexual nature or a religious nature or a combination of the two. Then we may be on the ground floor of the primary anxiety of the rest of history."

Joe ran on to Shapiro's station at the North-10,000 bunker.

On his return leg, Joe met no one. The valley floor lay empty in the semi-dark cast by a half-moon. Beyond the mountains on either side were storms, lightning muffled in clouds so far off they were silent. In his mind, he saw Anna step again out of the Rio, water and light flowing from her. In memory, the river was black and filled with coral, shell and turquoise.

SUNDAY

27

After non-denominational services at the Base Camp picnic tables, with the bomb in place at the top of the tower and only awaiting the arrival of General Groves, some men spent the hours before Trinity hunting antelope or searching the area for arrowheads or silver mines. Oppy searched for Fermi and Joe drove.

"We left dummy rigs of the detonators *and* the firing rig back on the Hill." Oppy spoke more to himself than to Joe. "Yesterday morning, the detonator dummy failed. Yesterday afternoon, the firing unit dummy failed. Truman is in Berlin expecting news of our great success and I already know that we will fail. If Fermi thinks we'll fail, I'll call it off."

"Fermi is checking blast measurements. He could be anywhere on the test range," Joe said.

"Then we'll cover the test range. Everyone here seems to think they're at summer camp. It would be good to speak to one serious person."

At the lean-to that constituted the North-10,000 MP station, Sergeant Shapiro said he hadn't seen Fermi.

"We did have some intruders last night, though. Could be locals."

"Local rabbits, local deer, local cactus in the moonlight?" Oppy asked.

"Could be." Shapiro backed off.

Oppy pointed into the brush and Joe swung the jeep off the road, manoeuvring to drive a course generally on the tower's six-mile periphery, where many of the last-minute adjustments to instruments were taking place, although it occurred to Joe that searching for Fermi might be Oppy's excuse to get away from the tower and the Base Camp. Maybe they weren't looking for anyone, maybe they were hiding. The bomb wasn't the only thing on the point of collapse.

"What time is General Groves coming?" Joe asked.

"Our general is arriving with presidential advisers this evening. Our failure will be well attended. We'll even have a reporter from the *New York Times* watching from a hill twenty miles away." Oppy glanced at Joe. "Do you have any idea what intruders the MP was babbling about?"

"Mescaleros."

Joe braked to avoid running over a sunburnt figure lying on the ground. The man was threading coaxial cable into a garden hose. His back and legs were covered with vaseline and dirt, and pinned to his shorts was a badge that showed he, too, was an elite scientist of Trinity.

As he stuffed the hose, he muttered, "In a circle of hell, men are doing precisely this right now. We can thank Foote and those other fucking Brits for this, because all the cable they insisted on importing and using here has melted under the New Mexico sun and has to be insulated again with 30,000 feet of hose. Have you ever run a catheter up the ass of a 30,000-foot-long snake?"

Further on, they found more physicists digging up the cables they had buried the day before, because they'd buried them taut and, under the weight of the earth they'd thrown back on, the cables had snapped. Two other physicists stood mournfully at a silver barrage balloon. The helium balloon was designed to carry neutron counters aloft; however, Trinity's elevation was so high and the air was so thin that the balloon clung to the desert floor. On a gentle rise stippled with piñons, a radiologist had strung wires on the branches and was hanging white mice from the wires by their tails to determine the effect of the blast on living organisms. The first mice hung had already perished from the heat.

"He's been out in the sun too long himself," Joe said after Oppy had sent man and mice back to the Base Camp.

"It all looks so sane on paper. Do you have a drink, Joe?"

"Sorry."

"Since when don't you have a flask? You're looking fit all of a sudden, unlike me. Two days ago, I touched the plutonium. I told Harvey it was shaking. He said I was shaking." Oppy took a deep breath. "So, Mescaleros?"

"Just what Groves was afraid of, I guess. They still think this is Stallion Gate. They still chase horses out of the mountains and round them up here."

"I recall the mustangs we saw."

"The trackers come in around dusk and stay until dawn. They're bound to see the shot unless I cut them off."

"That means you wouldn't be getting back until morning. You may miss Trinity entirely."

"You don't want any roasted Apaches, do you?"

At the West-10,000 bunker, Oppy left the jeep to talk to meteorologists releasing weather balloons. The balloons bounced as they rose, as if they were rolling up an invisible hill.

Behind the bunker, Ray Stingo was riding on a Sherman tank, taking a practice spin, treads flattening cactus. The tank had been painted white, the cannon removed and the machine-guns replaced with automobile headlights. Air bottles for the crew were clamped to the side armour. Behind the turret was a rack of rockets.

Ray jumped from the tank.

"Isn't it amazing, Chief? Lead-lined, air-filtered, air-conditioned. This baby's the first thing in after the blast to collect samples. The way they do it, they're going to ride up to the crater and shoot rockets with scoops on one end and cables on the other. They just pull the rockets back. That's a garbage truck!"

"Sounds like a professional endorsement."

Joe studied the thin seam of black above the mountains. They were the clouds from last night. Patient clouds.

Ray got in the jeep.

"Christ, there are only eight hours to go to the fight. Turns out your old pal Hilario's insisting on a minimum $1,000 bet from every spectator just to hold down the traffic. That's a Texas crowd, Chief."

"That's good. It helps the odds. What are they now?"

"Still two to one. There's a lot of confidence in the boy. I don't like the crowd, Chief."

"We'll cover the bets. Don't worry about the crowd, we have the MPs."

Ray watched Oppy coming back through the brush.

"I'm so fucking nervous I could piss a marble."

"That tent over the picnic tables where they had church this morning," Joe said. "You think you can appropriate that for the fight?"

"Sure. Why?"

"It's going to rain."

As Oppy went by the tank, it made a ninety-degree turn, rolled over an ironwood tree and headed for him. Ray was gawking up at the sky. Joe was caught on the other side of the jeep by Ray. Oppy turned and watched in a defenceless stupor as the tank clattered, dipped, rose. Joe was prepared to save Oppy from nuclear mishap, not a de-fanged, albino Sherman tank. As it looked over Oppy, it stopped. A hatch popped open and a head wearing a white cotton cap and goggles peered out.

"From this crude lab that spawned a dud," the tanker declaimed with a heavy Italian accent, "their necks to Truman's axe uncurled. Lo, the embattled savants stood and fired the flop heard round the world."

The ditty of gloom was popular on the Hill. The tanker pulled his goggles and cap to reveal cheerful eyes and dark, receding hair. It was Fermi.

"Actually, I would estimate the chances of igniting the entire atmosphere at one in three thousand. Acceptable. The chances of incinerating New Mexico at thirty to one. The bomb will work." He tapped his bald spot. "The problem is suntan lotion.

Teller bought the last bottles so he wouldn't burn from watching the blast. Edward really thinks the bomb will work." Fermi pulled down his goggles and cap. "Now I play with my new toy."

The hatch closed. As the tank rolled into reverse, Ray ran to catch up.

At four in the afternoon, three hours before the fight and twelve hours before Trinity was scheduled, Oppy and Joe climbed the tower. Leads coiled round the grey sphere of the bomb to two detonator boxes. Extra wires, crates and pulley ropes crowded the shed. Joe slipped out on to the platform. A pair of artillery spotter's binoculars hung on the hoist and Joe used them to scan the test site.

Oppy followed Joe out.

"I feel as if we're two men mounting the gallows together," he said. "Everyone else is so confident. Did you see the standing orders for today? 'Look for four-leaf clovers.' "

Joe could see woolly patches of buffalo grass, rabbit brush and yucca spears. Also, manmade burrows where crusher gauges had been buried and standing pipes with crystal gauges and threaded stakes of electrical wire running from South-10,000 to the tower base. No clover.

Down at the ranch house where the core had been assembled, a man was swimming in the cistern. It was a concrete cistern with double tanks for the cattle that used to run on the ranch. The man swam back and forth tirelessly, disappearing under the brackish water and surfacing at the other end. He climbed out, dried himself and dressed in white coveralls, cap, short boots and gloves, then got into a Dodge coupé. Joe watched Harvey drive to the tarmac road and turn to South-10,000.

Everywhere Joe looked, vehicles and men on foot were quitting the six-mile radius of the tower. On the West road, a jeep with four flat tyres carried a full load of GIs. Further in that direction, darkening clouds rose over the tents of volcanic peaks. Against them and against the mist of the Oscura, Trinity was a last lit, golden strand. But dust devils were moving

in, spinning around abandoned instruments, and thunder was becoming more regular.

"There's an invisible world out there. A new map, a cartology of Geiger counters, seismographs, radiosondes and gauges. Joe, I've been thinking about those Mescaleros. If you start chasing them, you might not come back for a day or two. You and I have been through so much, it would be tragic if we didn't share this climactic moment."

Joe wished the tower were higher, the glasses stronger, and he could see Hilario rolling down from Santa Fe. The lieutenant-governor probably had a state trooper driving. The crowd would be coming from the Texas line, cowmen with fist-sized wads of money. Pollack would just about be sliding into his Cadillac.

"I'll make sure I'm back on time."

Oppy leaned on the rail.

"The future is here, tonight. The world will revolve round us. You don't think the MPs will be able to watch for Apaches?"

"MPs don't know where to look."

Joe imagined Roberto and Ben hiding in a Model T. Maybe a pickup truck poking along the highway, with Felix at the wheel, a couple of cows in the back. Anna might be in Chicago already, among the concrete towers rising by the lake.

"That's their problem. I want you with me," Oppy said. "Until the test is over. Forget the Indians; you're staying with me."

Joe scanned the range. "I don't think so."

"What do you mean?" Oppy asked, as if he'd heard Joe wrong.

"I'll tell you what I see here. I see dirt, brush, rats, snakes. In the real world, in New York, the future is already happening. A warm blue evening. Someone noodling on the keyboard, scratching on sheet music. The horn section is spitting. Ever hear a horn section spit? Mezzo forte. The bass man is tightening his pegs. Same in Philly, Kansas City. Even Albuquerque. Everywhere but here . . . I see Groves."

Through the binoculars, Joe had found Harvey's Dodge

248

again. Coming the other way was a convoy of jeeps. The lead vehicle had a flag with a single star. Brigadier General Leslie Groves had arrived at Trinity and Joe and Oppy had to climb down immediately to greet him at Ground Zero.

"You think the crackpots have finally pulled it together, Sergeant?" Groves answered Joe's salute.

"Yes, sir."

Groves had the familiar leaden voice, the same slow, stoop-shouldered walk, but he had become sleek since winter. There was more silver in his wavy hair and moustache, a more certain angle to his grey eyes. He hadn't been to the test site since he chose it and he was too heavy to scale the steps and inspect the bomb in its shed, but he led Oppy and Joe and a dozen colonels and majors round the tower base with the confidence of an engineer whose blueprints had merely been followed.

"Looks like a privy." Groves eyed an eight-foot wooden crate that stood on end at the tower base.

"That's what the men call it." Oppy pointed to the cable running into the top of the "privy". "It protects the firing switch. We wanted to keep dust out. There –"

"You mean rain," Groves said. "The weathermen have let us down. I brought VIPs from Washington, that reporter from the *Times*. I hope they can see something."

"They will."

"My other concern is tower security."

"At this hour people are staying away from the tower," Oppy said.

"Obviously, you're a scientist, not a security officer. This is exactly the opportunity a trained saboteur would be waiting for. I want a light on the tower and some men down here with submachine-guns. Security and secrecy are our first priorities from here on." Groves turned to his aides. "Can you think of anything else?"

"Mescaleros, sir," Joe said. "The local Apaches."

"I remember. We saw some when we came in December. I thought you were going to take care of that, Sergeant."

"Yes, sir. If I could be detailed a couple of men of my

choosing, sir, I think I could keep the site secure from at least that threat. Mescaleros like to come down from the hills around dusk. I should get started now, sir."

"Then get moving. I'll assign someone else to the Director."

Oppy caught up with Joe at the jeep. He spoke in a low voice, his back to the officers.

"What are you up to?"

Joe started the engine.

"I almost got the chance once to tell Harvey that if he wanted to walk away from you, he shouldn't talk, he should just go."

"This is it, this is what we all worked for."

"You worked for. This is your bomb, not mine."

Joe swung away from Oppy and the tower and aimed for the North road. He only went twenty feet when he hit the brakes and stopped.

"Oppy!"

Oppy was heading back to Groves. He turned at the sound of his name. Suddenly he seemed pathetically out of place against the tower, the desert, the men in uniform.

"Good luck!" Joe shouted and stepped on the accelerator again. He'd pick up Shapiro and Gruber at the guard station. Ray should already be in Antonio. Joe could see the first lightning over the Oscura, but he was finally in the clear.

28

Joe couldn't get away from the right-hand jab. He circled to his right, the way he'd shown Shapiro, and walked into a hook. Heard a hoarse grunt and recognized his own lungs, lungs ten years older than the kid's, ten years of cigarette fumes encased in ten years of beer fat, the sort of fat that showed only when a 195 lb kid hooked to the ribs. He liked the way the kid kept his eyes and shoulders level, jab high and cocked. The eyes intense and watery, pale in the headlights and black water in the dark. Feinted the jab.

The next thing he knew, Joe was sitting on his ass. He didn't know whether he'd been hit with a right or a left. All he remembered was seeing a fist coming and being too slow to get out of the way. Being down brought a new perspective, closer to his leaden feet and the pounding sac of his heart. The wet tarmac had a diamond glitter. Ray had appropriated the mess tent from the Base Camp and the cars were parked under it in a ring of light. Canvas drummed in the rain. Joe rolled away from a rabbit punch and up to his feet. Who's here? Everybody's here. Texans, New Mexicans, soldiers. No scientists, but it wasn't their fight.

"Time!" Hilario shouted.

Ray sat Joe on the bumper of a jeep and pressed a towel against Joe's ear. The ear stung, so it was cut. Fists were taped, but no gloves. There was going to be a lot of cutting.

"Ought to be a real ring, ought to be a referee. This is like a fucking dogfight."

"Dogfights are very popular here."

251

Hilario's perch was a patrol car, befitting his official status. He looked like a white lizard on a black stone. Though there were some familiar faces from Santa Fe, the crowd was mainly cattlemen from Amarillo and El Paso. Creased faces, hats of doe felt and big thumbs on rolls of cash. Faces more comfortable in a country fair tent than any arena. Sporting men who expected some blood for their money, made from wartime contracts. Hilario was the perfect timekeeper for them because he only stopped a round when he thought the time was right to bet again. He had no shred of fairness, but he had an instinct for drama. Across from Hilario, Pollack watched from inside his white Cadillac. The MPs hung back, as Joe had told them to.

"Time," Hilario advised.

The kid came out popping the right jab again. He had a bullet head of close-cut dirty hair, more dirty curls on wide shoulders and down the back of a thick neck. Small nose and round brow designed for a fighter. Narrow chin with a sandy stubble. Thin lips with a broad smile. Nineteen years old, maybe twenty. He had a stomach of snake-white muscle and, in the middle of it, a pink root of glossy scar tissue that spread up from his belt. Either an accident or an operation by a butcher. Joe slipped the jab, hooked, crossed, threw another looping hook without hitting the boy once. The boy jabbed in return and found the fault line in Joe's eyebrow. It was a seam full of promise and the kid found it twice more before Joe covered up. He attacked the ribs, trying to get Joe's guard down so he could pound the brow again.

There were different philosophical levels to a fight. Joe felt it was important to understand where an opponent's strength came from. Some boxers just had arm strength, some had to come forward off their legs. The kid had speed and balance, but Joe suspected madness, more even than the typical washed-out, brainless Texan madness. It would take time to locate the source, but a fight between big men should have the pace of a long and penetrating conversation.

The kid backed Joe against the grille of a truck. When

Joe clinched, clamping the kid's fists under his arms, the kid snapped his blunt head forward and butted Joe in the temple. Joe dropped to a knee, but there was no rush of red on to the ground, so the brow was okay. He rose, backpedalled, jabbed until Hilario called time.

As Joe sat down, Ray swabbed his forehead with petroleum jelly.

"He's trying to cut you."

"Tell me something I don't know." Joe ran his tongue round his mouth and counted teeth.

"Captain Augustino's here, sitting over in the bar."

Shouts and hands indicated the changing odds. Three fingers. Hilario wrote a chit for a sombre Navajo in a velvet shirt. Shapiro had moved closer, and looked like he was sucking a cyanide pill or had bet on the wrong fighter. Across the court, the kid didn't want to sit and rest. He bounced on his toes and stared at Joe.

The kid had madness and speed. Joe sidestepped and the kid was there. When he stepped back, the kid was ahead of him. The scar on the stomach had turned a dull red as if alive all by itself and it occurred to Joe that it might be the mainspring, the potent source of that insanity. It looked like the sort of a tear a steer horn would make. No matter how good the kid got, and he was better than good, he'd never have a career fighting with a split stomach, he couldn't even get drafted. How would an over-the-hill professional, a fake Indian chief, look to a kid like that? No wonder his lips twisted in an effort as he wound up for the hook, chest cords popping and driving off the back leg, bringing his weight through without lunging or losing his balance, merely delivering as much hate as his fist could carry to the old damage above Joe's left eye. Fighting was a subtle matter, sooner or later a case of one man dominating first the centre of the ring and then, corner by corner, the rest of it. Even under a tent in the rain, there was a centrifugal pattern to the steps, the feints, the mental concentration. Hate was a good thing to bring to a fight. Then Joe's brow popped under nothing harder than a touch. One

253

moment he could see and the next moment his eye was a well of blood. The kid was all over Joe, ignoring Hilario, who was shouting for time so he could get one more round of bets down, until Joe made the kid step back with a jab.

"What time is it?"

Ray pinched Joe's brow closed, taped it, daubed it with jelly, then wiped Joe's face.

"Eight twenty, eight thirty. You don't need a clock, you need a zipper."

"The last money. Bet it, spread it around."

"With you bleeding to death, we can get pretty good odds."

"Bet it."

Joe stood alone. Headlights merged in the centre of the courtyard and insects spun over the white haze as if it were a pool. Across it, the kid stood and squinted back. Had that jab been the first tap of knowledge? There was a lot of sound from such a small crowd. He'd always had the sense that towards the end of a fight the paying public wanted to climb into the ring to deliver the last decisive blows. He remembered how once on the mesa a horse broke its legs and he and some other kids had had to stone the animal to death. It took a long time to kill a horse with stones.

The kid went right at the cut. In the middle of the court, Joe backpedalled and jabbed. Against the cars, he covered up, locking his fists against his cheeks, his elbows over the solar plexus, accepting the punishment on the ribs until he could escape. The kid winged combinations and then single shots. An effusion, an undiminishing supply of rage, a hook to the kidney, to the ear, then the cross to the cut. Like a busy sculptor working on a statue he passionately hated. Joe staggered, ducked, clinched, backpedalled until Hilario called time again.

On the hood of the patrol car, Hilario's pockets were misshapen from the money he'd stuffed into them. He watched Joe thoughtfully. Looked at the kid.

Ray rubbed Joe's back, massaged his arms.

"Drop the fucker."

The kid came out with another rush of punches, each punch a complaint from a small, withered soul. Joe answered with a fluid jab twice as fast as any other he'd thrown, but soft, just enough to tell the boy, I understand. Understanding was contagious. The kid circled instead of wading in. Good as he was, the kid had never fought more than three rounds before. This was the fourth. He still hit hard, but he leaned on the jab and wound up for the hook. Joe slipped the hook and countered to the heart, a probe, a gesture of rising interest in the boy's condition, also an announcement: we are at a new level. The kid jabbed for time, for an opportunity to rethink the changing context. His jabs were short. Joe snapped a jab off the kid's nose and for a moment the little eyes were glass.

The kid answered with a jab-and-cross, tearing the tape from Joe's cut. Joe's eye filled with blood that sprayed as he ducked. The kid came in to finish the cut. Left-handers when they punch tend to slide to the right. A matter of physics. One of Newton's Laws. The more they tire, the more they slide out of control. Moving low for a big man, Joe slipped a hook and rose, driving arm and fist of the bluntest curiosity into the boy's unguarded stomach and red cicatrix. The kid arched, half of him still following the parabola of his swing while the other half tried to bend away from Joe, who hit the coralroot scar again and continued to move in, staying low, pursuing the softening, collapsing midsection. In the air, the kid had no place to go. Joe hooked from the ground up, his own body rising.

Inevitability came in grunts and the sound, when Joe hit, of a stake being driven into sodden earth. When Joe stopped, the boy went from weightless to gravity-bound and sprawled in the headlights like a figure under water. The suddenness of the end brought a quiet to the tent. Joe pressed the back of his hand to the pulsing blood of his cut. Ray and the MPs started collecting money. Hilario was collecting, too.

Joe had left his clothes in the café kitchen. He washed, taped and dressed himself by the sink while Ray cleared the table of cans of peaches, lard and beans and counted the money by denominations. The long kitchen table was covered with stacks of notes.

"Chief, you should've seen Shapiro and Gruber. They went through those cowboys like Gestapos, took everything but their watches. Done." Ray took a step back from the table like a man getting a better view of a big Rembrandt. "My God, I've never seen this much money before. $66,000 for you. That's as good as a title fight. You should open a bank."

"I had something else in mind." Joe tucked his tie into his shirt and gingerly touched the tape on his brow.

"Well, here's to Chief Joe Peña." Ray found two glasses in the sink and filled them with Black Label. "The greatest heavyweight in the Army. Your night, Chief."

Pollack slipped through the kitchen door. His hair was freshly straightened and looked combed with a razor. He wore a canary jacket and a diamond ring on each hand. Dressed like a man about to travel at his ease, he made a slow, respectful circuit of the table. Then he laid down three folded papers.

"Deed. Receipt. Liquor licence." Pollack touched a stack of green notes briefly, to establish the fact of them. "Congratulations, you own a nightclub. I wish I could stay to show you the ropes."

"You're leaving tonight?"

"I said I was going to be on the dock when Eddie Jr came in. That's a three-day drive. Kansas City, Pittsburgh, New York. If he can come back from Italy, I can be there on the dock." Pollack counted out $50,000 and stuffed the bills in a money belt while Joe checked the papers. They were already signed.

"I never thought I'd say goodbye to the Casa Mañana or New Mexico, Joe. Something else happening here tonight? Lots of Army trucks sort of hidden off the road."

"It's a bombing range, you know."

"Thought I recognized some soldiers from the Hill."

"Maybe." Joe tucked the papers into his shirt.

Pollack draped the money belt over his arm. He'd never put

the belt on in front of anyone else, he had too much dignity for that. Just like he didn't go cross-country in a train because he never wanted to be mistaken for a porter.

"You're going to be okay, Joe. From now on, everyone's going to be okay."

"Thanks for everything." Joe shook hands gently because his fist hurt so much.

At the door, Pollack hesitated.

"That was the last fight for Big Chief Joe Peña?"

"Yeah."

"Good. I thought this time he cut it a little close."

"Son of a bitch," Ray said when Pollack was gone. "You own the Casa Mañana? You son of a bitch, you pulled off a deal like that?"

"I've got to go." It was nine o'clock. Joe counted out $1,000 and pushed the rest of his money with Ray's. "Hold this for me for a couple of days. Forget about the garbage business. I'm going to turn you into a maitre d'. After the test you're driving people back to the Albuquerque Hilton? Go to the Casa and stick by the cash register until I show up."

"Serious?"

"If anyone here asks tonight, say I was off to hunt Apaches."

"You're serious about me?"

"People are going to be lining up to grease the palm of Raymónd the maitre d'."

"In a tux?"

"You better be."

"That's better than garbage."

"Sometimes it happens that way, Ray. Some things actually work out."

"But it's a surprise," Ray insisted.

"Yeah."

The tent stood in an empty courtyard. The motel cabins were dark because their occupants were the MPs who were on the highway monitoring traffic, chasing the losers back to Texas, ushering fresh truckloads of GIs towards Trinity. The only vehicle left in the court was Joe's jeep, its top up to the rain.

257

Squalls were raiding parties of lightning and thunder that moved under a half-moon across the valley. There was no sign of any jalopy or pickup truck and it occurred to him that Ben and Roberto might not show. No. It was Joe Peña's night, he thought, and, as if in answer, the rain briefly let up. Joe Peña's Casa Mañana. He walked across the courtyard to the jeep and the drops seemed to part before him like a curtain, as if the world were opening up for him.

Joe got into the jeep. In the dark, on the seat next to him, was a muted yellow glitter with the shape of snakes. Two lightning wands.

"The boy didn't have a chance, Sergeant," Captain Augustino said from the rear seat. "You suckered him. That boy didn't know who he was fighting."

"You saw the fight, Captain?" they looked to Joe like Roberto's wands.

"I didn't need to."

"Lost some money?"

"No, I bet on you."

"You found the medicine men you were looking for?"

"They're very elusive. Found the wands where they were hiding. Magic." Augustino tapped a cigarette on a silver case. It looked like the same case the captain's wife had had and he tapped on it the same way his wife had. Couples did do things the same way, Joe thought. The match flame made the wands start from the seat; otherwise, the flame cast a soft, confidential glow within the jeep, an illusion of golden warmth against the water that laced the windshield. Augustino leaned forward, his sallow face lit by a smile of mutual understanding, his eyes full of something close to admiration. "I'm not going to put the Army in the position of saying that a medicine man can call fire down from the sky. Even if it is attempted sabotage, a medicine man doesn't know any better."

"I have to go look for Mescaleros. Groves' orders."

A car with its lights out turned into the courtyard and stopped by the café on the other side of the tent. A Plymouth two-door.

258

"Sergeant, I find amusing something so puny as a boxing match on a night like this, but I suspect the general would call it a dereliction of duty."

Augustino saw the car as well as Joe. Augustino knew the cars from the Hill as well as Joe, and this was Teller's car. There seemed to be only one person inside. Her white hands held the steering wheel.

"You'd have to arrest half the MPs on the site. You're not going to do that."

"True, I do have other matters in mind."

Amazing he could recognize her even by her hands. In the dark, he could see her grey eyes look around the courtyard and stare at the jeep.

"Since these aren't my sticks," Joe said and nodded to the wands, "and since you aren't going to do anything about the fight, I better start looking for those Apaches."

"Good hunting, Sergeant."

Joe started the jeep's engine. He'd leave the courtyard and wait on the highway for her to catch up.

"Just one question," Augustino said, "and then you can go. One question, fair enough?"

"Ask."

"Have you ever seen Harry Gold and Oppenheimer together?"

"You're back on that kick?"

"You know Harry Gold, also known as Heinrich Golodnitsky?"

"Yes."

"And you've never seen him with our Dr Oppenheimer?"

"No."

Something dropped on the wands. Augustino produced a flashlight and shone it on a photograph of Oppy and Joe and Harry Gold. The three of them were standing on the corner outside La Fonda.

"I think I've earned another question, Sergeant. Have you ever seen Harry Gold with Dr Anna Weiss?"

Joe sat back and wondered where a photographer was that

day in Santa Fe. The captain dropped a second picture. It was of Joe and Harry Gold and Anna Weiss on the same corner. She wore the silver hairpin she'd bought on the *portal*.

"The tour bus," Joe said. "The dudes with the cameras."

"Yes. We had a pair of buses following him. Considering the fact they couldn't stay near him all the time, we were lucky." A third picture slipped to the seat. In this one, Joe and Gold were alone and Joe's hand was on the newspaper under Gold's arm. "You see, a Soviet courier doesn't just coincidentally bump into Julius Robert Oppenheimer, the Director of a secret US Army project, or Anna Weiss, a member of the project. That's why you said 'No' to me. That's why you lied to me."

"I was talking to Gold. Dr Weiss joined us to talk to me."

"That's all you have to say. You witnessed a meeting between Anna Weiss and a Soviet courier. You did the right thing in telling me."

Joe cut the engine. The rain had a steadier hiss now, a long-drawn, patient sound on the tarmac. Even at a distance and in the dark, he could see two heads rise from hiding in the back of the Plymouth.

"You missed Fuchs," he told Augustino. "Gold met Fuchs at a bridge a few blocks from the plaza. They switched newspapers. I was trying to get the newspaper from Gold, to see what Fuchs gave him."

"I'm not interested in Fuchs."

"He's the man Gold came to see. I saw them meet."

"I'm not interested in Fuchs."

"When you saw Gold on the *portal*, he was carrying a copy of the Santa Fe newspaper. At the bridge –"

"I'm not interested in Fuchs."

How often does a man see an example of love? A chance taken for him? Even if the danger was so much greater than she knew.

"Leave Dr Weiss alone," he said to Augustino.

"That's up to you. It's her or Oppenheimer. You choose."

"I need some time."

As she waited, the windshield fogged before her face. Beads of rain idly coalesced and ran.

Go, Joe thought. Thank you, now go.

Augustino said, "Tonight. You know all the tests on the Hill for the last two days point to an ignominious failure here. We are on the eve of an historic débâcle, Sergeant. Billions of dollars wasted. A chance to end the war lost. That's why Julius Oppenheimer is coming apart now, because he knows the bomb won't work. He knows the first question General Groves is going to ask is, who's to blame? Oppenheimer is a master of escaping blame. His wife is a communist, his brother is a communist, his friends and students are communists, but he says he's not a communist and here he is running our most important project. I didn't make up Harry Gold, Sergeant. Harry Gold came here with a message. If Trinity fails, it won't be a failure of American science; it will be the result of Soviet orders. When it fails, as it will tonight, I will do my part. My men are in Santa Fe, waiting to arrest Gold. I will arrest his co-conspirator. That's been my mission all along."

Run, Joe pleaded in his mind. Go!

"No one is going to believe any charge against Anna Weiss."

"No one will defend her. A refugee from a Nazi mental home? A scandal? The wives on the Hill will rise as one to burn her at the stake and Kitty Oppenheimer will throw the first torch. Sergeant, I have some small experience in security, and I can promise you that in the atmosphere following the failure, everyone will be relieved that someone was blamed."

"On what proof?"

"Gold, Weiss, you. Courier, contact, witness. The evidence does point to this sordid triangle."

Finally the Plymouth slipped forward, lights still out, a shadow reluctantly turning in the café driveway, the sound of its motion covered by the rain. Joe watched the car's tail-lights, a red blur fading. After ten seconds, an Army sedan with its lights out rolled from behind a motel cabin across the courtyard and followed. It was half a mile to the highway.

For the first time, Augustino paid attention to Anna, now that she was gone.

"We assume she is taking those two fugitive medicine men to the border. I've told the officers not to arrest her without my direct order, but you certainly have incriminated her. And you will incriminate her more. You will incriminate her as only a lover can. How did she escape from Germany? While here, did she ever work to impede the development of the bomb, or prevent its application, or influence others to do so?"

"What do you want?"

"Gold, Oppenheimer, you. That would be perfect."

Joe took a deep breath. "Let me see the picture again."

Augustino picked up the top photographs and played the flashlight on the picture of Oppy standing with Gold and Joe in front of the hotel in Santa Fe. In glossy black and white, Oppy was angry, Gold wistful. With Joe cropped, the two men might have been holding an animated conversation.

"It seemed like a chance meeting," Joe said.

"I need more than a chance meeting." On to the picture Augustino dropped a white business card that said in raised letters, "Harry Gold". "I want this card in Oppenheimer's pocket – trouser pocket, jacket pocket, it doesn't matter. See, I have proof enough for myself. What I need for others is some minute piece of evidence, some concrete fulcrum of incrimination."

"When you knocked out Gold at the Casa Mañana, you weren't just searching him. You were taking out the card."

"Yes. When I took you out of the stockade, I told you you had a mission. That morning of the hunt when I let you live so you could bring Oppenheimer and General Groves down here, it was so you could carry out that same mission. To deliver that card. Or a card like it. Or evidence like it."

"What about the information you were always asking about?"

"Sergeant, you're much too truculent to be a reliable informer. You do the important things well, though. Oppen-heimer and Dr Weiss. So, what is your choice?"

The rain came harder, more at an angle. He thought he could feel her turn south to Mexico.

The card was cheap pasteboard. Frayed at the corners. It fitted neatly into Joe's palm, slipped easily into his pocket. He started the engine again.

"Back to the tower?" he asked Augustino.

"To our patriotic duty."

29

At 10 pm an anti-sabotage light was hung on the first landing of the tower for spotlights six miles away to train on. The weak beams that penetrated the rain lit an open jeep in which Eberly sat, drenched, a submachine-gun across his knees. Jaworski and Foote, in soaked clothes and dripping hats, had opened the door to the standing crate called the "privy" at the tower base. Oppy watched them, a damp, dead cigarette in his mouth, his porkpie hat wet through. The door of an Army sedan opened as Joe and Augustino drove up in the jeep.

"Get in here, Sergeant," Groves shouted. "Finished with the Apaches?"

"Yes, sir."

"Looks like you found them." Groves glanced at the tape on his brow as Joe slipped on to the rear seat with him. The car was small and steamy. The general's uniform seemed to be turning into towelling.

"Yes, sir."

"The problem isn't wild Indians." Groves rubbed condensation off the window to see the three men at the box. "Dr Oppenheimer is, you understand, a highly-strung individual. Anything can set him off now. He has to decide whether to call off the test or not and all the crackpots at the base camp want him to. That's why I brought him here, so he could make a calm, rational decision."

Joe looked through the window at Captain Augustino, who had stayed in the jeep. Was this the moment to say, "General, your head of security wants to arrest your project director as Joe

Stalin's secret agent?" No. Joe had figured it out. Augustino's whole plan depended on the test. There wasn't a chance in hell of the test being held in this weather. All he had to do tonight was stall. Tomorrow, when people were sane and dry, Joe would nail the captain's ass to a board.

"It is raining, sir."

"It will clear. Dr Oppenheimer doesn't need any more scientific cross-chatter, he needs some sensible advice. Fermi was talking about the end of the earth and we have GIs running all the way to Tularosa. Talk to him, he listens to you. Calm him down. Keep him away from pessimists."

As Joe left the car, the steel tower turned chalk white. Faded. Two seconds later, thunder rocked the valley floor. Close, he thought.

"All summer and all spring it hasn't rained." Oppy raised his face to the drops. "Here we are, four hours from Zero Hour, and it's pouring."

Inside the "privy", wet electrical tape unravelled in black curlicues from coaxial cable. While Jaworski cut loose strands, Foote wound the cable with fresh tape.

"Snakes and sunstroke we anticipated in the desert," Foote said. "Humidity took us by surprise."

"How about lightning?" Joe asked.

"I told you how lightning knocked out a rehearsal." Jaworski snipped away. "A power surge from lightning certainly could set off the high explosive."

"Nonsense." Foote wiped the tape with Kleenex. "The tower is grounded."

"Shut up!" Oppy said. "The bomb is a dud. You know and I know it, everybody knows it but the general. How can I think with you two nits picking at each other?"

The ladder leaned against the first landing of the tower. Oppy climbed the ladder and rose up the tower rungs towards the shed. Once past the second landing and the faint beams of the spotlights, he vanished into the dark. Foote silently finished the taping and checked that the cable firing switch was in the open position before shutting the "privy" door and padlocking it. Groves worked his way from the sedan while Augustino sauntered over from the jeep.

"Follow him," Groves told Joe.

"Sir, if I might suggest," the captain said, "why don't I assign Sergeant Peña to the security of the bomb itself. That will give the sergeant a plausible reason to be with Dr Oppenheimer."

"Whatever, get up there," Groves ordered.

Rain pulled at Joe and the cold steps swayed with him. At 100 feet, the tower seemed to be on a fixed tilt. The shed's sixty-watt bulb illuminated a floor of pulleys, cables and ropes, striped walls of corrugated steel and the bomb in its cradle. Since he had seen it last, the bomb had lost its lunar smoothness because two exterior detonator boxes had been bolted on. Cables connected the sphere's sixty-four detonator ports to the boxes, and out of the boxes' switchboard backs an equal number of cables hung down to the firing unit, a padlocked aluminium case between the cradle's feet. Out on the open platform, Oppy clung to the hoist with one hand and to his hat with the other.

"You look like fucking Ahab in the rigging." Joe stepped out with him.

From the platform it appeared that lightning was striking everywhere, as if the low clouds, black as smoke from a fire, were launching a climactic attack. In every arc of the horizon a bolt was hitting. One report of thunder overlapped and muffled another. A mile off, the silver barrage balloon that had been earthbound before was now lifted by winds. The balloon was anchored to a jeep, which dangled below, only its rear wheels touching the ground. The two men were trying to save the jeep, but the lightning built static charges that ran down the steel cable and exploded like cannon under the bouncing wheels.

"General Groves has dismissed the meteorologists." Oppy wiped the rain from his face and grinned. "The general is the new weatherman of the Trinity shot."

"It's your decision, though, isn't it?"

"That's what the general tells me." Oppy twisted his eyes

away from Joe. He bent his head and fumbled, and it wasn't until Joe saw the small flare that he realized Oppy was lighting a cigarette. "Thanks for coming back."

"Call it off," Joe watched the two men running from the jeep.

"It's not as if we could just do it tomorrow. To get to the same pitch, to ready the men and the equipment again would take a week at least."

"You said this bomb was a dud. You said you wanted an extra week, anyway."

"Like Ahab?" Oppy laughed.

"That's what you looked like."

"I did sail when I was a boy, you know. I had my own sloop and sailed all around Long Island." Oppy stared at the clouds. "This was the sort of weather I liked most, in fact. I'd run with the wind and go out on the tide race just to fight my way back in, one reach after another. There was one inlet in particular you had to clear. The riptide would curl around and try to take you into the breakers. It was the first time I knew I had courage. First time I proved it." Oppy cupped his cigarette from the rain. "It would take hours to clear the inlet and reach the bay. You see, it was the struggle that was important, the patience and the strength to find the right angle, Joe, the right piece of water and the right wind. As we're doing right now. Struggling."

A low, unbroken belly of clouds stretched from one end of the valley to the other, and the clouds seemed to be descending by their very weight, bringing a second, thicker night. Joe could see pinpoints of light on the ground where another party had abandoned another jeep and were running with flashlights.

"Did I ever tell you how I got out of Bataan?" Joe asked.

"No. You never told anyone. I thought it was a point of honour."

"No honour involved. It's a sailing story."

"On Bataan?"

"I got shot in the ass and in the back, then I caught some kind of jungle crud and a fever." Joe lit a cigarette from Oppy's.

"I had five Filipino scouts and we had a field piece we moved from hill to hill, holding the line though there wasn't any line to hold any more. When I got the fever and went off my head, the Filipinos ditched the piece to carry me. Problem was, there wasn't any place to take me. The last barges were gone to Corregidor and we were too far from the depots at Mariveles or Manila. They said the Japs would shoot me because I was too big. I knew the Japs would shoot me because I couldn't walk. So the scouts took me down to the water; there was no place left to go. They stole a fishing boat and put me in. I could just sit up and I was still trying to give orders. Like an officer, you know. It was low tide. I could see the shark net sticking out of the water, so I knew there were mines right below the surface of the water. There were mines off all the beaches." Joe let his voice drop the way Oppy did to make a listener lean forward. Oppy hunched closer. "As soon as it was dark, the Filipinos pushed me and the boat out. No motor, no oars. I couldn't believe my own scouts wanted to kill me, but that's what they seemed to be doing. I mean, if they wanted to kill me, I couldn't stop them. They could have brought my head in to the Japs and made some money. I tried to paddle back to shore because I could see ammo dumps going up in Mariveles, fuel dumps going up in Manila, and Long Toms, the 155mms, answering from Corregidor, the whole thing reflected in the water like the end of the world and I wanted to get back into it. Have you ever had dysentery? You pass out and you shit blood. I couldn't sit up any longer, no matter what was happening. I laid back in my own shit and piss in a drifting boat under the fireworks. There were holes in the shark net from when the Japs landed. We'd caught the Japs in the water when they first came and the sharks followed them and finished them off. Once the sharks were in, they didn't leave. They'd bump into the boat, give it a spin. It was a leaky boat. Sharks have an amazing sense of smell. I raised my head and there must have been fifty sharks around the boat, slowly swimming in a big circle. I did see the humour in the situation. I mean, how many New Mexico Indians get eaten by sharks? I kept thinking, if only I had a paddle, if only I had a gun, if only I had wings. If only I could kill myself, I thought, but I didn't have the strength to hold my breath. The main thing was to keep thinking, I told myself. Keep struggling. The problem was, every time I stirred so did the sharks. Those fucking Filipinos, they should have told me."

Joe stopped talking to watch the beam of a searchlight swing above the West-10,000 bunker. The beam no sooner found the erratic, diagonal ascent of a weather balloon than the target vanished into clouds.

"Told you what?" Oppy asked.

"To stop struggling. During the night, the tide came in and lifted the boat over the shark nets and when the tide went out I went with it into the bay. A gunboat picked me up and put me on a sub and that's how I escaped heroically from Bataan, by finding out that fighting the tide may not be a test of courage so much as a sign of stupidity, and that's the last time I went sailing." Joe held up a damp butt. "Son of a bitch went out."

"You're suggesting that fighting the rain is like fighting the tide? You're suggesting I'm stupid?"

"Was I?"

"I just can't decide how subtle you are."

"Well." Joe flipped the butt and watched the rain snatch it into the dark. "If the dud works, I think you got the right angle and the right wind now to carry radiation all the way to Amarillo."

Oppy turned away to lean on the rail. His clothes snapped around him like a sheet. At first, Joe thought Oppy was having a pneumonic spasm, but when Oppy turned back to Joe, he was laughing. Either tears or rain were running down his cheeks.

"You're right. I'll call it off." He wiped his face with his sleeve. "Let's go down together."

"My orders are to babysit the beast. You go."

After Oppy climbed down and drove away with Groves towards South-10,000, Joe went into the shed, made a seat for himself out of the ropes on the floor and lit a dry cigarette.

Half the shed was taken up by the bomb, its loops of cables, its cradle. The bomb that was dropped on Japan would be stuffed into a teardrop casing with tail fins just narrow enough to slip through the bay of a B-29. Otherwise, it would be the twin of this one. Same dull grey shell. Interlocking, inward-aiming lenses of explosive. Warm and silvery Dragon's heart. From the firing unit emerged the single coaxial cable that dropped through the floor and down the tower to the open switch in the "privy", a switch that wouldn't be closed for a week now if Oppy's estimate was correct. The FM receiver still mixed shelter communications with the Voice of America; Paul Robeson intoned "The Volga Boatmen" while someone read a checklist of gamma meters. A week until another test, Joe thought. He'd have Augustino's ass in a sling before then. He'd drive Groves back to the Albuquerque Hilton himself tomorrow and fill him in on the captain. Augustino could deny everything but the captain would be nailed by the same item he wanted to nail Oppy with.

At midnight, the word came over the radio receiver.

"Zero Hour has been postponed. Due to weather conditions, Zero Hour has been postponed from 0200 to 0400. Zero Hour is now 0400."

Two hours? Joe asked himself. Oppy only postponed the shot from 2 am to 4 am?

Well, fuck, the weather wasn't going to improve, Joe thought. Wind hit the tower broadside. The lamp swayed and the bomb in its cradle seemed to shuffle like a man on short legs.

TRINITY

30

While the rainstorm continued, the shot was postponed another hour, from 0400 to 0500. Through the platform binoculars Joe watched a heavy man in uniform and a gaunt man in civvies pacing in the headlights of a sedan outside the South-10,000 shelter. Not only was the rain as bad as before, winds had built. Joe knew Groves didn't take Oppy inside because everyone else wanted the test scrubbed. They made an interesting couple, Joe thought, out in the rain by themselves, circling a golden pool of water, almost male and female the way Groves patiently tended Oppy's nervousness.

At 0400, a bolt exploded by the tower. Joe held on to the platform hoist and remembered what Jaworski had said about the 5,000 lbs of high explosive in the shed, but the lightning blew nothing except the target light on the first landing of the tower. Joe climbed down the steps with another bulb. The searchlights trained on the target light half-blinded him and it took him a moment to notice that Eberly had climbed up the ladder from the ground. Beads of water ran from his poncho, nose and Adam's apple and from the barrel of his submachine-gun.

"I thought you ought to know, Chief. There's a regular field radio by the 'privy'. Captain Augustino called and told me to go to your jeep and make sure there were a couple of yellow sticks in there. And he told me to shoot you if you tried to leave the tower. I don't get it. If he thinks you're a saboteur, why are you guarding the bomb? If you're the guard, why should I guard you? This is the Army system?"

"The Augustino system." If Joe was dead, he was an arsonist, by the lightning wands in the jeep. A spy, by Harry Gold's card in his pocket. "Don't shoot, I'll be right back."

Joe descended the ladder and ran to the jeep. The photos were gone, but the wands still lay on the front seat. He grabbed them and returned to the ladder.

Eberly had seen everything. As Joe reached the landing, Eberly said, "I hate the Army."

From the platform, Joe saw what he expected. Oppy and Groves were no longer outside South-10,000. Headlights approached on the tarmac road. In the shed the radio said the shot had been postponed again to 0530. Joe hid the wands behind loose ropes.

"Five thirty in the morning is the best possible time." Oppy's jacket hung like a sopping rag, but he strutted within the confines of the shed and around the bomb with a new, jaunty confidence.

"Captain Augustino return with you?" Joe asked.

"He's down with Groves, yes. See, at 5.30 we have the dark that's necessary to photograph the blast accurately and then quickly we have the daylight to bring in the tank and perform the rest of the recovery process."

"You mean, 5.30 is the last possible moment you can run your goddamn test if the weather clears."

"Also, the best moment. We should have thought of it before."

Oppy stopped to cough as if he were emptying his lungs. A paperback book stuck out of his jacket pocket, a collection of poems, *Les Fleurs du Mal*. If Joe wanted to plant Gold's card, that was the pocket.

"That's your pose for the countdown, a carefree appreciator of poetry?" Joe asked.

"You know your Baudelaire? It's perfect." Oppy opened the door to the platform. *"I am like the king of a rainy country, wealthy but helpless, young and ripe with death."*

"It's pouring. Your cables are going to short, your cameras

274

won't see shit and the observer plane won't even find the tower."

"That's what everyone else says."

"Then call it off."

"The general says the weather will clear. The general wants optimum conditions –"

"The general needs Trinity. The general needs Trinity because he's never seen combat and the Army is going to dump him back to colonel if he doesn't produce a bomb."

"I say it will clear."

"You say it will clear? Now *you're* the weatherman?"

"I'm a scientist. We should hold out until the last –"

"You're going to tell me about your fucking sailboat again? We're a hundred feet up with a bomb in the rain, we're not reliving your happy childhood."

Oppy leaned against the door and turned to Joe.

"The dude from Riverside Drive? Do you remember him?"

"Yeah."

"The one you turned from Jewboy into cowboy? But the world demands success on a somewhat grander scale, Joe. I need Trinity. I need to end the war before it ends without me. That's why we'll try tonight."

"Augustino wants you to try tonight."

"The captain was the one who suggested we return to the tower. Groves wanted to get me away from the crowd." Oppy crossed the shed and rested his hand on the bomb. "I wanted to see it again."

"Augustino says it's a dud and you're Stalin's master spy. He's taking you straight from Trinity to jail. Call the shot off and I'll take care of Augustino for you."

Oppy began pacing again.

"If it works, he can't touch me."

"You don't have to take the chance."

Oppy stumbled over ropes. Two yellow wands shot across the floor, glittering on the oak planks. Their appearance was so startling they might have been a pair of golden serpents that had climbed from the tower.

"These are from that crazy medicine man. Augustino said you were involved."

"Augustino brought them."

Slowly, as if he were approaching something alive, Oppy stooped and picked up the wands. "The captain hasn't even been up here to the shed. I can't believe it was you."

"You don't understand. And if you weren't so damned clumsy –"

"There is something rich and laughable about you working with me and Harvey and Fermi at the same time you were working with a medicine man." The wands sparkled and twisted in the light of the bulb as he raised them. "Chief Joe Peña. What an incredibly stupid time for you to turn into an Indian."

"Give them back."

"Do you really think I'm going to let the effort of all these good men be endangered by a . . . tribe?"

"It's not just you, it's Anna, too. Augustino knows she quit the Hill."

"Of course. I told him. The last thing I needed was a certified lunatic threatening the success of the project and whoring with a soldier."

As Oppy tried to slip by, Joe hit him backhanded. It was like slapping a fly. Oppy landed, bent double, on the ropes. The wands flew on to cables, his hat and paperback under the bomb cradle.

"I'm sorry," Joe said.

Oppy clutched his chest and gasped rheumatically for air. Some men go through their lifetimes without being hit, it occurred to Joe. They say anything, do anything, and never expect a fist. But they're willing to blow up the world.

"I'm really sorry," Joe said.

He checked the wands. The yellow, micaceous skin was not even chipped. He retrieved Oppy's hat and book from under the bomb cradle, then knelt by Oppy and gently placed the book back in Oppy's jacket.

"You bastard." Oppy looked at the .45 on Joe's belt. "What are you going to do next, shoot me?"

"Listen," Joe said. "Forget the wands. You don't want to tell Groves there is some crazy Indian up here or he'll send up Eberly with a submachine-gun and what'll happen to your precious bomb then?" He pulled Oppy to his feet. He put the hat on Oppy's head and steered him through the door. "Most of all, don't say anything to Augustino. In an hour, the test will be called off and I'll explain everything then."

"I thought you were my friend. Captain Augustino warned me, but I trusted you."

Lightning hit a nearby bunker. Oppy rocked unsteadily on his feet.

"It's Fuchs," Joe said. Through the thunder he doubted that Oppy had heard him. It didn't matter.

As Joe helped Oppy get started down the steps, he could see Groves standing anxiously at the base of the tower. When Oppy reached the ground, he shook off whatever the general was saying and shuffled towards the sedan. As soon as the two men were in the back, the car set off towards South-10,000. The only figure Joe saw among the two jeeps left was Eberly, trudging miserably in the mud, keeping his vigil. Joe returned to the shed and opened his palm. "Harry Gold" said black letters. Putting the book in Oppy's jacket pocket, he'd considered, just for a moment, planting the card. Such moments were short. He laid it on the FM receiver because his trousers were damp from the rain. Another bolt hit close by. The bulb in the shed flashed blue and died.

Rain increased to triple time. Waltz time, Joe thought. Inside the shed it was dark, but all around the tower lightning glowed like the stems of flowers in a black garden. Joe used spare rope from the floor to tie the yellow wands, serpent heads up, to the detonator boxes. The Voice of America had briefly signed off and for the first time the site radio could communicate on a clear frequency. Base Camp asked if anyone had any information about a missing mess tent. Early breakfast was being served and the French toast and powdered eggs were getting wet.

Joe felt unexpected pleasure seeing the wands stand on their makeshift altar. As lightning closed in on the tower, the shed seemed to rise and plunge into each crash. The fierce, brief glow at the door made the sphere levitate and the wands jump, bright as gold, to life. The shadow on the wall was a head of coiled hair wearing a crown of wands. A dancer's shadow, kicking up thunder.

Everyone insisted he was Indian. So, why not? Put some finery on the atom, a brace of electric snakes, and let it dance on 100-foot legs. Dance in the desert and shake the earth. He wished he knew the right prayer or song. There had to be some music for this, or something he could improvise. Good music and good religion, he assumed, were both born in times of stress. Too bad Roberto didn't make it up the tower.

It was about seven hours to the Mexican border, staying under the speed limit. Traffic between El Paso and Juarez was an all-night affair. Anna would be putting Ben and Roberto on the trolley for Juarez about now. Or driving them across. It would be safer for her to stay over the border herself. He could picture her in a serape.

"*Thirty minutes to zero hours,*" the receiver said.

He strapped on his belt and .45 and decided, orders or no orders, it was time to go. "This desert's jumpin'," he hummed. Lightning hit east of the tower, but the flash at the door was blocked by a man in a poncho.

"I didn't hear you come up," Joe shouted over the thunder.

"Not in this storm, Sergeant." Captain Augustino squeezed into the shed as it went black again.

"I thought you went with Oppy and General Groves."

"Private Eberly drove them." Water dripped as Augustino pulled the poncho's cowl from his head. "You gave Oppenheimer the card, Sergeant?"

The captain hadn't brought the submachine-gun, Joe thought. He would have a regular issue .45 under the poncho.

"There's not going to be any Trinity, sir."

"Dr Oppenheimer thinks there is. General Groves thinks there is. I think there is. You didn't give him the card?"

"In his jacket." Joe shifted to block the captain's view of the receiver and the card lying on it even though the shed was dark. "The pocket with the book."

White light flooded through the open door, filling the shed like a well, touching bomb, cradle, wands, cable with a dizzying clarity, and in that shaft of light outside Joe saw not a drop. It wasn't raining any more. As the light faded into sound, the wings of Augustino's poncho spread. Joe drew his .45 but all Augustino held was a cigarette lighter. The captain brought the lighter to the bomb so that the flame reflected dully in the steel sphere and glittered on the wands. He pulled the wands free of the ropes to examine them.

"Magic, Sergeant?"

"I'm down to that, sir."

"We're all down to that. I have just seen scientists literally on their knees in the bunkers praying to this tower. Magic is in the air tonight." He snapped the wands in half. "Why take chances? See, Sergeant, I'm willing to give everyone the benefit of the doubt. Medicine men, physicists, they're all the same to me. I think that as a race we only move from cave to bigger cave, from fire to bigger fire. And, outside, always something to frighten us. By the way, you may not have noticed, but the weather has changed."

31

Thunder became a receding tide. The last bolts were perfunctory and muffled. On the floor, the broken wands looked dark, dead.

"You never gave him Harry Gold's card," Augustino said. "I saw it."

"That's right, sir." Joe took the damp card from the receiver. He prodded the captain out on to the platform. "Thirty minutes to go. We'll just drive about six miles out and hide behind a camera bunker until the test is over, sir."

Rain had stopped and the wind had shifted. A half-moon sailed from cloud to cloud, and the cloud shadows flowered across the valley. A searchlight reached six miles from West-10,000, but the target light was out again, so the beam was wide of the tower. Suddenly, the receiver in the shed sang, "*Oh, say, can you see?*" The question echoed from every direction because the Voice of America was signing back on ". . . *by the dawn's early light*" reverberated over cactus and staked cables, to volcanic cones on one side, to the foothills of the Oscura and back, echoes overlapping in the night ". . . *what so proudly we hail.*" Joe laughed. At the top of the steps, Augustino smiled and shouted to be heard.

"We can still put the card on Oppenheimer." He pocketed his lighter and jumped down a few rungs. "You can still save Anna Weiss. Last chance."

"Keep your hands in sight, sir."

Augustino lifted his hand to show a nickel-plated .22, just the sort of shiny little item an officer would carry, Joe thought.

"While you were boxing, Sergeant, I found your uniform and firearm and I emptied your clip."

Joe aimed at the captain's eyes and squeezed the trigger. The .45's hammer slapped an empty breach.

Augustino went on, undisturbed, "Anna Weiss is at the border right now. A phone call can still catch her. You never should have touched Mrs Augustino."

Augustino fired. A head shot. Joe's hair whipped to one side, spewing blood. A heart shot. Joe turned, as if he'd thought to dodge, and dropped.

The first shot had dug across the cranium and mass of hair. The second penetrated the heavy muscle of the chest and scored the ribs. As he fell to the platform, Joe reached and took Augustino by the throat, and Augustino fired wide.

"*Oh, say does that star . . .*" swelled across the flat as head-lights arrived at the base of the tower. It was the arming party jeep. Engine and headlights stayed on while the men jumped out. There was a hurried rattle of a lock, a creak of door hinges.

As Augustino pressed the bright muzzle of the .22 against Joe's forehead, Joe pushed the captain off the steps so that he hung straight out from the platform in Joe's grip, 100 feet above the ground.

"Arming lead connected." Jaworski spoke into the field radio at the "privy". From the speakers in the dark flowered a tremulous ". . . *home of the brave. Good morning and* buenos dias."

With his free hand, Augustino held on to Joe's wrist to keep from being strangled. I could break the captain's neck, Joe thought.

". . . *Latin American broadcast from Station KCBA in Delano, Cali –*" vanished in a squawk of dials. Over the loudspeakers and from the receiver in the shed, Harvey answered, "*Understand arming lead connected. Check.*"

"Firing switch closed and ready," Jaworski said.

"*Firing switch closed and ready,*" Harvey answered from the receiver and speakers.

Both Joe and Augustino were quiet. It was a strange pause

on the edge of the platform, Joe thought, like two murderers hushing themselves for midwives in the next room.

"There's another jeep here," Jaworski said.

"*Everyone's accounted for,*" Harvey answered.

"Joe?" Jaworski asked.

"*Augustino called in ten minutes ago and said he took him out,*" Harvey said.

"Then why is there a jeep here?" Jaworski demanded.

"*There's no one there.*" A new voice came on the receiver. Oppy spoke more in a wheeze. "*If the firing switch is closed, leave as fast as you can. If you have a breakdown, you're going to have to run.*"

"Then we'll take the other jeep, too," Jaworski said.

"*No.*" Oppy took a moment to decide. "*Leave the jeep. Lock up and leave.*"

A door swung shut. A hasp snapped closed. An engine revved, reversed and spun in the dirt back to the road and, as if holding one communal breath, strained and gained speed towards South-10,000.

Alone, alone, now all alone, Joe thought, the two of us.

"Give me the card," Augustino said.

"The gun." Joe reached with his other hand.

Augustino swung himself in to the steps. As the captain fired, Joe knocked the barrel up. Both shots went high and into the night. Augustino forced the barrel down to Joe's head again, but the gun clicked when he tried to fire. It was a small automatic and only carried five rounds. It was like ending a long dialogue with a stutter.

Augustino dropped the gun and clawed at Joe's hand, breaking free and twisting himself not towards, but away from the tower. He stared at Joe with eyes like lamps. The captain hung in the air so long without support, Joe thought that he might fly. Then he fell, turning over once, twice, before he hit the ground.

While Joe climbed down with one numb arm, the Voice of America played "The Nutcracker Suite". The jeep was where

Jaworski had left it. He still had time to drive clear, but as soon as anyone saw new headlights at the tower, the test would stop. Joe worked on what he'd say to General Groves. More searchlights burned from West-10,000. Excuse me, sir, for the setback to the war effort, the loss of millions of dollars, the death of the captain. It was hard to believe no one saw him descending the tower, and by way of explanation the pilot of a B-29 observer plane broke into the Tchaikovsky to say he couldn't find Trinity at all. Conversations about gauges and counters went back and forth in the dark across the valley, like the ruminations of a god. Anna had to be safely in Juarez, accepting the fact that safety in Juarez was a relative matter. On the final landing of the tower, Joe stopped and felt inside his shirt for the papers from Pollack. The Casa Mañana was there, folded, tucked away. He was more in shock than pain. The head wound had stopped bleeding and became a mat of damp hair. He could imagine the reaction he'd get when he arrived at the bunker. Going down the wooden ladder to the ground, Joe heard a new sound, like a finger stroking the teeth of a comb. Not the lost B-29. Once a year, rains brought a generation of toads. Waking in their desert burrows, gathering around temporary pools, the amphibians sang and mated and spent their whole conscious lives in a single night. This was the night.

Joe slipped painfully behind the steering wheel of the jeep and with his left hand reached for the key. It wasn't there. It couldn't be gone; orders were for keys to be in the ignition at all times. He felt around the floor. Under the seat. Joe got out of the jeep and felt on the ground. No key.

Joe had been the last man to drive the jeep. Augustino had been the last man in it. The captain lay, arms and legs outspread, face tightly pressed against the ground, as if turning from the glow of lights. He pulled out the dead man's pockets. No key.

The field radio. Joe went to the "privy", the heavy crate that held the firing switch. The radio was gone. Of course. Jaworski was an old soldier, he knew to take the radio with him, just in case.

The crate's door was padlocked. In the shadows of the tower legs, Joe found no loose bars or hammers. Coaxial cable ran out of the top of the eight-foot crate and up the tower, and from the bottom as a buried conduit. In either case, out of reach. Leaning on the crate and trying to push it over, Joe was surprised to learn how weak he was.

How big the valley is, he thought, as he staggered back from the tower. Mountains stooping to the plain. Far-off electric echoes over the music of toads.

He started to run.

32

The wide excavation road ran straight to South-10,000. Yucca lined the shoulders.

There was a perfume to the air, the scent of cactus flowers, the stir of moths and bats.

The bullets must have been .22 shorts, he thought. Running had started the bleeding again; he was aware because of the cold. Loudspeakers barked. Mainly, he heard his heart and lungs and the sound of his shoes on tarmac.

He was better than a mile from the tower now.

A Very light hung like a new star. There was a short siren. Five minutes.

He tried to remember what Jaworski had said about hiding, about depressions and the flash. But he was too close and he could see nothing through the brush except baked, flat earth. And toads, a soft, resolute migration of them, everywhere he looked.

It was unfair. A whole year encased in hard dirt, waiting for it to be mud, to squirm freely to the surface, to see the moon and sing in passionate chorus at the rim of a brief, desert pool, only to be fried by General Groves.

The Voice of America wandered in and out, like a spectator that really couldn't keep its mind on the event at hand. Now it was playing "Sentimental Journey".

A hare darted in front of Joe, looked back in alarm and dashed off at an angle.

There was a long warning siren for everyone to go to the trenches behind the shelters and the base camp. Only a few men, including Harvey and Oppy, would actually stay in South-10,000. Three minutes.

Never knew my heart could be so yearny, Joe confessed.

More and more the toads were underfoot, singly and in groups crossing the roads, stopping to sing. Sometimes the whole ground seemed to move. One hopped before Joe and he saw Groves plopping on his belly, toes to the tower.

The final warning rocket sputtered overhead.

In fact, the song of the toads was a powerful, sonorous trembling. Cello and flute at the same time.

"Do not look at the blast," Harvey warned. *"When you do look, use your red goggles or a welder's glass."*

A last warning gong beat frantically.

The Voice of America slipped into classical strings, rousing sleepy Latins everywhere. Mexicans, Peruvians, Tierra del Fuegans lifted their Polaroid all-purpose red goggles and looked north.

"Ten."

Cirrus and stratocirrus fluttered in the dark. Rattlers stiffened to attention.

"Nine."

He glanced back and the tower floated in a cloud, with impatient, circling beads of light.

"Eight."

He felt Oppy sway, eyes on a door that would safely catch the image from a periscope. Breath held, a burnt, unravelling string through the heart. Fuchs watching from a hill twenty miles away, the only man there standing for the blast. Harry Gold strolling on the Alameda, patiently looking south.

"Seven."

Dolores had left pots in the fire. A gust worked between cedar coals and clay, shooting sparks around Rudy. There was a bootlegger's truck in the corral, and rabbits packed like snow in the hutch.

"Six."

Billy and Al put their hats on their hearts, not noticing that from dark kivas everywhere, figures stole to the surface.

"*Five.*"

The car crashed the gate and the band rushed for the parade ground, striped clowns with trombones, saxophones, clarinets. In Harlem's Palais des Sport, the French heavyweight swooped to the rafters, his satin shorts as bright as a macaw.

"*Four.*"

A piano toured the Rio Grande, its lid raised as a black sail.

"*Three.*"

Thinking Woman wore an embroidered Mexican dress with her turquoise necklace and silver pin, finally enough colour, Anna said, for her.

"*Two.*"

It was a slit trench for coaxial cable that had never been filled in. Maddened by the nearness of their destination, a thousand toads scaled the high shoulder of earth and abandoned stakes, and at the crest sang with pulsing throats. Those on the other side slid deliriously into the miracle of water.

"*One.*"

Last step. Last heartbeat. Last breath.

"*NOW!*"

From the eye of the new sun, a man diving.

Martin Cruz Smith
Gorky Park £2.95

'Superb . . . from the opening pages where three frozen and mutilated corpses have just been discovered in the snow of Moscow's Gorky Park to the grand finale' NEW YORK TIMES

'Brilliantly worked, marvellously written . . . a genuinely frightening, genuinely original vision' SUNDAY TIMES

'Straight to the top of the international thriller class' GUARDIAN

'Chief investigator Renko – vulnerable, decent, brave and smart – takes his place alongside the best creations of Le Carré
NEW YORK TIMES BOOK REVIEW